# THE WOLF HUNT

Ayelet Gundar-Goshen

# THE
# WOLF
# HUNT

TRANSLATED FROM THE HEBREW BY
SONDRA SILVERSTON

PUSHKIN PRESS

Pushkin Press
Somerset House, Strand
London WC2R 1LA

The original title in Hebrew is *Relocation*, published
by Achuzat Bayit, Tel Aviv in 2021.

First published by Pushkin Press in 2023

1 3 5 7 9 8 6 4 2

Hardback ISBN 13: 978-1-78227-988-4
Trade Paperback ISBN 13: 978-1-78227-991-4

Offset by Tetragon, London
Printed and bound by Clays Ltd, Elcograf S.p.A.

www.pushkinpress.com

*For my mother,*
*and for Yoav*

# THE WOLF HUNT

PART ONE

# RELOCATION

# 1

I LOOK AT the tiny fingers of a newborn baby and try to understand how they could possibly grow into the fingers of a killer. The dead boy is named Jamal Jones. In the newspaper photo, his eyes are as dark as velvet. My boy is named Adam Shuster. His eyes are the color of the sea in Tel Aviv. They say he killed Jamal. But that's not true.

# 2

MY NAME IS not Leela. It's hard for Americans to pronounce Lilach, so everyone here calls me Leela. But my name is not Leela.

With Mikhael, it's easy. They just call him Michael. He never corrects them. It's not polite. Unlike me—I always say "Lilach" the first time and then let my new acquaintance turn me into Leela without making an issue of it but without cooperating either—Mikhael started saying "Michael" a long time ago. He claims that with his name, it doesn't matter, it's almost the same thing. But four and a half months after Jamal died, when they hooked Mikhael up to the polygraph and asked him what his name was and he said Michael, I know that the needle jumped.

When we make love, I call him Mikhael. I called him Michael once, and it felt as if I were having sex with someone else.

When our son was born, we gave him a neutral name—Adam—that would work in both Hebrew and English. A name that would slide down the throats of the Americans like good California wine and not stick in the esophagus like Lilach and Mikhael, names that give us away the minute they read them on our passports: *Not from here.* We raised a child in America. We stored our Israeli-ness in the closet, along with the soccer trophies Mikhael had been saving since high school—for the memories, not because they were of any use. We raised an American child who went to high school with American children, and now they say he killed another American child.

## 3

JAMAL JONES. YOUR face is kind, but your size is intimidating. Your shoulders are broad, so broad that they seem to surprise even you. Perhaps it happened all at once, that growth spurt during one summer when, without warning, you changed from a short, skinny kid into a giant of a teenager. But your face didn't keep up with your limbs. Your body stretched and swelled, but your eyes remained the eyes of a child, and your lips, without the shadow of a mustache, retained the sweet pout of a child.

On the street at night, I would be afraid of you. I wouldn't linger to look into your eyes, which seem kind and pleasant in the newspaper photo. I would probably walk faster, put a hand in my pocket to be sure my phone was there in case I needed it. I would cross over to the illuminated side of the road and wait for your silhouette—that of a broad-shouldered Black man—to walk past me and disappear around the next curve.

If Adam was with me, I would be twice as stressed. Not only a woman on the street with a Black man behind her, but a woman with a small child she has to protect. And it wouldn't matter that you're the same age. You're a man, Jamal, and Adam is a child, short and skinny, his shoulders slightly stooped, like a chick that hasn't yet managed to raise its wings. That's why I can't understand. Your picture in the paper. The kind eyes. The broad shoulders. To think that, while all this time I was afraid of you, maybe it was you who should have been afraid of me, of what I was capable of giving birth to.

Now I'm afraid all the time, Jamal. Afraid of everything. But then, I wasn't so afraid yet, only rarely. I remember: Every night, all three of us took off our slippers and put them on the hardwood floor before going to sleep. In my double bed, I would read the news from Israel on my phone until Mikhael said, "It's late," and closed the blinds with the press of a button. Beyond the blinds was the yard, and beyond the yard was a green, quiet street that led to a green, quiet avenue in one of the greenest, quietest, safest cities in America.

## 4

ON THE FIRST night of Rosh Hashanah, a man with a machete walked into a Reform synagogue in one of those greenest, quietest, safest cities in America. There were two hundred twenty worshippers and fifteen catering-company employees inside the synagogue. In the large hall, usually used for bar mitzvahs, tables were being set for the Rosh Hashanah dinner. Propped up against the wall were high chairs for babies and young children because, even though most of the regular worshippers were senior citizens, young families came for the High Holidays, so they were joined by grandchildren and great-grandchildren. The prayers on the top floor had just ended, and people were beginning to trickle down the steps. In the hall on the first floor, workers were spreading white cloths on the tables and placing plates of sliced apples and jars of honey from Israel on them.

Later, on the news, they said they had been lucky; the man who attacked the synagogue in Pittsburgh was armed with a semiautomatic rifle and had managed to wound several people and kill eleven congregants before he was stopped, but here in Silicon Valley, just four were injured and only one person, a young woman, was killed. I understand what they meant on the news. But I knew that as far as Leah Weinstein's parents were concerned, that was definitely not luck. Their daughter had been standing right next to the door when the man ran inside with his machete.

In the photo on the news, she looked younger than nineteen, perhaps because of the makeup. She had a round face and soft brown eyes, and the makeup, instead of making her look older, actually emphasized her youth. In pictures taken a short time before the attack, you see her at the door of the synagogue in her white holiday dress. Her arms hug her body in the gesture of someone who doesn't really like to be photographed but knows she must be because the family insists. A well-brought-up girl. But when that man ran into the synagogue with his machete, Leah Weinstein did not act like a girl. She pushed her grandmother back and faced him, and that was the last thing she ever did.

I saw the video several times in the days that followed the attack. The plump young girl in the white dress stands in the lobby beside her grandparents. In the background, you can hear the voices of the synagogue choir singing a medley of holiday songs. It's difficult to pinpoint the precise moment when the joyous hubbub of song and speech turns into screams of terror. At first, you hear some sounds from outside, but you really can't know for sure yet because those are the shrieks of young girls, and sometimes it's hard to distinguish between screams of laughter and screams of panic. Then all at once, there's no mistaking it anymore: Smiles vanish, people scramble for shelter. The man in the hoodie bursts inside, and they trample one another in their mad dash to get away from him, all but Leah Weinstein. Instead of fleeing, she pushes her grandmother back, and perhaps because that movement is different from all the others, it catches the man's eye, leading him to her. In the video, he bends over her for a moment, only a moment, then brandishes his machete and continues running. The person who videoed all that, one of the worshippers on the upper floor, kept the camera on the attacker as he moved forward. That's why you can't see exactly what happened to Leah in the minutes that followed, although the screams of her grandparents are clearly audible, as are the screams of the young boy standing next to them, who hadn't known Leah before then but saw the girl in white suddenly collapse, covered in blood. By the time she was loaded into the ambulance, Leah had already lost so much blood that nothing could be done for her.

We were at home when they reported the attack. I remember exactly where each of us was standing: Mikhael was at the barbecue grill outside, along with his brother, Assi, who had arrived that day from Israel with Yeela and their twin boys, Tamir and Aviv, for a visit. Adam was in the pool behind them with his cousins. Yeela and I were in the kitchen, trying to salvage a honey cake that hadn't risen. Mikhael suddenly burst in with his phone in his hand and said, "There was a terrorist attack," and when Yeela asked with concern where in Israel the attack had taken place, he shook his head and said, "Not in Israel. Here."

We listened to the news all through dinner. After dessert, the kids went upstairs to watch something on the computer and we sat in the living room and watched the TV reports. Late that night, when we were already in bed, someone sent a WhatsApp video of what had happened in the synagogue. I didn't know if we should watch it. I told Mikhael that maybe it was disrespectful to the people who had been there. After all, it wasn't an action movie. Those were real people, and that was the moment when their lives were destroyed. But Mikhael insisted we watch it, said it was important.

"We're not watching it to be entertained," he said, "we're watching it to try and understand what happened there and to think about what to do if it happens again." We viewed the video once. And then again. When Mikhael started to play it a third time, I said, "Enough."

Later that night, my mother called from Israel, wanting to hear more details. The text I'd sent her right after we found out about the attack wasn't enough for her. I assured her again that we were all fine and told her what they knew here.

"They said on the news that he was Black," she said. "Since when do Blacks attack Jews? That's always been white people's job. An attack on Erev Rosh Hashanah," she went on. "That means he planned it ahead of time." She added that she'd sent a holiday gift for Adam—he should get it in a couple of days.

"Did you see the video from the synagogue?" she asked.

"Yes," I said, "it's horrible."

My mother sighed on the phone. "Just don't tell me later that it's saner to raise children there."

Afterward, I had nightmares that I couldn't remember when I woke up, but I knew that the girl from the synagogue was in them. In the morning, I asked Adam not to watch the video if someone happened to send it to him. He asked whether Mikhael and I had seen it. I said no.

On the morning of the funeral, Mikhael and I dropped Adam off at school. We didn't know the family and weren't members of the Reform synagogue, but we wanted to show solidarity. When we arrived, we saw other Israelis who had come to offer support.

Someone told us that Leah Weinstein had graduated from Adam's high school two years earlier and was going to college in Boston. Her parents had bought her a plane ticket to come home for the High Holidays. Israelis stood together in the cemetery parking lot and spoke Hebrew, and not far from them, American Jews were speaking quietly in English, and in both groups, the same thing was being said: How could this happen here in Silicon Valley? Then we entered the cemetery. Leah Weinstein's parents wept bitterly. She was their only child.

That evening, we picked up Adam from school and drove to the synagogue to light a candle and leave a flower on the sidewalk. The street outside the synagogue was crowded with people, along with a few news crews. A TV reporter with a blond bob spoke to the camera, her expression grim. We all listened to her as if that outsider had been given the authority to tell us who we were, what had happened to us.

"Paul Reed was born and raised on the east side of town. When the neighborhood was flooded by high-tech people who had come to work in the Valley, the rents also climbed in the poorer neighborhoods, and the Reed family had to move to Oakland. An hour before he left home with a machete in his bag and took a bus to the synagogue, Reed posted an antisemitic rant on Facebook. His parents say that, over the past few weeks, his mental state had deteriorated. He had been hospitalized twice in psychiatric institutions."

"He's not mentally ill," Assi muttered. "He's an antisemitic shit and a terrorist. They better not turn him into a lunatic who's not responsible for his actions and then release him."

"Nobody will release him," Mikhael said, "but we have to consider that the guy was institutionalized twice. He could just as easily have attacked a mosque or a bank, which means that what he did in the synagogue was not really an antisemitic act."

Assi waved his hand dismissively. "If your lunatics here in America can attack anywhere, why do they somehow always end up in a synagogue?"

The reporter looked away and listened to something said to her through her earpiece, then she put her grim expression back on and turned to the camera. "Eyewitnesses claim that they saw two suspicious people near the synagogue before the attack. The area is being searched. The FBI has yet to determine whether Reed acted alone or was part of a hate group liable to strike again."

That last sentence caused a stir in the crowd. Yeela and Assi exchanged glances. Adam said, "Mom, if it's a hate group, then it makes sense that they'll come back to strike again, because right now, there are a lot of Jews on the street."

Mikhael put a hand on his shoulder. "That reporter is causing hysteria for no reason. I'm telling you, ninety-nine percent of analysts say that these attacks are carried out by mentally ill people acting alone."

"We can't know for sure," I said and saw the same doubt in the eyes of the people around me. The row of lit candles cut us off from the street. Police barriers fenced us off from the other side of the lawn. Tensing at every sound, nervously looking around, we huddled together on the grass like sheep at night, searching for the wolf.

## 5

THE ANXIETY THAT began that night intensified in the days that followed. Even after the FBI determined that Paul Reed had acted alone, the Jewish community refused to calm down. Perhaps because this was a case of not only panic, but also humiliation: The outdoor security-camera video showed Reed charging into the synagogue observed by at least ten men who did nothing, too paralyzed to act. The video from the indoor security cameras showed the kippah-wearing worshippers fleeing to the side as Reed, screaming, races straight ahead, a lone, single-minded man doing the thing he'd set his mind on.

Perhaps that's why, when one of the Israeli parents suggested that we start a self-defense class for the young people, people eagerly agreed. Einat Greenbaum told me about it when we came to pick up our kids from school three days after the attack. "It's the father of a boy in the middle school," she said. "He has experience in Krav Maga and volunteered to teach the kids."

When Adam got into the car, I told him enthusiastically about the class. He said right away that he wasn't the slightest bit interested. I wasn't surprised. He never liked things like that. A mother once told me that the world is divided into two kinds of children: Those who choose to learn karate and those who choose to learn chess. Adam went for chess, and I'd actually been happy about that. But after Rosh Hashanah, after the video of Leah Weinstein, I suddenly regretted that he had never formally learned how to fight.

"There are only three sessions," I told him, "and you'll learn things that will serve you for the rest of your life."

Adam stubbornly refused all the way home and asked me not to nag him about it. I knew there was no point in insisting. The best way to make a kid hate a class is to force him to attend. But the images from the synagogue—the possibility that it could have been Adam—haunted me. I knew Mikhael was right, it was only mass hysteria, but I still wanted Adam to go to that class, just as I'd wanted him to get a hepatitis vaccination—not because the disease was an immediate threat but to be on the safe side.

"Do it for me," I said as we turned onto our street, "so I won't have to worry so much."

"You're really forcing me," he said. "It's not fair."

"At least think about it," I pleaded, hating him in my heart for making me beg.

"Okay," he said as I parked in front of the house. "I'll think about it."

That night, all the adults sat in front of the TV again, something we didn't usually do, and Adam joined us. CNN showed the synagogue security-camera videos. Assi watched and muttered, "Why didn't anyone stop him?"

"It's not so easy to stop someone like that," I said as I put a plate of the sunflower seeds they'd brought from Israel on the table. On every visit, Assi would schlep three kilos of sunflower seeds with him and present them to us with the pride of a doctor introducing antibiotics to a remote tribe.

Adam sat on the couch next to me, shifting his gaze back and forth between me and his uncle. The guest-room door upstairs opened, and Tamir and Aviv ran out. I heard their strong, confident steps on the stairs, and I knew that Adam would never have run down the hallway of someone else's house with such freedom. They came into the living room, sat down beside Adam, and buried their heads in their cell phones. I thought they weren't listening, but a few moments later, Tamir looked up and pointed to the TV. "That would never happen in Israel."

"But there are terrorist attacks in Israel," Adam said.

"Sure," Tamir replied. "But there's no way a terrorist walks into a place and no one tries to stop him."

I wanted to say something about the class but stopped myself. I ordered Indian takeout. I thought we'd stay up late, but by nine o'clock, our guests were already beat from the jet lag and said they were going to sleep.

"The kids get up early," Assi said proudly.

Tamir and Aviv were training to join an elite combat unit.

Every day they were with us, they went running in the morning an hour before we all got up. When Adam woke up and went downstairs, he would find them making protein shakes in the kitchen, sweaty and panting after a long workout. There were athletes at his school too, boys who charged each other on the football field, but he had nothing to do with them. For him, they were distant creatures, like grizzly bears. Tamir and Aviv were his cousins. Every morning, he encountered a reflection of the life that could have been his. Their damp, post-workout smell lingered in the kitchen after they'd gone. During our meals together, they asked Mikhael about the elite combat unit he'd served in. His discreet answers only excited them more. After a few days, Adam began asking as well. He had never shown an interest in it before.

On the following days, the presence of the twins, strong and tan, loud and brash, filled the house. My son trailed after them like a dog hoping to be adopted, and though they let him follow them around, they never invited him along on their own initiative. He admired them, eagerly drank in every word they said in their up-to-date Hebrew, which he didn't always under-stand. They liked him, I think. From the minute they arrived, they treated him like an old pal. Instead of *Adam*, they called him *Edamame*. That made us all laugh.

Before they came, I was afraid Adam would be an outsider, just as he had been during their last visit two years ago. The twins had been immersed in their own private world then, always laughing and whispering in the latest slang, which Adam wasn't familiar with because, even though we spoke only Hebrew at home, our usage had grown old-fashioned without our noticing it. Tamir and Aviv spoke like sixteen-year-old Israeli kids, and my son spoke like his forty-year-old parents, so that's why—but not the only reason why—during their entire stay with us, Adam walked around like a stranger in his own living room. This year, I tried to prepare myself: *Another family is coming to live in our house for two weeks. They'll see what we have in our fridge, go into our bathroom after us, wash their hair with our shampoo until we all smell the same. They'll notice the minor tensions in our household, and we'll see the cracks in theirs. Arguments between couples will be hushed. Arguments between parents and children will be loud. Other arguments will not take place.*

That's how I prepared myself for every eventuality, except the most unforeseen one—an attack that would unite us, because even though nothing happened to any one of us individually, something had happened to all of us together.

"I think we can talk to him about the class again," Mikhael said to me a few days later, after Adam had spent a couple of evenings with Tamir and Aviv. I wanted Adam to learn self-defense, but I think my reasons were different from Mikhael's. When we got into bed, he said, "Maybe now he'll finally agree to do something athletic. It could be healthy for him, physically and socially."

My stomach clenched. It was the first time Mikhael had spoken about Adam that way, as if there were something wrong with him that had to be fixed. I knew it was because of Tamir and Aviv. It wasn't the way they carried themselves, because they slouched, almost deliberately, and dragged their feet. No, it was the way their bodies gloried in a comfortable slackness that amplified their strength. Mikhael noticed this about Assi's kids—it was impossible not to. Thirty years ago, he and Assi used to pee together on the kibbutz fields in a never-ending competition: who peed farther, who peed longer, who could hit the bushes. They compared their children now the way they had compared their pricks then. And Mikhael, the strong, smart, levelheaded one, was losing.

## 6

I COULD NEVER say exactly when that fence had been erected—Mikhael and I on one side, Assi and Yeela on the other—but it was obvious to me that the fence was made of money. At some point along the way, money became something we didn't talk about. And not talking about something makes you realize it's important. When we'd first arrived in America, before Mikhael moved up in the company, we talked freely to Assi and Yeela about money. I complained to them about the insane cost of preschool in the States, and they grumbled about the interest Israeli banks charged on mortgages. But as the gap grew larger, we talked about it less frequently.

The worst times were when Assi told Mikhael about his idea for a start-up. He'd speak enthusiastically while looking around suspiciously, as if at any moment someone would snatch away his brilliant brainchild. Mikhael would listen, ask a question or two. I think he did it out of politeness, but for Assi, Mikhael's questions were gasoline poured on the fire of his hopes—he would light up immediately, wave his arms as he spoke, plan the presentation they would both give to the investors. It used to happen every time they visited us, but since the loan, it occurred less often.

The annual visit always passed quickly. We made great shak-shuka for breakfast. In the evenings, we picked up Adam from school—Tamir and Aviv were shocked by how seriously people took their studies here—and went to eat in the best restaurants in town. Every time the check came, Mikhael whipped out his credit card, saying, "It's on me." His intentions were good, but I think the gesture caused damage. The loan Mikhael had given Assi three years earlier sat between them, unmentioned. Fifty thousand dollars to get his sure-to-succeed initiative going.

When everything collapsed, Assi paid back what he could. He wanted to pay back more, but Mikhael told him there was no need. I thought Assi would love Mikhael forever for saying that. But apparently something inside him would always hate him for saying it.

Even after the loan and the collapse, our joint vacations happened at their usual times: Rosh Hashanah at our place, Passover at theirs. The present visit wasn't supposed to be different from the others, but the attack on Rosh Hashanah, although we weren't directly involved, affected everything. Assi talked about it constantly. At every opportunity, he said he thought it was just getting started, that antisemitism in America was only beginning to rear its ugly head.

Tamir's and Aviv's induction into the army at the end of the year was another ever-present part of our conversations. How many sit-ups they did. How many kilometers they ran. On Saturday, when they were packing for their flight back to Israel, cramming their suitcases full of things they'd bought, I was surprised at how relieved I was.

The next day, I woke Adam early for the first session of the self-defense class. He'd been sound asleep and didn't want to get up. Mikhael drove him, yawning and grumbling, to the old rec center on the edge of town, and I picked him up two hours later. Waiting for him in the parking lot, I worried that he'd get in the car and announce that once was enough for him, but when he opened the door, he was surprisingly positive. The sleepy kid who had entered the class that morning emerged with a rousing dream—a terrorist would come to the synagogue and he would be the one to stop him.

I didn't have to wake him for the second class. He woke up and got ready by himself. When I came to pick him up, I saw the boys leaving the center together, chattering away in English, walking shoulder to shoulder to the parking lot. I think that was the first time I realized that I had never seen my son as part of a group. He'd had friends over the years. Not many, but he'd had them. Quiet, polite boys. I knew that he would have preferred his teenage years to be different, and I noticed how little they resembled what we saw on TV. But I didn't worry. High school might seem an eternity when you're there, but in reality, it's very short. And then you have your entire life ahead of you. Only after everything went off the rails did I understand how wrong I'd been, how clueless about his longing to be part of a noisy crew of kids walking together down the street, each drawing strength from the presence of the others.

The difference was the instructor. He didn't let the boys make the natural though unspoken division into a central group surrounded by hangers-on and rejects. At the very first meeting, he told them he didn't care about well liked and not well liked, about popular and unpopular. If anyone tried to attack them, they were one another's only hope. They had to be united because tomorrow morning another piece of shit like Paul Reed might come along, and the only way to stop him was through cooperation. Adam's eyes glowed as he told me that. It sounded a bit pompous to me, like the speech given by the commander of an officers' course, but I kept my cynicism to myself. For Adam and the other boys, that class was what might stand between them and another massacre in the synagogue. They gave themselves over to it totally. And when the three sessions were over, they asked for more.

"Does he have any maneuvers left to teach you?" I asked.

"Of course he has more maneuvers to teach us," Adam said. "Besides self-defense, there'll be Krav Maga, assault course training, orienteering..."

If it hadn't been for the synagogue attack, I might have raised an eyebrow and said that the class was beginning to sound like a combat-unit boot camp. But the fear still pulsed under my skin. It calmed me to know that Adam was continuing the class. It made me happy to see him fitting in with the other boys, and I liked the fact that the instructor taught them in Hebrew. When Adam said he needed a compass for the next session, I smiled to myself and hurried to order one. It was great to see him finally blossoming, part of something larger.

I was afraid that after another meeting or two, he'd drop out of the class and withdraw into himself again. I worried that a sixteen-year-old boy's natural laziness would keep my son in front of his laptop at home, especially since it took twenty minutes to bike to the rec center, so I was pleasantly surprised when he persevered despite the distance. Once, he had spent his afternoons alone in the amateur chemistry lab he had set up in our garage. Now he barely went in there. He would come home sweaty from the bike ride, cheeks red and eyes shining. And I knew it wasn't only because of the ride that his whole body was like that. It was because of something else.

Only after Jamal Jones died did I discover that they were a fairly large group. Ten teenage boys. They met every Sunday at noon. Under the gentle caress of the California sun, they navigated, camouflaged, attacked, and neutralized, then went home to eat schnitzel for supper and study for their math tests.

One rainy Sunday, Adam came home completely soaked.

"You should have called," I said. "I would have picked you up."

He laughed. "We trained in the rain. Uri said there are no umbrellas in war." That was the first time I heard the name—Uri—and the way Adam said it: with profound respect, almost awe, as if merely uttering it were a great honor.

"You'll catch cold," I said, but he swore that he hadn't been cold for even a minute. And he didn't rush to take off his wet clothes. Pride kept him warm.

Over the following weeks, Mikhael and I heard more and more about Uri. His name punctuated every one of Adam's sentences. Rumor had it that Uri had been part of the IDF general staff. The boys in the class said that after leaving the army, he joined the Mossad. Uri didn't talk about that and wouldn't answer questions. I had already encountered that reticence of former elite combat-unit members, the quiet way they moved around in the world, with the pride of modesty. And the truth was that the less information he volunteered, the more the boys were drawn to him.

"Maybe Uri is still in the Mossad," Adam told us one evening. Mikhael stepped in at that point. He was squeezing oranges while I was making potato pancakes and Adam was setting the table. Adam said that maybe Uri's entire stay in the United States was part of a secret mission, and Mikhael, with that ironic half smile of his, said, "You think he's recruiting the future generation of Mossad agents?"

Adam laughed. Mikhael sliced an orange in half with one stroke of the knife and went on in the same amused tone: "Maybe the whole idea of the class is just a cover story. Maybe next time you meet, he'll send you all into a forest to kidnap a senior Hamas member who traveled to San Francisco."

I waited for Adam to laugh or offer a sarcastic response of his own. Nothing prepared us for the hurt, sullen silence that prevailed for the rest of the meal.

Only later, when TV voices had dulled Adam's angry silence and Chandler and Joey got us ready for bed, covered us with a blanket, and kissed us good night, only then did Mikhael say in a sleepy voice, "I think I know him."

"Who?"

"That Uri. I think he was three years behind me."

"And what was he like?"

Mikhael didn't say anything for a while. I thought he'd fallen asleep. "Brilliant. They said he would be chief of the general staff."

I turned to face him. "And look at what became of him, a Krav Maga instructor in Silicon Valley."

Mikhael ran a warm, heavy hand over my thigh. "You mean a Mossad agent in California." In the darkness of the room, I heard the smile in his voice, which made me smile too. And so, smiling, we fell asleep.

7

I THOUGHT I recognized her standing next to the fruit display, but I wasn't sure. She was looking down at the cherries and holding the handle of a half-full shopping cart. It wasn't until she looked up that I knew for certain. Her eyes were very red and her pupils were dilated to the size of blueberries. Leah's mother noticed me looking at her. I turned around quickly. As I began pushing my cart toward the dairy section, I heard her behind me.

"Excuse me," she said in a thin voice. "Can you please help me?"

I turned around and said, "Of course." I didn't know if I should tell her that I knew who she was. That I'd been at the funeral. That I was so sorry.

"I'm just a little dizzy. Can you please help me get to the benches outside?"

Only then did I see how she was gripping the handle of the cart. She wasn't shopping for fruit; she was clutching the cart to keep from falling. I left my own cart and hurried over to her. "Come with me."

She hesitated, as if even after she'd decided to ask for my assistance, she wasn't sure that she actually required it, that she really needed a stranger in the supermarket to help her walk. But a moment later, when I reached out to her, she gave in and placed her cool palm in my hand.

"I took a pill," she said as we slowly made our way down the aisles toward the glass doors. "I thought it would put me to sleep for only a few hours, but I still seem to be a little woozy." Her pupils were enormous. I don't think she noticed that she was leaning on me as she walked.

"The thing is that I have to make a pie. A reporter is coming over this evening. I wanted to make the pie my daughter asks for every time she comes home from college."

"What kind of pie?"

"Blueberry. I'm not such a great cook, but that pie always comes out so delicious."

The glass doors opened. I helped Leah's mother sit down on the bench, hurried back inside, and returned with a glass of water.

"I don't think you should drive home on your own," I said as she took small sips.

"Sometimes when I'm driving, I hope I'll have an accident. My daughter died fifty-one days ago."

"I know," I said. "I was at the funeral." Then I added, "We're from Israel."

She turned to look at me. "That was very nice of you. Israelis hardly ever come to our synagogue. It's nice you came to the funeral."

She squeezed my hand with hers, which was still cool, and took another sip of water. "It's not that I think I'll see her again if I die in an accident. I'm not one of the lucky ones who believe in heaven. I just hope that then it won't hurt anymore."

I didn't know what to say to that. I hurried back inside again and got her another glass of water. Leah's mother took it but didn't drink.

"Would you like me to drive you home?" I asked.

"Our rabbi said that Pete and I should start going out more. I told him that I'm always smelling Leah's clothes. I go into her room, open the closet, and smell her clothes."

I asked myself whether I should call Pete to come and get her. I didn't know what kind of pill Leah's mother had taken, but she definitely didn't look like someone who was going to bake a pie today. "Maybe you should call your husband?"

"Why not." But she didn't move. Her purse was slung over her shoulder, but she didn't reach for it. "Her scent is fading away."

A red-haired woman standing at the supermarket entrance looked at us with interest. I didn't know whether she was an acquaintance of Leah's mother or just recognized her from the news. I hoped they were friends and she would come and sit down on the bench so I could get away. But the redhead went inside, and other people, although some of them looked at us, didn't stop.

Leah's mother took her phone out of her bag and called her husband, who said he'd come right away. Talking to him seemed to revive her a bit. She asked my name and my husband's and wanted to know how long we'd been in America. "Do you have children?"

"Yes," I said. "One." I waited for her to ask what his name was, but she didn't. We spoke for another few minutes. She looked better. When a metallic-blue Jeep turned into the parking lot, she straightened up and said, "Here's Pete." After a moment, she added, "I can't thank you enough." And a moment later, she said, "You know, sometimes it hurts so much that I think it would be better if she had never been born."

★　★　★

Adam was sitting in the living room when I came in. He asked why it had taken me so long. I didn't tell him about my encounter with Leah's mother, but that night, I told Mikhael, who sighed and said, "That poor woman."

"I hope they put off the meeting with that reporter," I said. "I really don't think she's in any condition to be interviewed right now."

But Susan and Peter Weinstein didn't cancel the visit of the reporter, the one with the blond bob. They didn't want people to forget their daughter. The speed with which Leah's face was fading from the screens seemed unfair to them. They had things to say about her. She had been so bright. So sweet. She had saved her grandmother. They thought the reporter would want to hear those things, but what she really wanted to talk about was Paul Reed. The murderer interested her much more than the victim. And perhaps what hurt Susan Weinstein the most was that, for the reporter, Paul Reed was a sort of victim. He was pushed out of the neighborhood where he grew up. When he was seven, white people bought the house he'd been born in for almost nothing and then charged much higher rents. In Oakland, the boy was exposed to drug dealers who dragged him down, and when some combination of drugs and genetics caused his mental collapse, Reed did not receive the treatment that might have stabilized his condition because it cost too much money. When the reporter said those things during the interview, Susan Weinstein exploded.

"It's not my fault if Black people would rather get high while other people work hard. The Jews worked to get ahead in this country. We paid full price for our house. We're not racist in any way—my father marched with Martin Luther King Jr., and believe me, King would be ashamed to hear that a Black man with a machete charged into a synagogue like a wild animal in the jungle."

The interview appeared on the news. The sentence about the jungle was widely quoted. Two organizations demanded that Susan Weinstein apologize for her racist remarks. Mikhael and I sat in the living room and watched Leah's mother speak to the camera, her forehead sweaty and her pupils dilated.

In the weeks that followed, I was tense every time I went to the supermarket, afraid she would be there. But I didn't see her again. They say she stopped leaving the house.

## 8

HOW LONG WERE we asleep? How long did we walk, work, and speak in such total oblivion? The terror caused by the attack subsided, absorbed into our daily lives. Paul Reed and Leah Weinstein were still mentioned on TV, his picture alongside hers, but terrible things continued to happen—a baby disappeared during a family vacation in Florida, a policeman shot a Black man who was out on a morning run in Wisconsin—and those things gradually overshadowed the synagogue attack until the day came when it wasn't mentioned at all. The memory of Rosh Hashanah grew distant.

Every morning, I drove Adam to school, and I drove him back every afternoon. On the drive home I used to ask him how his day had been, only to be met by a wall of shrugs. But motherhood is one long climb up a wall. Instead of asking directly, I started asking more oblique questions— *What did you learn today, who did you talk to, what was fun, what annoyed you?*—questions I'd found on a parents' forum, questions formulated by well-groomed psychologists whose pictures appeared in the corner of the screen along with their phone numbers. Like the rigorous screening at Ben Gurion Airport, when they check to see if there's a bomb concealed in your innocent-looking bag—that was how I scrutinized his face every afternoon, searching for a clue. *Are you happy, my son? What happened to you during those long hours we were apart? Did anyone make fun of you? Hurt you?* I tried to read all that in his face, and I was so totally focused on getting answers to those questions that I never once asked, *And you, my son, did you make fun of anyone? Did you hurt anyone?*

At some point, even those questions stopped. I continued taking him to school in the morning and driving him home in the afternoon, but I no longer tried to understand what was happening to him in between. There was some relief in that. Not constantly struggling with that alienation but letting it grow. When I stopped trying to know, find out, understand, investigate, I could just enjoy the time we spent together in the car, lean back in the driver's seat and listen to music. He decided what we'd listen to on the way to school and I decided what we'd listen to on the way home. I could act appalled by the foul language in hip-hop, not because it really appalled me but to let him enjoy an adolescent victory over his old-fashioned mom. On the way home, I played the Beatles, Pink Floyd, David Bowie. I thought a lot about which songs to choose—what he could relate to, what he might like. Everything I wanted to tell him, I told him in those songs. And he listened, even if he didn't always understand. Once, on the way to school, after witnessing an argument between me and Mikhael, he played "Life on Mars" between one hip-hop song and another, and David Bowie sang in the car. I knew he'd done it for me, to cheer me up, and I hid my emotion behind my sunglasses.

That's how it was—hip-hop on the way to school, Beatles on

the way back, and in between, silence. He was in school, I was at home, Mikhael was at work. Three rivers that did not touch until the evening, when we joined into a single sea for a dinner that was sometimes noisy and sometimes quiet but always, always took place in total oblivion. Oblivion we were startled out of at eleven o'clock on a Thursday night, when Adam called Mikhael and said in a trembling voice, "Dad, can you pick me up? Someone died here."

## 9

WHEN HE CALLED, we were watching an episode of *The Simpsons*. It wasn't an especially good episode, but neither one of us suggested changing channels. We'd already had so many hours of Marge and Homer that they seemed like another couple in our social circle, and you don't toss a couple of friends out of your living room just because, one night, they don't happen to be as funny and interesting as usual. And there was another reason: A large, dark silence lay in wait for us behind Marge and Homer's chatter, like a panther staring out from the blackness. We hadn't exchanged a word since Adam had left the house two hours earlier, closing the door behind himself in anger. (He didn't slam it. My son has never slammed a door. He has a sort of angry gesture that stops itself a moment before the door actually slams, producing a noisy but controlled sound, a miniature rebellion.)

He hadn't wanted to go to that party. Mikhael pressured him. He wanted Adam to spend more time with his classmates. Ever since Adam had started the self-defense course, his social life had improved, but most of the boys there were younger than he was, and apparently Mikhael thought they weren't enough. When he heard about the party, he bribed Adam to go. He offered incentives like the ones he offered his employees.

"I know you're not crazy about going, so let's decide that today you go, and over the weekend we'll do something really great, maybe a drive up to Bear Valley?"

I didn't like Mikhael's way of engineering people's behavior. His system of incentives seemed like something you'd do with sea lions, not people. But Mikhael insisted, saying that the entire American economy worked that way so there was no reason it wouldn't work with our reclusive son.

I heard about the party by accident. I'd stopped at the supermarket to buy a few things and bumped into Ashley's mother. She asked if we wanted to drive the kids to the party and they'd bring them home. "What party?" I asked, and I saw her eyes widen in surprise.

"Josh's party. Adam didn't tell you? All the sophomores are invited. I'm sure they're all invited."

We were standing in line waiting to pay. The more she repeated that everyone was invited, the more I realized she wasn't so sure that Adam was included. But at home, when I asked him, he said, "Yes, at Josh's place. Everyone's invited."

"So, are you going?"

"I don't feel like it."

"Why not? I'm sure it'll be fun."

"Why are you so sure?"

Though Adam's look was hostile, there was a drop of curiosity in it, as if part of him really wanted me to explain. Then Mikhael interrupted us. In a confident voice, that vice-president-in-charge tone that always put me off, he offered Adam the party/Bear Valley deal.

Adam spent the next few hours in his room, listening to hip-hop behind his locked door. Then he went out for a run, as he'd been doing every evening since beginning the self-defense class. I heard Kelev whimpering at the door and was angry at Adam for not taking him along. I put on my coat, clipped the leash to his collar as he quivered with excitement, and went out into the frost. Hoping to bump into Adam, I'd prepared an angry rebuke (*If you want a pet, you have to take responsibility*—a mother's remark), but he wasn't on the street. On the way back, I saw a small light in the garage window and went inside. Adam was bent over his chemistry set beside the small cabinet, and he straightened up as soon as he saw me.

I asked why he hadn't taken Kelev out. I told him that he had to learn to consider others, that I was cold, that I shouldn't have to walk around outside in this weather just because he didn't take care of his dog. He mumbled that he was sorry, and when I noticed how troubled he looked, I thought I'd been too hard on him. It never occurred to me that maybe it wasn't my rebuke that troubled him but the chemistry set and the cabinet and what was inside it. Only when the police knocked on our door several weeks later did the question pop into my mind, like a closed eye suddenly opening: *What were you doing that evening in the garage, Adam? What was in the cabinet?*

## 10

**TWENTY-EIGHT MINUTES** after Adam called, we pulled up in front of the Hart family's house, brakes squealing. We weren't alone. Other parents had received similar phone calls from their kids. "Mom, Dad, someone collapsed and died." Every minute, another car raced onto the block and pulled up to the curb. More and more adults stepped out. Worried mothers. Worried fathers. Only a short time ago, a young girl had been murdered in our city, and the news of another dead youngster struck exposed parental nerves.

Ashley was sitting on the fence, wrapped in a coat that belonged to her mother, who nodded at me but remained beside her daughter. A few girls were crying along the pathway to the front door. Makeup smeared their young faces. Their dresses were very short, despite the cold. After all, they'd planned to spend the evening inside the house, which was lit with colored party lights, dancing in the living room, or drinking in the kitchen, or in Josh's parents' bed (they were out of town), or in Josh's older brother's bedroom (he was in college), or in Josh's bed. They had planned to fool around, kiss, maybe suck. They'd planned to get drunk, vomit in the toilet or the bathtub or, if they had no other choice, in a potted plant. They had not planned to stand outside on the path to the front door, exposed to the freezing wind, while inside, a boy's body lay on the living-room floor.

A group of boys was gathered at a nearby bench. They smelled strongly of weed and alcohol. Some of them were crying. Not uncontrollable weeping, like the girls, but restrained, embarrassed crying, and they kept wiping their faces with their hands. Others were standing on the bench on their tiptoes for an obvious reason they made no attempt to hide—to steal glances at the body inside the house.

Yellow police tape cut across the yard. I was surprised at how familiar it looked to me, that yellow tape, what a sense of déjà vu it aroused in me, after an endless number of crime scenes and bodies in movies and TV series. As if in a dream, I walked across the lawn, past the patrol cars, and around the yellow tape, crushing autumn leaves under my feet. Red-and-blue lights glared from the roofs of the police cars onto the wet grass and bounced off the windshields of the parents' cars, which kept coming. For a moment, it seemed as though they were the flickering lights of the party, especially since, with all the commotion, no one had bothered to turn off the music.

Strong, insistent bass sounds came from inside the Hart family's home. You could almost believe that the grim-looking police officers were there because an angry neighbor had called to complain about the noise, not because a stammering teenage girl had called to report that a boy had collapsed and died.

I looked around, searching for my son. I saw Mikhael at the other end of the street. He was wandering through the crowd looking for Adam, and when he caught my eye, he shook his head. I shook my head in reply—*No, I don't see him either*—and continued walking. A woman in an evening dress supported a tall boy who was vomiting on the grass. His vomit stained her foot, shod in high heels despite the cold, and sprayed her sheer stockings. Another mother, wearing slippers and a windbreaker over pajamas, passed me and asked without stopping, "Have you seen Cora, a redhead?" I shook my head and began walking faster. *Where are you, Adam?*

Suddenly I was afraid for him for no real reason. I knew very well that it wasn't Adam lying inside that house. After all, Adam had called us. He was the one who told us to come. And yet, the seconds ticked by and he wasn't here. More and more kids fell weeping into their parents' arms, even the toughest boys. When their dads or moms got out of their cars, they suddenly broke down and melted into their embrace.

I was looking around so much that I stumbled into a rosebush, and the thorny branches pierced the fabric of my pants, scratching my skin. "Adam!" I shouted. "Adam!" The streetlights barely penetrated the tangle of bushes. The flashing lights of the patrol cars, the crying of the teenagers—it had all become muted. Everything but the booming bass, which, from this side of the house, sounded like the rumbling of thunder. I kept searching. Maybe Mikhael had already found him. Maybe they were standing on the street in front of the Hart house wondering where I'd disappeared to. But something inside me knew he hadn't. Something deep and primeval pushed me forward, made me more and more frightened, as if at any moment, someone would tell me that there were in fact two of them, two dead teenagers; as if the direction of time and our clear knowledge of his voice when he called and said, "Someone died here," no longer protected him, and somehow, this house had harmed him.

I took another step. At eye level, there was an open window, the wooden shutters gaping. A transparent curtain moved in the icy wind. But it wasn't because of the wind that I froze. It was because of him. Because of his face.

The dead boy lay on the living-room floor next to the open window. He was wearing light-colored jeans and a white sweatshirt, and his face was so twisted in anguish that for a moment, I couldn't breathe. I'd seen dead people before. I'd been at the deathbeds of my father, my grandmother, and a dear friend who had died of cancer. I'd attended American funerals with open caskets. But nowhere had I seen a face that showed such suffering. Only later, when I looked at the newspaper photo, did I discover how much beauty there was in the boy's features before death came and made him so ugly.

I looked away quickly. The body of the dead boy was large, sprawled half on the carpet, half on the wood floor, in a remarkably natural pose. As if he had stretched out, as comfortable as a cat, and was ready to leap to his feet at any moment. His shoes were exactly like Adam's—red, white, and black Air Jordans that Adam had asked us to buy him for his birthday. They cost a fortune, but he'd pleaded, so I finally agreed, and I was furious when, a few weeks later, he told us he'd lost them in the pool's locker room. Maybe Adam had wanted to emulate this boy, the way he'd wanted to buy the same brand of clothes that Tamir and Aviv wore. These were the kind of trendy shoes that kids who spent hours on YouTube and TikTok pestered their mothers to buy for them. At that moment, because of the shoes, it suddenly hit me: *That's someone's son lying there.*

I was dizzy. A policeman and an idle paramedic who were standing in the living room turned and looked straight at me. I turned away, heart pounding, ashamed. Inside the house, someone finally turned off the music. I pictured the faces of Adam's few friends. No, the boy in the living room wasn't one of them—I was certain of that. A Black boy had been at our house a few times, but he was much skinnier and wore glasses, and I think his family moved to San Diego anyway. That's what Adam had mumbled when I asked why he didn't come around anymore. I had never before seen the boy lying on the living-room floor, not even all the times I'd driven Adam to and from school. But they were likely the same age, in the same class.

A large wooden ladder was leaning on the wall next to the window. Maybe Adam had climbed up to the roof. A crazy idea, but I felt I should go up to check it out. I wasn't thinking straight. The sight of the dead boy had rattled me. I hesitated next to the ladder for another moment and, from the corner of my eye, saw an abrupt movement inside the house.

A Black woman had pushed past the policeman, who was trying to get her to go back outside. She was tall and broad-shouldered. Her face, heavily made up, had strong, striking features. She was wearing a pink dress with large white flowers and pink high heels. Her ankles looked swollen. Her steps were small for someone of her height, and her eyes darted from side to side, surveying the room. The dead boy lay beyond the couch, but she didn't know that. From where she was standing, she couldn't see him. The policeman knew where the boy was lying and tried to block her path, but she continued moving forward. One moment she was fine, and then she walked past the couch. All at once, her beautiful face contorted. I saw it happen. Her expression broke in half, and what I saw there was even more horrible than what I'd seen on the dead boy's face, making it clear beyond any doubt that he was her son.

I thought she would run to him. Hug him. But she just stood there and stared, looking so hollow that I started to run away. I forgot the ladder and my stupid idea to climb up to the roof and ran the length of the house to the dark backyard with its huge barbecue grill in the middle. I tripped on a hose and darted around two garden gnomes just to get away from that window. I almost ran into a stack of wicker furniture. There were more rosebushes behind it.

And there he was, my son. At first, I almost didn't see him, curled into a ball among the bushes. He was sitting on the ground, hugging his knees to his chest, his head hidden between them, his entire being constricted.

"Adam?"

When he looked up, I saw that he was crying, tears streaming down his badly shaved cheeks. He leaped up into my arms and buried his head between my breasts, squeezing me so hard, it almost hurt. The intensity of his crying terrified me. I had never heard him sob that way before. "It's okay, it's okay," I mumbled, but my words only made him cry harder. I stopped speaking and held him. I whispered, "Shh, shh, shh," the way I used to as I stood beside his crib when he was a baby. And it worked. A few minutes later, he calmed down. "Let's go," I said. "Dad must be worried."

I didn't want to walk past that window again. I led him along the other side of the house to the noisy, illuminated street, now more crowded than before. We had almost reached it when the front door opened and two policemen came out, supporting the woman in the pink dress.

Everyone froze and stared. Someone near us whispered, "That's Jamal Jones's mother." She walked slowly down the pathway, wobbling on her high heels, which clacked with every step—*clack-clack-clack*. She didn't look at us. Her eyes were somewhere else. The clothes were the same—a pink dress with large white flowers—but the woman inside it in no way resembled the one I'd seen earlier. *Clack-clack.* Now she passed very close to me and Adam. I heard Adam's breath catch in his throat. His whole body shook. Jamal's mother walked past us, escorted by policemen, and reached the end of the path. People turned their heads to look at her as if she were a celebrity, a politician, someone important. And now it occurs to me that maybe we all gazed at her that way because the woman on the lawn was someone we were all afraid to be. We looked at her with pity, but also with curiosity about what it was like when the thing you feared most came to pass.

She was about to get into the police car when she suddenly stumbled and collapsed onto the ground. A cry of alarm rose from the crowd. Someone screamed, "She fell!" The policemen picked up Jamal Jones's mother and consoled her. A blond woman got out of her parked car and shouted, "I'll drive with you." I don't know how the policemen answered her, because at that moment, Mikhael grabbed my hand. "There you are!"

I was surprised to see how calm he looked. Sad, yes. Concerned, definitely. But not panicked. Amid the general, contagious fear, my husband was one of the only people who saw the event for what it was—a teenage boy had collapsed and died at a party. Tragic, but not a danger to anyone standing there on the street.

He let go of me and put his hand on Adam's shoulder. "Are

you okay?" Adam nodded that yes, he was okay. I thought that Mikhael's presence reassured him more than mine.

"The car's there," Mikhael said, pointing up the street. But Adam didn't seem to be in a hurry to leave. His classmates were crowded on the Harts' front lawn, consoling one another. They cried. They hugged. Some of them whispered in choked voices. Some were silent together. Others held hands. Adam looked at them.

"We can wait a while," Mikhael said gently.

Adam shook his head. "I want to go home."

Mikhael opened his mouth to say something but changed his mind. He kept his hand on Adam's shoulder and put his other hand on mine, and so the three of us walked along the illuminated lawn and down the street to our car.

Suddenly Adam broke away from us and began to run across the street. One minute the three of us were walking together, and a minute later, he was gone. Mikhael and I watched him, confused, as he sped toward a man with a buzz cut wearing a padded jacket. They hugged in that tight, masculine way, something we had never seen Adam do. When the man tapped his shoulder in what seemed to be a prearranged signal, Adam broke free of the embrace and turned to us.

"Mom, Dad, this is Uri."

## 11

AS SOON AS he opened his mouth, it was clear. Something in his voice, the way he pronounced his words, compelled us—no, not *compelled*; compulsion arouses resistance, and this was just the opposite; his voice made us *want* to follow him. His voice was like the music of the Pied Piper of Hamelin. Mikhael had a similar trait. He always knew how to manipulate people. But with him, it was engineered, as if, at any given moment, a program in his head calculated what needed to be said in order to make someone do what he wanted. But with Uri, it was a warm quality. His voice melted something in your body, relaxed the muscles of your opposition. And all he said to us was the most common, meaningless thing: "So you're Adam's parents." The minute he said it—in Hebrew—it was as if a protective wall had been built around us and we were no longer a family meeting their son's teacher in California but a cohesive group of Israelis led by their commander, Uri.

Mikhael spoke first, praising the self-defense class. "Adam talks about you all the time."

Uri listened. He didn't return the compliment the way an American would. He didn't say, for example, *Your son is amazing, really something special.* That's what Adam's computer teacher had told me at every elementary-school parent-teacher conference and what his middle-school chess teacher had said at the end of every lesson. Uri just listened, then nodded, and Adam looked at that nod with awe, the way you'd look at a lunar eclipse.

Maybe that was why I suddenly spoke to him, skipping the hello-I'm-Lilach-nice-to-meet-you and saying instead, "I understand from Adam that you were in the elite commando unit too."

Uri and Mikhael exchanged a brief glance, one very familiar to me. And there was that slight quiver of discomfort in Mikhael's shoulders that happened every time someone mentioned his service in the unit too specifically or too loudly. As if his military ID had been branded into his flesh with a white-hot iron along with an order for eternal secrecy, even twenty years after his discharge. Seeing Uri also make that movement, which I knew so well from Mikhael, was almost funny. A slight straightening of the back, visible even through the jacket he wore. But his voice gave away nothing. It was as steady and pleasant as it had been before as he said, "You must be cold. Let's go over to your car."

As if to make it clear that Uri's voice commanded not only people but also the forces of nature, we were buffeted by a freezing gust of wind, the kind the Bay Area is famous for. On the Hart lawn, parents and children shivered. The crowd would certainly disperse within a few minutes. It was too cold. Too late.

On the way to our car, Adam spoke excitedly about Uri's class, telling Mikhael details of their last orienteering exercise. *Have you really forgotten the dead boy down the street, my son?* I didn't know whether he was talking so much because he'd forgotten or because he wanted to forget. Maybe he hoped his words would blur what had happened, just as, when he was a child and woke from a nightmare, he'd run to me and yell, "Mommy, tell me a story! Tell me a story!" and wouldn't go back to bed until new images came to cover up the ones that had frightened him awake. I tried to catch Mikhael's eye, to wonder silently with him about the animated way Adam was talking. But Mikhael was fascinated by what he was saying about the class, and his gaze shifted between Adam and Uri.

*They look alike,* I thought, *the stranger and my husband.* But with Mikhael, the sculptor's hand had halted in the middle of its work. His face was pleasant, but something had been nipped in the bud; it was unfinished—he was almost handsome—while with Uri, the hand had persevered for one moment too long. He was too chiseled. Too handsome.

From minute to minute, Uri, Adam, and Mikhael's lively conversation seemed less and less appropriate to the circumstances, a desecration. Perhaps Uri thought so too, because I suddenly noticed him trying, with subtle, almost invisible gestures, to make Adam lower his voice and get into the car, as if he were removing him from the scene. I walked over to the driver's side and opened the door. I hoped Mikhael and Adam would follow me, but they lingered. I sat down and closed the door. They were still standing outside. Though the closed window muffled their voices, I heard Mikhael ask, "The same year as Amos, right?" Uri mumbled something in the secretive tone members of the unit always used, whether they were speaking to each other in the alleyways of Beirut or on suburban streets in Silicon Valley. I put the key into the ignition and pointedly turned on the stereo. The Beatles.

I didn't see the patrol car until it was right beside us. Mikhael, Uri, and Adam apparently did see the red and blue lights approaching, but I was too immersed in the music coming from the stereo to notice them. The police car was crawling along like a funeral hearse. Two white policemen in front, Jamal's mother in the back. The window was open. They evidently wanted to let her get some fresh air after her collapse. And through that open window, the cheery sounds of the Beatles, loud and in your face, drifted over to the woman like an obscene joke.

I quickly lowered the volume. Adam and Mikhael finally got into the car, their eyes accusing. I turned off the stereo completely. Mikhael opened the window and leaned out to Uri. "Where are you parked?"

"Near the house." He didn't have to say which house. We all knew that, from now on, Josh Hart's house would be *that* house. And from now on, Jamal Jones would be *that* boy.

"Get in. We'll drive you to your car."

It was only two hundred yards along the dark street, but Uri nodded, got into the car, and sat next to Adam. His bulk filled the back seat. He smelled strongly of rain. When we reached the Hart house, he signaled for me to stop. "*Yalla*, let's hope for a quiet night." He took his keys out of his jacket pocket, patted Adam on the shoulder, nodded to me and Mikhael in the rearview mirror, and got out.

When he closed the door, the car filled with a strange silence. Adam curled up into his coat. Mikhael rested his head on the foggy window and closed his eyes. I drove thirty feet, braked, and waited for a car in a driveway to pull out so I could continue. I saw the boys begin to leave the yard. A police car was still parked in front of the house. Through the open door, I could see policemen talking in the entryway. And Uri.

I leaned forward, not quite sure what I was seeing. Yes, it was him, still holding his keys. His expression was very somber as he spoke to a short, broad-shouldered policeman, who replied to him with a reverence that surprised me. Uri listened, nodded, and disappeared into the house, the door closing behind him.

## 12

THE NEXT DAY, the sky was remarkably blue. The winds that had blown all night had driven the clouds away. It was one more advantage we had over our neighbor San Francisco: There were no homeless people. No drunks. No fog. Of course, there were people who felt homeless in their own homes, but they slept in double beds, not on street benches. And there were people who drank from bottles opened at noon, but when those bottles were finished, they were hidden in trash bags meant for recycling, not smashed on the street. And of course there were clouds, something gray that hung inside the houses, an actual chill in certain rooms, but not in the sky outside. That sky was as blue as it was in a real estate brochure.

When we first moved here, Mikhael said that the birdsong in the morning reminded him of sounds in the kibbutz. I thought that was terribly funny. I told that to everyone who called from Israel to ask how we were doing, strange conversations that always began enthusiastically and ended limply. Once, people making international calls spoke quickly. The minutes cost so much that they wanted to cram as much as they could into the conversation, the way you cram clothes into a suitcase you have to close right away. There was something liberating about it, as if you could give the conversation your all because you had limited time. But with Skype, you don't stop talking until you have nothing left to say, and you're surprised at how fast that happens. Gradually, people stopped calling. First Tamar, then Rotem, and finally even Noga. They became holiday, birthday, and a-visit-every-other-year friends.

On the morning after the boy, the tulips in the vase were neither more nor less red than they'd been the day before, when Jamal Jones was still alive. That, of course, was as logical as it was monstrous. I decided to call the retirement home to say that I wouldn't be coming in today. I wanted to ask Lucia to put a note on my door so the residents wouldn't be upset when they found it closed. They wake up early, and when they go down to the lobby on Friday morning, they like to see that I'm already there. My salary at the home wasn't great, but I liked the work. Elderly people can't sit in their rooms all day. They need to go out, see other people. I was in charge of organizing cultural activities. I brought lecturers. On Fridays, I taught a class on cinema, which I was now planning to cancel.

"I don't understand," Mikhael said. "Why can't you go in as usual? We're letting Adam skip school and he won't get up until noon, so what is there for you to do here?"

Nonetheless, I called to cancel, but the conversation with Lucia made me change my mind.

"I was going to talk to you about Martha," she said, and added with a nonchalance that sounded insincere to me: "Never mind, I'll get you up to speed next week."

Of all the residents of the home, Martha was the one who never missed a class. She didn't speak much, but her eyes always smiled at me when I came in, and every time I sat down next to her, she ran her hand across my back, a kind of caress.

Before leaving the house, I glanced toward Adam's room one more time in case he opened the door. I tried to wipe away the memory of the look in his eyes when we came home from the Harts' the night before.

When I entered the lobby of the home, I saw that all the residents already knew what had happened at the party. It had been on the news.

"It's so sad when something like that happens to a young person," Armando said evenly. "Old folks like us, it's okay, it's fine, but children shouldn't have to go that way."

"And to think that not too long ago, that young girl was killed in the synagogue," Nyla said as she leaned over the cleaning cart. Martha ran her fingers through her white hair, then ran her hand over my back and asked quietly how I felt. Her fingers reminded me of my grandmother's.

"I think I'm okay," I said. She gently touched my back again and asked if the boy who died at the party was white or Black or Latino.

"*Negro,*" Armando said firmly in Spanish. "I saw his picture on the news." I looked over at Nyla to see if she was offended. She was putting empty plates into the cart and, with a forgiving smile, said to the Puerto Rican man with the walker, "Careful, Armando, if you say *Negro* on the street, a lot of people will get angry at you."

Dwayne laughed out loud. He was the oldest resident, but his energy sometimes made him seem like the youngest.

"It's really a good thing that word isn't used anymore, because since people stopped saying *Negro*, everything has changed for us, right, Nyla? Since they stopped calling your kids *Negroes,* you're not afraid anymore that a white cop will put a bullet in them in the middle of the day!" Dwayne laughed again. He liked to laugh, because he could show his beautiful new teeth, the envy of all the residents. His son had paid for them before boarding a plane to his home in Maryland.

Nyla rolled her eyes. Armando and Dwayne and Chan and Martha were stuck together in this old building, too poor to choose a more luxurious retirement home for themselves. Old age had united them. I believed that was why they were never offended by one another. The true enemy was death, or maybe it was youth: their children, who thought they were better than them.

"Tell me, Leela," Dwayne said, "Lucia said that the dead boy went to school with your son. But what was a Black boy from the east side doing in a school in your neighborhood?"

"They don't have a local high school there," I said, feeling a bit uncomfortable, "so they scattered the kids among our high schools." When Dwayne didn't say anything, I added, "It's good for our children to meet kids from underprivileged neighborhoods."

He regarded me for a moment without replying. Then he said, "Darlin', I wish some retirement homes in your area would take in us elderly folks from underprivileged neighborhoods," and the other residents laughed. "The diapers there must be made of silk."

"Let's go," I said, smiling despite myself. "Time for class." Martha remained sitting in the lobby, staring into space, until Dwayne offered her a hand in a gallant gesture you don't see much these days. A few minutes later, they were all inside. When

I'd planned the weekly meeting, I'd intended to screen *East of Eden* and talk about the plot as a version of the story of Cain and Abel and about how the first murder was motivated by envy, not evil. But now I was assaulted by the sights I had seen yesterday. Dwayne's smiling face turned into the face of the dead boy lying on the living-room floor. The man sitting in front of me had recently celebrated his ninetieth birthday. Jamal Jones would never turn seventeen. I shortened the introduction, hurried to screen the film, and slipped out of the room three minutes after it began.

When I walked into Lucia's office, she understood right away. "Go home," she said gently. She stood up from her desk and walked down the corridor with me, her hand on my shoulder.

"What did you want to tell me about Martha?" I asked.

"It can wait."

"Lucia, what's up?"

She stopped at the door of my office, looked behind her to make sure we were alone, and said, "I'm going to refer her for a neurological evaluation. Recently, the staff has noticed signs of cognitive decline."

I tried to protest. Martha had smooth cheeks that reddened every time she spoke, as if the fact that someone noticed her existence was proof of a hidden crime she had committed. I could imagine how much a meeting with the doctor would humiliate her. The cruel simplicity of the list of questions—"What day is today? Can you touch your nose with your finger? What's the name of this place?"—that would determine whether she'd stay or go.

Lucia shook her head. "We don't have the manpower necessary to guarantee that an old woman suffering from dementia won't end up wandering down the highway. You know that."

Residents diagnosed with cognitive decline were given a

farewell party before being moved to a "memory-care" institution. The most terrible parties were those where the departing residents smiled because they didn't understand that they were being sent away. But Martha wasn't like that. She planted flower seeds in window boxes. She brushed my back with her hand whenever we met. She wouldn't want to go.

"It's only an evaluation," Lucia said. "She might pass it with flying colors."

"I'll go to the appointment with her."

Lucia looked at me skeptically. "I'm not sure that's a good idea, Leela. We have to think about how that would look to the other residents. We don't want them to start being jealous."

"Her family lives far away," I persisted. "There's no one to sit with her in the doctor's office."

"Let me think about it," Lucia mumbled and left. I'd been in America long enough to know when I was being turned down.

I got my bag from my office and locked the door with the plaque that said LILACH SHUSTER, CULTURAL COORDINATOR. If my doctoral adviser could see it, he would definitely ask whether this was the glamorous job I'd moved to America for. The first time Mikhael received an offer to relocate, I'd refused to go. I didn't want to leave everything, especially given the horror stories I'd heard about women wasting away in Silicon Valley after exchanging their desks for kitchen tables. "Those women gave up on themselves," I'd said to Mikhael. "I don't want to live like that."

As I walked toward the exit, I saw Martha at the end of the corridor. She had left in the middle of the film and was taking small steps forward with her walker. Her robe had opened slightly, exposing the wrinkled skin of her thigh. I watched her as she looked around the hall. The troubling thought occurred to me that maybe she didn't know where she was.

When she saw me, her eyes lit up.

"Here you are, Leela. I saw you leave and wanted to see if you were all right."

## 13

**WHEN I GOT** home, Adam was still sleeping. I sat and drank the coffee Mikhael handed me until Kelev's whining became impossible to ignore and I had to take him out for a walk.

He ran quickly, despite his limp. When Adam had found him, the vet said that, given his condition, it might be better to put him to sleep. But Adam insisted, and today Kelev was just as fast as the neighborhood dogs. But it was still a bit strange walking with him. He wasn't the kind of dog kids wanted to pet. That was because of the scars—one across the width of his nose, one under his ear, and an especially ugly one on his back—where the boys had burned him. There was no fur there, and the flesh was pink-purple. It repulsed me a little to touch it, but Adam pet him there all the time. *His scar isn't ugly,* he once told me, *only the people who gave it to him are ugly.*

One day about five years ago, my son came home battered and bruised. I was so alarmed that it took me a minute to realize that he was holding something even more battered and bruised. A small, quivering puppy. Adam had heard the whimpering coming from the woods when he was riding his bike home from school. He saw some boys torturing the puppy and knew that if he didn't do something, they would kill it.

"And you didn't think that they might kill you too?" I'd asked.

"Mom, don't get carried away." His unemotional tone. His lack of concern for his own injuries. His devotion to nursing the puppy back to health despite the vet's initial doubt that it would survive. We paid for all the medical treatment, for a titanium bone to be inserted into Kelev's leg to replace the one that had been crushed. When the puppy woke up after the operation, Adam petted him gently, carefully. I asked what he wanted to name him.

"Kelev," he said, the Hebrew word for "dog."

"That's it, just Kelev?"

He gave me that rare, mischievous smile of his and said, "Why not? The way *Adam* means 'human being' in Hebrew. And like you always say, the fact that someone is born a human being doesn't mean he'll act like one."

They were inseparable, Kelev and Adam. They went every-where together. Once, before Adam had his own laptop, I saw that he had used mine to read a long article about extending the life span of dogs. His interest in the subject never flagged. He asked Mikhael how long dogs lived. He tried to argue, saying that those were probably old statistics, that they definitely lived longer today. I loved seeing my son and the dog together. Kelev's ugliness constantly reminded me of the beauty of what Adam had done.

When I came home after walking Kelev, Adam still hadn't gotten up. "We have to wake him," I said to Mikhael, "so he won't sleep all day and stay up all night."

I went upstairs and knocked lightly. A long minute passed before he opened the door, and when he finally did, it was obvious that he hadn't slept a wink. His face was very pale, his eyes were red, and he was wearing the same clothes he'd worn to the party the day before. He stayed in these clothes the rest of the day. The following morning, just as I began to wonder if we should say something, he finally took a shower and threw the shirt and pants I'd started to despise into the washing machine. During the next few days, he rarely left his room, and we let him stay home from school.

The parents' association had sent out an e-mail with the details of the funeral service, which would be held at the graveside, and they'd attached a poor-quality picture of Jamal taken a few years ago. That morning, after I knocked on Adam's door, opened it, and told him to hurry up, we didn't want to be late, he stared at me from his bed and said, "I don't want to go."

I almost told him that I didn't want to go either, that all morning, I'd been waiting for my temperature to go up, for my throat to start hurting, for anything that would keep me from having to look at Mrs. Jones's face again. Instead, I said, "Adam, it's important for his family that we go." And also because I'd read that it was essential for us so we could begin working through our grief. That's what it said in the first article that came up when I typed *Teenagers coping with a classmate's death*. Perhaps Dr. Angela Harris had paid Google to make her article appear first. I stayed up until three in the morning reading the next four articles as well, like a student cramming for an exam she has to take the next day. *By the time my son gets up, I'll have an answer. When he opens his eyes in a world where a schoolmate can suddenly collapse and die in the middle of a party, I'll be there with scientifically proven coping strategies.*

"I don't want to go."

His left eyebrow trembled slightly, a tic that sometimes appeared when he was upset. I told him it was his choice. Mikhael and I were going in any case. He could eat breakfast and decide whether to join us or not. I went downstairs. I put the cornflakes on the table. I waited.

## 14

**AN HOUR LATER,** Mikhael, Adam, and I parked in the packed Albert Creek Cemetery lot.

Almost everybody from Adam's school was there. When I got out of the car, I was surprised to see a police cruiser parked at the far end of the lot. Adam, who was still in the car, stared at it and didn't make a move to get out.

"Let's go," I said. "It's about to start."

The sophomore boys who'd come to the cemetery were standing together under an enormous plane tree, which was both close enough to and far enough from the gaping hole. They spoke quietly, occasionally glancing at the crowd that had gathered around the coffin itself. But none of them actually moved closer, as if standing near the open grave was limited to adults only, in accordance with some obscure law. Adam glanced at the tree.

"Go be with your friends," Mikhael said. "We'll be here."

I nodded to a few American mothers I knew. One of them said it was just terrible. Another one asked in a whisper, "Do they know what happened yet?"

"It must have been cardiac arrest. In my niece's high school in Miami, the same exact thing happened." Ashley's mother spoke with absolute confidence. She always spoke with absolute confidence, whether you asked her about spaghetti sauce, the date of a math test, or the cause of a death at a party.

Shir Cohen strode across the grass. She nodded hello at me and continued on toward Gali and Hila. Gali was a postdoc at Stanford. Hila was a law professor. Shir had a small start-up. Somehow, the children of all three of them were on the same math track, so they could pretend that it was our children's academic interests that differentiated us, not the faint scorn that women with real jobs felt for women like me.

I turned away and looked for Adam under the plane tree. It took a moment for me to see him. His eyes were still cast down. Unlike the others, he didn't even glance over at the grave. Maybe it was a mistake, bringing him here. Maybe Dr. Angela Harris was wrong and there was no reason to take a sixteen-year-old to see another sixteen-year-old buried. I wanted to go over to him and suggest we go home. This had been a bad idea, we didn't have to stay. I began to walk over to the tree when I suddenly saw a figure in a padded jacket worn over a black, button-down shirt. "What's he doing here?" I said.

Mikhael looked at me questioningly. Then he saw Uri standing on the other side of the gaping, waiting hole. "Maybe he came to support his students."

There were two other boys in Adam's grade who were in Uri's class, Boaz Greenbaum and Yochai Karin. Both were taking more computer science courses than Adam, so they weren't in any of Adam's classes, the kind of thing Mikhael didn't know and I always did. Einat, Boaz's mother, volunteered at the Jewish Community Center and at first had tried to drag me into lighting Hanukkah candles and planting trees in the park on Tu BiShvat. Eventually she gave up on me and asked Moran, Yochai's mother. She already volunteered at the Israeli Community Center but agreed willingly. I saw them not far away, standing next to each other. Einat Greenbaum's arms were crossed over her breasts, and she wore a delicate gold necklace with a small Star of David. But if that's why Uri was here, to support his students as they buried a friend for the first time, why didn't he go over to them? He didn't even glance at them. Instead, he was looking, nearly staring, at us. Mikhael began to feel it too. Not at Yochai or Boaz, or even Adam. At us.

A lot of people dressed in black stood between him and us. The crowd moved like a huge, many-legged tarantula. Some of them were looking around; some were checking their phones; others were whispering. Those small movements, heads rising and lowering and turning, made us and Uri alternately visible and invisible to each other. Nonetheless, there was no mistaking it. And Uri didn't even seem to be trying to hide the fixed way he regarded us. His presence there, the way he examined our faces, felt like an intrusion.

The funeral began, freezing the distance between us and Uri. Standing at the grave were Mrs. Jones, wearing a black dress that looked too small for her, and two boys who supported her, one on either side, and wore black suits. A gold cross lay between her breasts.

"You know about the boys' father?" Einat Greenbaum, who was now standing beside me, whispered, gesturing with her head toward the boys. "He's not here. He converted to Islam after they got married." I wanted to ask how she knew things like that, how some people always know things like that as soon as a tragedy strikes, but right then, the minister began to speak. His speech was well written, but his voice didn't quaver even once, and it was clear that he hadn't really known Jamal.

"Your smile lit up the hallways. You were a ray of light for your friends. I promise you, Jamal, you will always be in our hearts."

One of Jamal's brothers began to cry. The other, younger brother, looked at him in surprise. He was old enough to attend the funeral but not old enough to understand that he would never see his brother again. He looked at the coffin in confusion, as if he expected Jamal to push it open, climb out, and announce that the game of hide-and-seek was over.

The minister continued speaking about the tragedies that were happening to us, one after the other. I stopped listening. I looked at Jamal's mother. Her eyes were totally blank, like those of a figure in a wax museum. But her hands were alive, a strange quirk; her fingers moved back and forth, as if she were playing the piano. I looked at them, mesmerized. Back and forth, gently but also confidently, so you could almost hear the music she was playing. At that moment, I turned around because of a loud sob.

It was Josh Hart, the only boy not at the plane tree, standing close to his parents, who had been called back urgently from their trip.

*Someone died*—that must have been what he told them. *Someone died in our living room.* Josh's complexion was green, maybe because of the shock. Mr. and Mrs. Hart were pale. He was head of a lab at Google. He had a broad forehead and a kind face that seemed tormented now. She kept looking around, her expression apologetic, as if she wanted to say, *But it's not our fault, he just happened to die in our house.* Between them was Josh, who had his father's broad forehead and his mother's blue eyes, and I thought, *This is a family used to having their picture taken at vacation spots, arms around one another, not in the Albert Creek Cemetery, standing over a gaping rectangle.*

Josh sniffed again. His mother opened her bag and handed him a tissue. *I should be beside Adam,* I decided, *the way she's beside her son.* I walked quietly toward the plane tree. So many kids, but where was Adam? I saw Ashley, Boaz, Yochai. The boy I'd seen vomiting the other night. The girls who'd worn miniskirts, standing on the Hart lawn, were now clad in dark formal clothes, their mascara smudged again. A group of boys taller than me were standing at a bench and I tried to look over their shoulders to see if my son was concealed there. But he wasn't there or anywhere else near the tree. I looked over to where Uri had been standing earlier, expecting Adam to be beside him. But Uri was alone, separate from the crowd.

I left the group of teenagers and walked away from the open grave along the narrow cemetery paths. As I moved farther from the funeral, the birdsong and the rustling in the treetops grew louder. If it weren't for the white stone slabs, I might have thought I was taking a walk in a nature reserve or a park. A man in a gray jacket came toward me on the path. Since it was too narrow for both of us, he stepped aside to let me pass, and that's when I saw the police badge attached to his belt. For a moment, I considered asking him what the police were doing there, but although he acknowledged my presence with a brief nod, his eyes were fixed on something straight ahead. I kept walking.

When I turned around again, the man in the jacket had disappeared. There were tall cypresses and oak trees all around, and a low stone wall up ahead. I saw them there, next to the wall. At first I thought it was Adam standing next to another boy with short hair, legs firmly planted. But a moment later, I noticed how thin the legs were inside the tight jeans. How slim the shoulders were. The figure turned its head, and then I had no doubt—under the sloppily cut bangs was the face of a girl, her expression intense. Sculpted lips. A small, impudent chin. Huge eyes.

Instinctively, I stepped back. I didn't want to spoil the moment, and even though I didn't know what was happening between them, it looked very private, almost secret. I had never seen Adam with a girl, and his body language made it clear that the situation was new for him too and he was surprised by it. I walked away quietly. My mind was working fast. She hadn't been at the party, that was certain. I would have remembered that face. Maybe she was in a different class, or a different school. A mother's thoughts, like prying hands feeling an opaque bag to guess what was inside: Oranges? Apples? Hand grenades?

Even though part of me was angry—*It's disrespectful, what he's doing, slipping away from a classmate's funeral to meet with a pretty girl*—part of me, I'm ashamed to admit, was glad. Because although Mikhael and I tried not to make a big deal of it, we were a bit worried, had even asked ourselves if it was really just shyness that held him back. But there he was, standing next to a girl and, yes, it was disrespectful, but it was also understandable. After all, boys don't stop acting like boys just because another boy is being buried in the ground. With that thought, I walked away toward the large lawn, and I would surely have gone back to stand beside Mikhael if a strangled sound had not stopped me.

I turned toward the stone wall again. Adam and the girl were now arguing in hushed, restrained whispers. I was too far away to hear the words, but there was no mistaking the body language, the tone of the conversation that drifted over to me through the rustling treetops. They were arguing. Her hands were on her hips, her legs in a confident, defiant stance. And he stood there with his arms crossed, fists thrust under his armpits, jaw clenched. At that moment, he reminded me so much of his father, because that's exactly how Mikhael stood when we fought. For years, Adam had watched us fight, and now, in a perfect imitation of Mikhael's posture, he shook his head in clear refusal as the girl spoke to him. Fragments of words from the stormy conversation between them reached me, her thin voice rising in a question, his curt voice in reply.

And then, without warning, the crack of her hand slapping his face as hard as she could.

## 15

I DIDN'T ASK Adam about the girl. I didn't ask about Uri's appearance in the cemetery either. The next morning, when I told Mikhael about the slap, he frowned and asked twice, "You're sure?" then thought for a while. He finally said, "Maybe he told a sick joke, the kind boys tell when they have to cope with moments like that, and she didn't think it was funny." After another brief silence, he added, "In any case, it's between them. He doesn't need to know you were there and saw them."

"Right," I said, "but you should have seen how she looked at him."

"How?"

"Like she was afraid of him."

Confused, he asked, "But you said she was the one who slapped him, right?"

"Yes, but that's how she looked at him."

He rubbed his morning stubble, appearing skeptical. "Lilach, you yourself said you were too far away to hear what they were saying, so how can you be so sure?"

"I'm telling you, Mikhael, that girl was afraid of our son."

Adam was still asleep. Mikhael and I were having coffee in the backyard. We'd just finished Skyping with Assi and Mikhael's parents, who called every Saturday night after their family dinner on the kibbutz, which, because of the time difference, was when we were having our morning coffee. They asked, "So how are you?" and we said, "Everything's fine," and Mikhael told them briefly about the boy from Adam's class who had died at a party the week before.

"Another dead kid? What's happening there in America?" Assi's face wasn't visible on-screen, but his voice filled the yard.

"Oh my God," Dina said, "an Israeli?"

"No, not an Israeli," I replied.

"What's his name?"

"Jamal."

"Jamal? What kind of name is Jamal?"

*You answer,* I signaled to Mikhael, *it's your family.*

"It's a Muslim name, Mom."

"You have Arabs in the school?"

"Not Arabs, Mom, Black Americans."

"Black Muslims?"

Mikhael didn't say anything. I think he didn't buy her pretended innocence. He knew that, like a bulimic who shoves a finger down her throat to vomit, his mother shoved a finger down the throat of political correctness until the bile rose.

"It's the drugs," Moshe said. "There in America, it's a national disaster. I saw it on television."

"Actually, here they're saying it was cardiac arrest," I said, without mentioning that my source of information was Mrs. Fuchs, Ashley's mother.

Moshe shook his head. "What are you talking about, a sixteen-year-old with cardiac arrest? It can only be drugs. Poor kid."

Then Dina asked if Adam was okay, and I said yes, that he and the dead boy weren't good friends or anything. "It's so sad," she said, and she stood up to get the dessert. I heard Assi ask, "Is it chocolate?" and Dina shout to Moshe not to touch the cake, he knew it wasn't good for him. Mikhael managed to ask his father when he planned to get an angiogram, and Moshe said, "We'll talk when you come," and when Mikhael persisted, Moshe said, "Okay, bye, son," and turned off Skype.

(Sometimes I wondered if those conversations, which should have brought us closer together, didn't do exactly the opposite. For us, it was daytime, for them night. We were drinking our morning coffee in California, and on the kibbutz, Assi's cigarette glowed in the dark of the balcony like a firefly.)

I poured us more coffee. Once again, it was just me, Mikhael, and the garden, but the air was thick with the sounds of the truncated conversation, and for a moment, I could actually smell Dina's olive pastry. The sounds still hung in the air—the Saturday-night dinner wineglasses clinking, the lemonade made from lemons that Moshe squeezed himself and the fresh mint he added from the plant outside, the political arguments, the rustle of newspaper pages when Dina read the weekly Torah portion—"So we have some substance, not just food!"—and everyone hearing but not really listening. Suddenly it was crowded, very crowded around our small garden table, and perhaps in order to soften the effect of the conversation with the family in Israel, that was when I told Mikhael what I'd seen the day before at the funeral.

I thought he'd be much more surprised about the girl and the slap. I'd hoped that together, we could try to understand what had happened there, near the stone wall in the cemetery. But Mikhael, having decided "It's an argument between kids," was not interested in guessing what it might mean. He closed the subject. Like in the apartment we had shared in Tel Aviv—I would open the window to look out and Mikhael would close it. He had spent his entire life in the air-conditioned temperature of seventy-five degrees. If there was a heat wave outside, or a storm, he knew only a muted version of it.

### 16

*WHERE DID YOU serve in the army? Where are you from in Israel?*

For almost twenty years of get-togethers with Israelis, at some point between the beer at the beginning and the coffee at the end, over plates filled with first-course salads or the crumbs of the three homemade cakes, those questions were asked. Mikhael was a champion at sidestepping them. He did it so well that the people he was talking to never even realized he was doing it. I, unlike him, replied directly and simply, maybe because my answers were direct and simple: I was raised in Haifa and went to the private Reali high school there. I did my military service at Sde Boker, teaching soldiers history in Ben-Gurion's former desert home. My uniforms were tight and my skin was tanned. I had a red bra, and when I wore it, I sometimes let the strap fall to drive the soldiers in the class crazy. They sat on the floor during my prepared lecture, my hips at their eye level, and with pitiful yearning, they stared at the outline of my pussy visible through the folds of my khaki uniform. When my lecture was over, the commanders barked like sheepdogs to get their soldiers back on the buses. As the roar of the motors grew distant, I delighted in the silence around me and walked down the dry riverbed to the Zin Valley. I almost always hiked there alone, but once, I met a geologist from Ben-Gurion University who had come to experience the wilderness.

"That's a rare geological slice," he told me, pointing at a rock I'd peed near two days earlier. "Everything is written in the layers of the rock, from the time of the Tethys Sea to right now. You can see exactly when each thing happened."

He was nice, that geologist from Ben-Gurion. Even weeks later, when I walked down to the valley, I hoped to see him and maybe sleep with him there, on the sand. I liked that he could pinpoint exactly when each thing happened because I never could. And when I met Mikhael, I sometimes toyed with the idea of taking him to the university, introducing him to that geologist and his colleagues in the department, and saying to them, *Okay, date this specimen for me. What happened first? What caused what?*

Mikhael himself didn't know. Until we met, he had never considered opening his adoption file. "What's the point?" he'd said when I asked during our trip to the Paran Desert. Then he pointed to the riverbed in front of us and said, "We don't have to pick up every stone in this wadi."

I knew that when he arrived on the kibbutz at the age of three, he was a foster child. Six months later, Dina and Moshe made an official request to adopt him. "He was such a sweetie," Dina gushed during my first visit to the kibbutz, "such an intelligent, considerate child." She told me that, in the years before Mikhael, they had fostered quite a few children, and the emotional boundaries had always been clear, but Mikhael crossed them quickly, all the way to their hearts. After a few months with him, they were certain he would stay with them forever.

I listened to her on that first visit and thought there was not one story here, but two. One they told and talked about, the Shuster family legend, and another, written in invisible ink, about a child who knew very well, with the intuition of abandoned children and dogs, what he had to do. And so, intelligent and considerate, never insolent or angry, he forged his path to them.

Maybe it all began there. Or maybe he had always been like that—I don't know. But there's no doubt that Dina and Moshe never regretted their decision. Mikhael was one of the most popular children on the kibbutz. When Assi was born a year later, he watched over him like an angel. Because in every community there are children who are a source of worry and others who are a source of pride, and Mikhael belonged to the second group.

When we decided to get married, I asked him again about his adoption file. "Soon we'll want children. It's important for the genetic tests." A week later, he called me at work in the middle of the day. "She's from Libya. He's from Romania." That evening he told me more. He spoke as if he were reading from a newspaper he'd found on the train and was just browsing before he put it back down on the seat. "She cleaned houses. She was sixteen when it happened." About his father, he said almost nothing. You don't have to pick up every stone in the wadi.

I think he wiped out his curiosity about himself. Maybe that was the first thing he ever did. But he had enormous, infectious curiosity about everything else, which made him a perfect student from the time he was a child. And he loved grades. How he loved getting back exams and seeing, next to his name, numerical proof that everything was fine. He never boasted. That's why he was so well liked, and when he came up against trigonometry in high school and then calculus in college, he didn't get angry or go crazy. And he certainly didn't give up. He simply began again. Again and again and again, until he succeeded.

I loved him terribly, but sometimes I wanted to take his face in my hands and tell him that he didn't always have to be so intelligent and considerate. And sometimes, deep down, I hoped for both of us that he would fail once, because otherwise, how would he learn that, even then, I would stay with him?

Mikhael loved programming. I think that, more than anything, he loved to predict all the possible moves in advance. When he had a good idea, he would open his laptop and type furiously, forgetting himself. I remember one breakfast: Adam in his high chair; Mikhael sitting at the table surrounded by half-eaten pieces of banana and apple, totally focused on typing. (Years later, when the detectives and police officers asked him, "How did you not see?," accusing him of being part of it—if I could have shown them what he'd been like then, sitting in front of the computer, totally absorbed, they might have understood.) And another time, after I'd put Adam to bed, I slipped into his study, silently took off my dress and underwear, stood behind him, my hips close to the back of his neck, and waited an entire minute until he finally realized I was standing there naked and turned his head away from the screen and touched me.

There were other people equally devoted to their work, Israelis who swore they would earn their first million by the time they were thirty-five. But with Mikhael, it had nothing to do with money. He loved the brilliant elegance of a good algorithm. The money came only later. But as soon as it did, it was hard to ignore. As a child, Mikhael had striven for good grades. He wanted all the teachers on the kibbutz to confirm publicly that Moshe and Dina had made the right decision. When college ended, the grades were over. The clear, numerical proof of his value was over. Then came the Silicon Valley money. And once again, at any given moment, he could check how much he was worth.

Mikhael didn't boast now either. He never talked about money. He never rolled up his sleeve to reveal, purely by accident, his sixty-thousand-dollar watch. Every month, he wrote a check, put it in an envelope, and sent it to Dina and Moshe, along with new photos of Adam.

Even when everyone began sending pictures by e-mail, then by WhatsApp, he continued to put several pictures into the envelope with the check. After his first promotion, he asked my permission and began sending another envelope every month. He didn't put pictures of Adam in that envelope, only a check. His familiar, straight handwriting slanted slightly when he wrote her name on the envelope. I tried to imagine her opening it, shocked by the amount. I always pictured her old. But in fact, she was only sixteen years older than Mikhael.

## 17

THAT SATURDAY, ADAM almost didn't come out of his room. I didn't bother him. As they say here, I gave him some space. On Sunday, I assumed he would sleep until noon again. But at nine, he was already up and freshly showered. He said he was going to the self-defense class. When he came back, it was late afternoon. I had just finished frying schnitzels. He stood at the kitchen counter and devoured them standing up, straight from the large tray covered with paper towels.

"Why don't you take a plate and sit down," I said.

"They taste better when you're standing up."

I asked if he was planning to eat dessert standing up too, and he smiled and finally sat down at the table.

"What's for dessert?"

"Mascarpone cream."

We used to make meals together, a hobby we'd shared from the time Adam was seven, when Mikhael and I began watching the Israeli version of *MasterChef* with him to keep up his Hebrew. After every episode, Adam asked if he and I could cook the dishes we saw on the program. On Fridays, we would write out the dinner menu together—I'd hoped it would improve his written Hebrew—and Mikhael would pretend he was eating at our restaurant. Long after Adam and I stopped preparing menus, we still cooked together.

Over the years, it happened less frequently—once a week, once every two weeks, once a month. I kept showing him pictures of dishes, tried to tempt him with sophisticated kitchen gadgets—a chestnut cutter was one of the latest—but about two years ago, Adam lost interest. Still, when I told him about the dessert I'd made, I saw a flash of appreciation in his eyes.

"Have you done your homework for tomorrow?" That was the last thing I wanted to ask him, but I didn't think I knew how to ask anything else.

"We didn't have any."

"But Ms. Gray always gives homework, doesn't she?"

"She didn't give any this time because of Jamal's funeral."

That was the first time he'd mentioned the name since the night of the party. I pounced on the opportunity. "Did you know him well?"

A shrug. A moment later, he put his spoon down and walked toward the stairs.

"But what about the mascarpone?"

"I'm not hungry."

"Were you friends, Adam?"

He stopped on the third step. For a moment, I thought I saw his back shake. "No," he said. "Absolutely not."

The next morning, I drove him to school. Before we left, he spent such a long time in the bathroom that I was beginning to lose patience, but when he finally emerged and I saw the razor cuts on his neck, I suddenly felt sorry for him. There were some boys in his grade who could grow beards, whose body hair was in harmony with their faces and gaits. But he still wasn't comfortable inside this new body of his. The black hair sprouting from his pores was still sparse, and perhaps that was why it was so confusing.

"Come on," I said gently, "we're late."

On the way, we listened to Kendrick Lamar. When we came to the traffic light before the school, I looked at his face. "You have a bit of blood here, on your neck."

We drove into the parking lot three minutes before his first class. "If you run, you can still make it." He opened the door, ready to jump out. (How much I loved to see him run. His limbs, which looked a bit clumsy when he walked, would move in perfect coordination.) But instead of getting out, he suddenly froze in his seat.

The police detective's face was plain and undefined, almost as if something had passed over his features and removed everything that might change it from forgettable to memorable. I couldn't decide if he was the same man who had walked past me in the cemetery three days earlier. His partner, a woman, wore her blond hair pulled into a tight, thin braid that swung every time she moved her head. They were leaning against their patrol car and examining the students entering the schoolyard. They didn't look tense, and that was good, because long years in America had taught me to worry, first of all, about school shootings. Every once in a while, some teenager would walk into a classroom with an automatic weapon and spray the teacher and students with bullets. We had drills for such situations here, the way Israelis in Israel have drills for rocket attacks.

I leaned forward over the steering wheel to see if there was a crowd in the schoolyard. Everything looked normal. "I think I saw that policeman at Jamal's funeral," I said. Adam didn't answer. When I turned to look at him, I was surprised to see how pale he was.

"Mom," he said without glancing at me, "I don't feel well."

His eyebrow was twitching again, the way it had on the morning of the funeral.

"Does something hurt?" I asked.

"My stomach. I think I'd better go home with you."

I agreed right away. He really looked terrible. I shifted into reverse and drove out of the parking lot. The male police detective watched us.

In the afternoon, Ashley's mother called to ask if I'd heard. Her voice blazed at me through the phone. "It wasn't cardiac arrest that killed him, it was drugs!"

"How do you know?"

"They did an autopsy. They usually do that when someone so young dies suddenly." She didn't say anything for a moment. Maybe she expected me to speak.

"Wow," I said, and that was fuel enough for her to continue.

"The police went to the school today and questioned everyone who was at the party. They sat with Josh Hart and went over the names of the kids who were invited. Ms. Gray told me that later in the week, they'll talk to all the students in their grade."

All the students in the grade except Adam, who stayed home for the next few days with a case of diarrhea. He was sick until the weekend, and on Sunday, he suddenly came out of his room and said he was going to his self-defense class.

"But you're still not well," I said.

"I feel better."

I was ready to argue with him about it. Remarks like *You have to let your body recover* were on the tip of my tongue, but Mikhael whispered, "He's been buried in the house for a week already, it'll be good for him to go out a little." And to Adam he said, "Just don't knock yourself out too much. Come on, I'll drive you."

That night, Uri called Mikhael. I was beside him when the call came in. We were sitting in the living room, waiting for the final credits of one episode to turn into the opening credits of another episode. When his phone rang, Mikhael glanced at the display, saw it was an unknown number, and frowned. No one from work would dare call him on Sunday, and no one from Israel called when it was so early there. I was the one in charge of our few social contacts here.

For a brief moment, he let the phone vibrate between us on the couch like a scared black mouse. Then he picked it up and answered. His eyebrows rose slightly when he heard who it was, but the warmth of the Hebrew he spoke gave no hint of his surprise. "Uri, how are you?" (Mikhael used his friendly tone, the one his employees liked so much because it made you feel that he was utterly devoted to you and only you.) "Yes, of course you can come by. Can you just tell me what it's about?" I couldn't hear the reply. Mikhael got up from the couch with the phone in his hand and went into the kitchen to continue the conversation.

I followed him. I watched as he moved the fridge magnets around, something he did when he was upset. "Great, I understand. So, tomorrow at nine. Bye."

When the conversation ended, he remained standing in front

of the fridge for a moment, staring at the door as if he'd forgotten why he was there, what he'd wanted to take out.

"What did he want?" I asked.

"To talk. He's coming over tomorrow morning at nine."

I looked at him, aghast. Mikhael was never late to the office, certainly not on Mondays. He left the house every morning at eight sharp no matter what. (In that respect, he was more American than the Americans. He didn't want any of the staffers who worked for him to think that the company had opened a Mediterranean vacation spot here. Once, when it still annoyed me that I was the only one who drove Adam to school, he tried to explain it to me. "It's like what they teach you in boot camp, that the soldiers in a unit can only pattern themselves after their commanding officer. If I start cutting corners and coming in late, everyone under my command will cut corners and come in late.")

"Why didn't you tell Uri to come over now, or tomorrow evening?" I asked. Mikhael remained standing in front of the fridge, moving the magnets around, rearranging them according to some inner logic known only to him.

"Because he suggested tomorrow morning."

"Okay, but for him, it doesn't matter. Einat Greenbaum told me that his company went out of business, so he's between jobs now. Who knows if he has any commitments besides that class he teaches."

Mikhael placed a star-shaped magnet next to a magnet of the three of us smiling. "He's coming tomorrow morning, Leelo." And then he added, "I think he'd rather come when Adam isn't here."

## 18

IN THE MIDDLE of the night, my mother called. The ringing, which cut off my dream, alarmed me.

"I have to hear from Dina that someone in my grandson's class died from drugs?"

"Mom, you woke us up."

"Sorry. I thought you were still watching TV." And she immediately unleashed a torrent of questions: Who and when and why, and why didn't I, and since we're already talking, when were we planning to come for a visit? At the end of the conversation, she told me to give Adam a big kiss and a hug. A moment later, when I thought she'd hung up, she added, "And a hug for you and Mikhael."

Seventeen years earlier, when I told her we were temporarily relocating, my mother refused to believe it was only a career choice. She asked if Mikhael had other reasons. "Mikhael?" I asked. "Other reasons?" I thought she'd talk about Ofri, but she didn't say a word about what had happened. Instead, she averted her eyes—something she almost never did; my mother was a look-you-right-in-the-eye person—and said she thought that maybe Mikhael's time in the army had...messed with his head? My mother never ended her sentences with a question mark—usually, a platoon of exclamation marks followed her to every discussion she had in the office and every conversation she had at home—and those two things, her averted eyes and the question mark at the end of her sentence, made it clear how much my announcement of our move had shaken her.

"*He* doesn't need people," my mother had said then. "*He'll* be fine. But you, Lali, you love having people around. How will you manage there with all those Americans?"

"Americans are people," I said.

"True, but a different kind of people."

"You're exaggerating," I told her. "And besides, I'll have Mikhael."

"So Mikhael will have a serious job and you'll have Mikhael?"

"Yes. He'll work in tech and I'll work at loving him."

She sighed and said that loving a man was a demanding, exhausting, and unsatisfying job. And working at loving a child was even dangerous. "Of course, you have to love them. But that shouldn't be your job. Because then your heart becomes hostage to someone else. And that's not a job, sweetheart, that's imprisonment."

On the day of our flight, my mother didn't come to say goodbye. She had an important meeting at the office. And maybe, I thought later, maybe she wanted to believe our move was because of Mikhael so she wouldn't have to think it was because of me, that I was the one who had decided to put an ocean between us.

"You fired me," she said to me after Adam was born a year later. "You simply fired me from being a grandmother."

I told her that wasn't true, because, really, if anyone had been fired, it certainly wasn't meant to be her. Leaving Israel had been like closing down an unprofitable factory, leaving behind locked doors and unemployed, helpless grandparents.

"Just don't tell me later that it's safer to raise children there," my mother said with a sigh on the phone now. "Things like that, with drugs, don't happen in Israel."

She hung up. She hadn't expected a response. That argument had been settled a long time ago. After Ofri, I'd felt as if I were seeing things as clearly as possible: We have a chance to rescue our son from the insanity of life in Israel, the most insane thing about which is that everyone is sure it's sane.

## 19

URI WAS LATE. Mikhael glanced at his watch at least five times. I wondered if it was because he was anxious to see Uri or because he hated being late to the office. It was different with my job. As it was, Lucia always complained with a smile that I invested too much time in the residents, much more than the hours I was paid for, so no one in the home raised an eyebrow when I called that morning to say I wouldn't be there until noon.

Finally, at ten after nine, a knock. Uri didn't ring the bell the way everyone else did. He rapped his fingers on the front door, a sound you immediately felt was unique to him. Mikhael hurried to open it. When they stood opposite each other in the doorway, the similarity between them struck me again. Both tall, broad-shouldered. But Mikhael was wearing a light but elegant jacket, the kind men wear in offices here, while Uri had on jeans and a flannel shirt.

"Coffee?" I asked. I made black coffee for the three of us and put some tahini cookies on a plate.

Uri and Mikhael waited for me in the living room. I heard them talking about the self-defense class, what they'd done yesterday, what they'd do next week. I knew Mikhael was waiting for me to come in so we could start, and finish, and he could go to work. When I finally walked into the living room, he didn't even wait for me to sit down before saying, "So, what's happening with Adam?"

Uri's eyes shifted back and forth between Mikhael and me. He leaned forward to pick up his coffee. The tiny cup I'd bought the last time we were in Chinatown disappeared almost completely in his large palm. "The truth is that he worried me a little yesterday." He spoke slowly, weighing every word. "At the end of the class, he looked . . . strange."

"He was sick last week," Mikhael said. "Maybe he's having trouble dealing with what happened—first the stabbing in the synagogue and now a boy from his school dying in front of him."

Uri put his cup down carefully. The delicate way he placed it on the tray only emphasized how easily he could break it with his fingers if he wanted to. "What do you know about the relationship between Adam and Jamal?"

The question surprised me. Uri's green eyes fixed on my face as he waited for an answer I didn't have. "They took biology together," I said hesitantly. "I don't think they were really friends because I'd never heard his name before."

"I actually had heard his name." Uri inhaled, and his exhale came out as a small sigh. "Adam didn't tell you that he was being bullied in school?" The question mark at the end of the sentence flickered for a moment before dying out, because the three of us knew that the answer was no. He hadn't told us.

"A group of boys there have been bullying him. He didn't talk about it much, but from what I gathered, Jamal was the worst of them."

"What do you mean, bullying him?" I asked in a shaky voice. "What exactly do you mean?"

He hesitated for a moment before answering. When he did, he spoke as carefully as he'd placed his cup on the tray earlier. "Pushing. Kicking. Maybe more than that, I don't know exactly." I held my stomach as if I'd been kicked myself. Uri kept speaking, but to Mikhael now. "But I think that what hurt him most was the verbal abuse, which happened online. Jamal made up songs about Adam and posted them on the class chat group, shaming him."

After a moment of silence, Mikhael asked Uri if he knew how long it had been going on. He said he didn't. His fingers played with the empty cup. *Maybe I should offer him more coffee,* I thought, but I couldn't get a word out. My tongue was heavy and numb in my mouth.

The boy whose picture I'd seen in the papers, the boy with the kind face and alert eyes, that boy had abused my son. I picked Adam up from school every day. He opened the car door and got in, his face expressionless, replied, "Okay," to my "How was your day?," and we both let David Bowie speak instead of speaking to each other. And that entire time, my son was being hurt and I didn't know it. His stooped walk, his introversion, all the things I saw as signs of a dreary adolescence were actually signs of something much darker.

Uri leaned forward and took a cookie. But he didn't eat it. He just held it and said, "Three weeks ago, I taught them a maneuver to prepare them for advanced hand-to-hand-combat training. I asked each one of them to imagine the person he most wanted to defeat, someone he wanted to kill. It helps them focus." Mikhael nodded. He knew those exercises from his time in the army. I said nothing. "Many of them imagined Hitler. Half the boys said later that they were thinking of Paul Reed." Uri leaned back, the cookie still in his hand. "A week after that, I spoke to each one of them privately. I asked Adam who he'd been thinking about during that exercise. Who he'd wanted to kill. He told me what Jamal was doing to him at school."

I felt an annoying itch on my thigh where the Harts' rosebush thorns had torn my skin through my pants, leaving me with scratches that still hadn't healed.

"I couldn't decide whether to tell you," Uri said. "I didn't want to betray Adam's confidence. That was a few days before the party." After a beat, he added, "I think he feels guilty. All those times he'd hoped Jamal would die, and all of a sudden, it really happened. Something like that can confuse a boy."

Mikhael nodded. "There was a work supervisor on the kibbutz who always yelled at me. I spent hours imagining how I'd get back at him. When my mother told me one day that he'd died of a stroke, I was sure the police were on their way to arrest me. As if I'd done it to him."

"Exactly," Uri replied, his eyes flashing, as if Mikhael's agreement had ignited something inside him. "That's why I thought we should talk." He added that over the next few days we should keep an eye on Adam, to see if he was processing what had happened. In general, the three of us should be in touch more, keep our fingers on the pulse.

"Yes, definitely," Mikhael said and looked at me. I said, "Yes, of course," and looked at Uri, who was now eating the cookie he'd been holding.

"Wow," he said. "This is great."

A few minutes later, both of them were gone. Before leaving, Mikhael gave me a perfunctory goodbye kiss on the cheek, the kiss of a man leaving for his office, and Uri gave me a strong, reassuring handshake. They were about to close the door when I suddenly asked, "Uri, that's all, right?"

I didn't know why I asked, but I knew I had to, the way that, earlier, when my thigh had started itching, I knew I had to scratch it right away or I'd go crazy. My need to ask now was just as powerful, because I was suddenly afraid to spend time alone in the house with my thoughts, and Uri, who must have picked up on my fear, said, "Yes," in the soothing tone of the Pied Piper of Hamelin, a tone you can't and don't want to resist.

Only long after they'd left, hours later, did the impression of his voice fade, replaced by another impression that grew stronger: of the lit-up entrance of the Harts' home, Uri disappearing inside, and the door closing behind him.

## 20

WHEN ADAM WAS a baby, we used to bend over his crib and try to decide who he looked like. The color of his eyes was mine, but the oval shape was Mikhael's. The same with his hair—deep black like Mikhael's, large curls like mine. So we studied each one of his features, measuring and classifying—his chin (Mikhael's), his lips (mine), and so on, his fingers, shoulders, ears. When he got a bit older, we moved from his physical features to his mental attributes, asking which one of us he resembled, to which one of us he belonged. Perhaps Mikhael was afraid that, just as high cholesterol was inherited, I would pass on to Adam my grandfather's concentration camp, the gene that has *like sheep to the slaughter* written on it.

When he was four, Adam began to come home from preschool with bite marks on his hands. From a distance, you might have thought they were scrapes, but close up, there was no mistaking it—another child's baby teeth had sunk into his flesh, leaving small, pinkish craters. When we spoke to the teacher, she assured me that they treated such things very seriously. It was a difficult age, she said. *The children feel so much but still don't have the words to express everything, so they bite and hit, and of course we react firmly and teach them that that's wrong.* We listened and thanked her for her time, but the minute the door closed behind us, Mikhael said to Adam in Hebrew, "You have to learn to hit back."

We had a terrible fight afterward. Not in front of Adam—when he was that age, we were careful not to let him see us argue. But he felt our tension on the drive home and sang children's songs to make us laugh. We tried to keep our anger caged, but we knew it was still visible. At night we let it loose.

"You want your child to be a thug who no one will go near?" I said.

"You want a wimpy kid that everyone in preschool walks all over?" he countered.

We said many things to each other before the argument ended the way most of our arguments did: I burst into tears, alarming

Mikhael, who was quick to console me. Later, when he slipped out of me, dripping onto my thigh, he said quietly, "I just can't bear to see him like that, covered with other kids' teeth marks."

"Would you rather see him biting them?" I asked.

Surprised, he turned to me and said, "No question about it. Don't tell me you'd rather see him being the victim?"

"You're asking me which I'd prefer, a child who hurts others or a child who is hurt by others. But maybe those aren't the only two options."

Mikhael sat up in bed. His naked body shone in the blue light that came through the window. He was beautiful.

"Leelo, those are exactly the only two options—there are those who do things to others and those who have things done to them. Children recognize it in an instant, and the truth is that adults do too, they just don't talk about it."

After we showered and went back to bed, he hugged me and said quietly, "I won't raise a victim. Being a thug isn't great, but you can educate a thug. Being a victim is for life."

Mikhael had received confirmation of the fear he'd lived with since Adam was born. That's what made him angry when he spoke to the teacher; that's what he refused to allow. He, Mikhael Shuster from the elite commando unit, would not raise a victim. The teacher hadn't understood that. Her name was Cynthia Wagner. But I understood it. And that's why, the next day, I registered Adam at a different preschool and hoped that would be the end of it.

But for Mikhael, it was only the beginning. He signed Adam up for a preschooler judo class. He bought him the white outfit and tried to get him excited about it. Adam went once and didn't want to go back. Mikhael left work early to take him there. He told him he'd buy him ice cream after every session. But Adam's aversion to the class only deepened. He sat on the sidelines while the other kids were on the mat. After two more sessions, the teacher himself said that maybe it would be better to wait a year or two.

Mikhael didn't give up. He watched a few instructional videos on YouTube, and one Sunday morning, he asked Adam to come and play with him in the backyard. He didn't mention the word *judo*. He said only that he wanted to practice a "physical game" with him; that's what he called it. But although Adam couldn't wait for Mikhael to come home from work and read him a story or help him build something with his blocks, Adam didn't want to go into the backyard with him. The more Mikhael insisted, the more Adam entrenched himself on the living-room couch and refused to move. Perhaps he'd seen that underlying his father's enthusiastic invitation was a deeper wish to change him. Mikhael turned it into a matter of principle. He, who always let Adam choose what game they'd play, ordered him in a quiet voice to come out to the backyard right now. At some point, Adam began to cry hysterically and refused to calm down. On that day, the boundaries between them were redrawn. They both honored them.

## 21

ON THE EVENING after our talk with Uri, we tiptoed around Adam. I didn't ask him to clear the table. We didn't remind him to take out Kelev. We didn't ask when he would finally straighten up his room. When we finished eating, Mikhael said, "I have something for you," and put a small, wrapped box on the table. Adam looked at it in surprise and reached out hesitantly. It was an Equinox watch, the kind you see in magazine ads: virile-looking men climbing mountains, or deep-sea diving, or parachuting out of planes, always wearing the watch. It was obvious to me that it cost a fortune and I think it was obvious to Adam too, and perhaps that's why he didn't put it on but only stared at it the way you'd stare at a magnificent, dangerous animal. "There's a compass on top," Mikhael said, and he moved his finger affectionately around the silver circle. "It'll help you with the orienteering Uri's planning for you."

"Uri?" Adam said, his eyes suddenly shining, and only then did I realize how dull his expression had been until that moment. "How do you know what Uri's planning?"

Smiling, Mikhael handed Adam the watch. "We talked a little today. The truth is we decided to go for a beer tonight."

I was surprised. Mikhael was not the kind of guy who goes out for a beer. Although he knew how to deal with people during the day, he almost always preferred to spend his evenings at home. He went, but only reluctantly, to the get-togethers I organized with the few couples we saw socially. Of course, he was charming during the evening—attentive, interested, amusing. But when we got into the car, he would take my hand and kiss between my fingers and say, "Bottom line, wouldn't staying in bed together have been more fun?"

Adam put on the watch and went out with Kelev. Mikhael mumbled something about an e-mail he had to send and went upstairs to his study. Through the window, I watched Adam walk down the street, earbuds in place. Thin. Short. He seemed to be slightly more stooped than usual. I cleared the dishes off the table and I'd begun washing them when a gust of cold wind blew through the window. *It's freezing outside,* I said to myself. *How did you let him go out like that?* I called his phone, but he didn't answer. I grabbed his coat and hurried after him.

Ashbury Lane was particularly dark. Two streetlights were broken and I could see only by the faint light of television screens glowing from the houses. I saw Adam trudging along at the end of the block, no sign of Kelev. *He took him out without his leash again,* I thought. *If Kelev dashes into the street or gets into a fight with another dog, Adam will run to help him and get hurt. He always forgets himself at those moments, forgets that he has a body.*

I hurried after him when he turned onto a side street. He'd definitely be surprised that I'd run after him like that. *Why'd you come all this way?* he'd ask. *I didn't want you to catch cold. I didn't want you to be sad. Did they really bully you, Adam? Since morning, I haven't been able to stop thinking about it. The idea that they hurt you. When you were younger, you used to come running to show me every little injury, demanding a kiss for every scratch and scrape. I would make a ceremony of pasting smiley-face Band-Aids on them and always add "a kiss to make it better," the secret incantation of mothers everywhere. And now I can't remember when you stopped showing me your injuries.*

The side street led to Sycamore Avenue. Adam turned onto it, and so did I, holding his coat out in front of me. I walked faster and reached out to touch the familiar, beloved back.

The boy turned around, took out his earbuds, and looked at me in surprise. "Yes?"

"I'm sorry, I thought you . . . " I didn't say, *I thought you were my son.* I stopped in time. The boy put his earbuds back in. I remained standing there and watched him walk away.

All the way back on Ashbury Lane, I thought about how I would tell Adam and Mikhael about it when I walked in. Maybe Adam would laugh at me, say, *Mom, you're completely cuckoo.* When I reached our street, he was walking toward me with Kelev on his leash.

"Mom?"

"You forgot your coat and I didn't want you to catch cold." He took the coat but didn't put it on. There was no point. We were already at our door.

At the table, we drank tea, and Adam rubbed Kelev's stomach

and stroked the scar on his back. Adam was the only one Kelev allowed to touch him that way.

"How do you feel?" I ventured.

"Fine."

"Did they talk about Jamal at school?"

"Yes, in homeroom. We wrote letters to his mother."

I recalled the face of the woman in the Hart living room the moment she realized who was lying behind the couch. "What did you write?"

"I didn't. I said I had a headache and asked to leave."

All the possible questions, and you had to choose one and hope it was the right one. "Why did you say that?"

He stopped petting Kelev. For a moment, the dog's head rose from the carpet, then fell back again. "Because I had a headache. I still do. I'm going up to my room."

He stood up and went. Kelev trailed after him up the stairs. I could have followed him to his room and asked more questions about Jamal, given him the chance to tell me what had happened in school. But I could guess what his face would look like when I came in. I was worried that he'd realize Uri had spoken to us and be angry.

I remained sitting at the kitchen table. I heard Mikhael getting ready to go out. He walked lightly down the stairs.

"Where were you before?"

"I went out to bring Adam his coat." After a brief pause, I added, "I got him mixed up with another boy walking down the street."

He smiled and kissed my head. "Don't wait up for me."

I waited up for him. I watched TV in the living room. Then I went upstairs to tell Adam to go to bed, that it was late already. He was sitting at his laptop. The blinds were closed. The smell of semen coming from the toilet paper in the wastebasket stunned me with its potency, but I knew the drill. We both knew how to pretend I didn't smell it.

"Go to sleep, Adam. You have school tomorrow."

It was after midnight when Mikhael finally got home. He came into our bedroom reeking of cigarette smoke and beer.

"How was it?"

"Finally, someone I can talk to."

I sat up in bed and asked how that joint outing had originated. Mikhael took off his shoes and replied that he and Uri had spoken briefly in the morning when they left the house. They'd clicked right away and decided to go out for a beer that night. I assumed that wasn't the only reason, that Mikhael had needed to talk more with the man who could help him understand what was happening with Adam.

"And how was it?" I asked again.

He said it was fun, just a little awkward at the end.

"Why awkward?"

"He's a programmer," Mikhael replied as he took off his shirt. "One of the guys who founded Orion, the company that folded not too long ago."

"And he asked you for a job?"

"Not in so many words. But I think he hoped I would offer to pass on his CV." Mikhael pressed a button and the electric blinds began to drop. I asked if he planned to recommend Uri to Berman. He shook his head. "I can't recommend someone I've never worked with. It's unprofessional."

He brushed his teeth in a few rapid strokes and lay down beside me. His large hand rested on my shoulder. The thing we had been trying to avoid all day lay on the mattress between us.

"Can you believe that Adam was bullied in school and didn't tell us?" I said.

Mikhael sighed in the darkness. "It's driving me crazy. All the way to work, I kept imagining it, and I wanted to beat the hell out of those kids with my bare hands. Later I read up on school bullying, and it turns out that it's very common."

I could picture him gathering data, searching for statistics he could rely on. "What kind of parents are we?" I whispered, partly to him, partly to myself, letting the tears I'd held back since the morning finally flow. "How could we not see it?"

He took my hand. "You can't see what he chooses not to show you. He didn't want us to know. It embarrassed him."

"But why should talking to us embarrass him?"

"For the same reason it embarrasses him to shower in front of you or be near you in the bathroom. Because he's not a child anymore."

I sat up. "We have to find a way to talk to him about this."

"That's what I thought at first," Mikhael said, "but I've decided that it's better to wait. In any case, the circumstances have changed—the kid who led the bullying is dead."

"But you don't think Adam needs to process what happened?"

"Maybe he doesn't want to process what happened," Mikhael said. "Maybe he just wants to forget."

Mikhael straightened the blanket over his body. The house breathed quietly. "I think you should recommend Uri to Berman," I said a moment later. "His concern for Adam, the effort he made to come here this morning—that says something about his character."

Mikhael didn't say anything. I didn't know if he'd already fallen asleep, but I added, "Think about it this way: programmers are a dime a dozen, but good people are rare."

## 22

MY MOTHER CALLED in the middle of the late news. It surprised me. In Israel it was nine thirty in the morning, and I knew she was usually with clients at that hour.

"Tell me, is Adam okay?"

"I think so," I said. "Why?"

"He called me yesterday. He never calls me."

"What did he want?"

"To talk about Paul Reed. He asked how we determine temporary insanity in the case of a murder. I think that attack in the synagogue is still bothering him."

The past few days, there had been a media frenzy about the possibility that Paul Reed would be found unfit to stand trial, but it had never entered my mind that Adam was interested in the case.

"We had a whole conversation about it," my mother said. "Like the good old days of Judge Ruthie."

Judge Ruthie was a game my mother invented when Adam was little to get him to talk to her on the phone. Before that, she used to read him books in Hebrew, choosing the most popular titles from the library in Haifa, the ones that might catch the attention of her grandson in America. Her voice filled our living room, dripping with forced enthusiasm. When he got a bit older, she asked us to let her know what he was reading so she could buy copies for herself. They managed to get through three Harry Potter books in English, reading aloud to each other. I think it was exhausting for her too. I had to promise to give him candy if he would go to the computer. And then she invented Judge Ruthie: Every week Adam was supposed to ask her about a particular legal issue, and she would pass judgment. I was sure it wouldn't work.

The first case was about whether a child had the right to raise a snake at home even if his parents were against it. Judge Ruthie ruled in favor of the child. She also ruled in favor of raising Adam's allowance. I thought I'd go mad, but Mikhael was amused.

"She finally found a way to be part of his life," he said. "A nonpoisonous snake and a two-dollar raise seems like a fair price to me."

Later on, they shifted to more theoretical issues. One evening, they spoke for almost half an hour about the judgment of Solomon. "You have a brilliant child," she told me that night. "You were like that at his age." I didn't know if that was entirely a compliment.

One day Adam announced that he was tired of playing Judge Ruthie. My mother said that was fine, she had a lot of work at the office anyway, and those conversations took a little too much of her time. But a few weeks later, she called and asked if we wanted to send him to her for Christmas break. Actually, she'd already bought a plane ticket. "Don't be angry, Lali. I can still cancel it and get a full refund. It's just that the price was too low to pass up."

Adam didn't want to go. She asked us to try to convince him. I said I'd rather not pressure him. Two weeks was really a long time.

"What are you talking about? As if your father and I didn't go away for two weeks when you were his age." They had traveled a lot even before that. A year after my sister, Nitzan, was born, when I was three, they took a three-week tour of Europe, and the pictures from that trip decorated the walls of the house in Haifa to this day.

"Times are different, Mom. Today a child doesn't leave his parents for such a long time."

She exchanged the ticket from California to Israel for a ticket from Israel to California. When I went to pick her up at the airport, she was upset. The gift she'd bought for Adam was so large, they hadn't let her board with it. I suggested we go to the mall in the evening, but she insisted on going right away. I think she was afraid to meet Adam with empty hands. He hadn't seen her for a year, and children don't hug strangers.

For two weeks, at night, my mother closed herself in her room and spoke on the phone to her office. In the afternoons, she encouraged me to go out and do whatever I wanted—she'd stay with Adam. There was nothing I wanted to do, but I didn't tell her that. When the two weeks were over, we drove her to the airport. Adam hugged her tightly. Maybe it was the sum of all the hugs he hadn't wanted to give the first few days she was here. She hugged him back, but she was looking at me. Perhaps she wanted to be sure I really understood what I'd taken from her.

My sister's call came twenty-six hours after we'd said goodbye at the airport. "Mom fell," she said. "She came back from the airport and tripped getting into the shower."

Nitzan said Mom had broken her hip, and for the next few weeks, she would need a lot of help at home. I got on a plane. I went back to sleeping in my old room. I left the door open so I could hear her if she wanted to go to the bathroom at night, but she insisted on going by herself. We fought about that almost every day. We fought about other things as well.

There are people who know how to be sick. They sink into their illness as if it were a comfortable bed and let you take care of them. My father had been like that. During his last days, he lay in bed like a large, tranquil baby. But my mother didn't know how to be sick. She was embarrassed when I had to help her in the shower, and no matter how much I denied it, it embarrassed me too. Her pink, exposed skin overwhelmed me. Her flesh was too palpable.

When I was a child and we used to bathe together, her nakedness and mine were taken for granted. But now we were both repelled by the renewed encounter. After my first week there, she said I should go home to Adam.

"You said it yourself—a boy his age shouldn't be away from his mother for so long."

"But what about you?" I asked.

"Nitzan will come in the evenings, and I arranged for my cleaner to come in the mornings to cook and straighten up."

We argued only a little about that. On the night of my flight, we hugged goodbye.

"Thank you for coming," she said. "That was so generous and unexpected of you." And again, I didn't know if that was entirely a compliment.

## 23

THE FIRST GRAFFITI appeared the next day at the entrance to the high school. The day before, the math-tutoring class had ended at seven in the evening, and the custodian locked the school doors after the last student left. At six in the morning, the words were already sprayed on the wall opposite the parking lot. You couldn't miss them: THE JEW KILLED HIM.

The school security guard, who arrived before everyone, called to inform the principal, who got in touch with the custodian and asked him to paint over the graffiti before the first students appeared. But it quickly became apparent that there was more graffiti. The words were sprayed over and over again on the inside of the wall around the school. In a corner of the gym, a Star of David dripping blood had been painted next to Jamal's name. The cafeteria had been vandalized as well. The principal decided there'd be no classes that day, but by the time the announcement was made, it was too late. Most parents and children were on their way to school or had reached the entrance. All of us stood in front of the words that had been sprayed on the wall in bright red. We didn't know what we were supposed to do. The school maintenance crew was hurrying through the crowd with ladders and pails and would have begun painting if an announcement hadn't suddenly blared out of the loudspeaker asking everyone to leave the schoolyard immediately.

The metallic voice was alarming, and we hurried, almost ran, away. Uniformed policemen with dogs passed by us and went inside to search the school. One of the fathers near me, a broad-shouldered American, asked when graffiti had become such a big deal, and Shir Cohen, looking worried, replied, "After Paul Reed, no one wants to take any chances. Who knows whether the person who did this also planted a bomb in the school?"

My heart was pounding. I looked around. All the parents and children had quickly covered the distance to the street, crossed to the other side, and stood on the grass. We all had the same expression on our faces, something between an embarrassed smile and panic, because at any moment, there could be an announcement saying that nothing had happened, it was just some disgusting graffiti. Or a terrible thing could happen, an explosion that would destroy the place, and both scenarios seemed possible and impossible to the same degree.

From where I stood, near Stacy Hart and Einat Greenbaum, you could see the words that had been sprayed on the wall opposite the parking lot. Ashley's mother took pictures with her phone.

"Just to think that someone is capable of linking the tragedy of Jamal Jones and antisemitic accusations." A few American mothers came over to me and Einat to say that it was really terrible. "Our hearts are with you," they said, and I knew they meant, *Our hearts are with the Jews.*

I was nauseated. I wanted to go home. I looked for Adam. He and Boaz had joined a few boys from a lower grade who were also in Uri's class and were sitting on a bench not far from us, talking quietly among themselves. Adam sat beside them, his left hand circling his right forearm in a grip that seemed too tight to me, almost convulsive.

Meanwhile, more and more parents had arrived and crowded together on the grass, shocked and protective, because even though such things happen in America, they didn't happen in this America. Apart from condemnations, I also heard speculation: Maybe it wasn't done by a single person but by a marginal group like the one Paul Reed belonged to. Maybe some boys in the school who didn't fully understand the significance of what they wrote had decided to be provocative.

The police search lasted almost an hour. The sun appeared from between the clouds and warmed the crowd that had gathered. The terror thawed slowly. The police finally came out and announced that we could go in. The school was clean.

Parents began to escort their children toward the front doors. Einat and I looked at each other hesitantly.

"I don't know if we should leave them in school today," I said, hoping she'd reassure me, tell me I was overreacting, but Einat was even more stressed than I was.

"After what happened in the synagogue, we can't allow ourselves to be complacent."

I called Mikhael and asked what he thought. "Of course Adam stays in school," he said. "If the police say the place is clean, there's no reason to panic." I still wasn't sure, but to my surprise, Adam was the one who decided. His face was gray and pale, but he insisted on going inside with his friends. I left him there and drove home, my heart hammering.


## 24


LATE THAT AFTERNOON, I called the principal and asked her to think about increasing security. I knew some other Israeli parents had requested the same thing from the administration and I assumed that the American Jews would do so as well.

There were only twenty Jewish children in a high school of four hundred students.

When I drove Adam to school the next day, I was glad to see a police car at the entrance. But as soon as we drove into the parking lot, the police detective with the braid headed in our direction as if she had been waiting for us. Adam got out of the car.

"Hi," she said, "you're Adam Shuster, right?"

Adam said yes.

I turned off the engine and joined them. "Hi, I'm Lilach, Adam's mother."

She shook my hand. She had a strong, confidence-inspiring grip, the kind people dream about acquiring, but either you're born with it or you're not.

"I'm Detective Natasha Peterson," she said and turned to Adam again. "I talked to your friends from biology last week, but somehow we didn't manage to meet."

"He was sick," I told her, "diarrhea and stomach pains, probably a virus."

"I'm glad you've recovered," she said to him, then turned to me. "I won't keep you, Mrs. Shuster. You must be in a hurry to get to work," and before I could tell her that I wasn't in a hurry to get anywhere, she spoke to Adam again.

"I'd like to talk to you today, if that's okay with you. This morning, I'm meeting with all the kids who weren't here last week."

"Okay, but can we not do it during my math class?" Adam asked. "We have an exam next week."

She smiled. She had a broad smile that I didn't completely believe. "If only my kids would take school as seriously as you. Let's meet at twelve in the guidance counselor's office."

Everything was arranged. Detective Peterson said goodbye and walked over to another car that had just pulled into the lot. Adam headed to the school entrance and disappeared into the yard. As I was about to get into my car, Ashley's mother came up to me, dying to hear how my son was reacting to the whole graffiti thing. When she finished being horrified by the antisemitism, she moved on to talk about poor Mrs. Jones.

Her eyes were suddenly alert. Tragedies affected her the way caffeine affected other people. "They're from the east side of town, you know." The words *so sad* and *terrible* came out of her mouth with solemnity—she set them afloat on the lawn as if they were ships sent out to capture listeners on other continents. "They moved here from Chicago after a nasty divorce," she added. "She works at the InterContinental on Nob Hill, as a maid." Ashley's mother sighed again and repeated the word *terrible*, and this time the sigh managed to capture another listener who came over to us, asked the same questions, sighed, and then wondered about summer-camp registration.

Shir Cohen, standing a distance from us, rolled her eyes at me. I went over to her. She gestured with her head toward Ashley's mother and said in Hebrew, "That woman produces rumors at the same rate Nike produces shoes."

I burst out laughing. That was a mistake—Ashley's mother turned around and saw Shir. "Mazel tov!" she shouted at her. "Martin told me. You must be so happy." Shir's face reddened slightly. She looked embarrassed. For a moment, I thought she might be pregnant.

"Going public is the scariest stage," Ashley's mother continued. "I remember how it was with Martin, all that suspense."

Shir responded with a polite nod and whispered to me in Hebrew, "Let's get out of here fast."

"So your company went public yesterday?" I asked as I walked her to her car.

"Yes," she said. "It feels like I haven't slept for a year." She had dark bags under her eyes, but the eyes themselves were shiny and full of life.

"And now do you have to go to the office or are you allowed to make up for lost sleep?"

"The truth is that what I want to do most is sit in a café. I don't remember the last time I went to a café in the middle of the morning. Are you busy now?"

We drove into the city and went to a nice place facing the water. She was smart and funny and maybe a bit lonely. Her husband, Zach, was an American Jew. They'd met at Berkeley. She told me that for the past few years, they had worked separately on their own projects, but at the moment, Zach's start-up was not in good shape, and even though he insisted it didn't change anything between them, she thought it had.

We wandered around the shops in Union Square. Shir wanted to buy presents for the kids—"Compensation for my not being at home"—and I decided to buy something for Adam. She told me that her youngest had been a bit anxious since the attack on the synagogue. She'd had nightmares that had only recently stopped, and now, with the graffiti thing, Shir was afraid they would come back. After that, she was silent, and when I didn't say anything, she asked, "How are things with you guys?"

I told her that Adam hadn't been anxious after the attack, but he was preoccupied with Paul Reed. For a moment, a desire to tell her more flickered inside me, but Adam had kept Jamal's bullying to himself—he hadn't wanted to talk about it even to us—and I felt that telling Shir would be a breach of trust, the trust he didn't have in me. Instead, I told her a bit about Uri's self-defense class. She'd heard about it, even tried to sign up Daniel, her oldest. "But he'd rather practice his saxophone. That's the only thing he's doing at the moment."

When we finished buying gifts for the kids, Shir said that now we were allowed to look for something for ourselves. We went into a Uniqlo store to try on clothes and found adjoining dressing rooms. When she came out, I zipped her up, surprised at her suntanned, supple back. She was a head taller than me, and fuller, and I thought she was checking me out the same way. I was once a very good-looking woman. Not as striking as my mother, who had turned heads throughout my childhood with her huge eyes and regal cheekbones, but definitely attractive. I wondered what Shir thought of my looks.

We came out of Huntington Park on the California Street side. I suggested we go somewhere to raise a toast to the IPO. When Shir hesitated, I said, "Why not? You earned it."

She smiled and said, *"Yalla,"* then added quietly that yesterday, after the stock issue, she'd been sure Zach would be waiting with a bottle of wine, but when she came home, he was already asleep. I suggested that we go to Mark Hopkins.

"The InterContinental?" she asked in surprise. "That's a tourist place."

"That's how I want to feel, like a tourist."

It really was a tourist place. You felt it the minute you walked in. Not only because of the ridiculous prices and the extravagant menu, but also because people took pictures of their martinis instead of drinking them. A family chattering away in Hebrew was sitting not far from us in the bar. Shir whispered, "Those Israelis, they're everywhere," then ordered an exorbitantly priced mimosa. "So why here, of all places? Are they paying you a commission?"

I laughed. Sitting on one of the Mark Hopkins fancy leather armchairs, mimosa in hand, I couldn't completely explain to myself why here of all places. Nonetheless, when I thought about the route I'd chosen for us that morning, a collection of seemingly random turns, I realized that they added up to a purpose.

Half an hour later, Shir said she had to leave—she still had to go to the office that day. I hugged her goodbye, then ordered another mimosa and drank it to the last drop. I paid the check and, filled with liquid courage, walked confidently back into the lobby and straight to the elevators that take you to the guest rooms. I was sure someone would ask me something and I'd have to stammer out an answer, but no one did. I was a white woman wearing expensive clothes, and it was only logical that I'd go to the bank of elevators, walk into one, and ride it to the top floor.

I went down one floor at a time, getting off at each one and checking the corridor. I said to myself, *Lilach, this is absurd, it's crazy. Step into the elevator and get the hell out of here.* But every time I entered the elevator, instead of the lobby button, I pressed the number of the floor below me.

When the door opened on the fourth floor, I saw her: Jamal's mother pushing a cart of bed linens down the corridor, her back to me. She stopped, swiped a key card, and opened the door to a room. When she went inside, I glanced at her profile to check again what I was already sure of. A beautiful, strong-featured face.

She disappeared into the room and I remained standing in the corridor. The door in front of me opened and a slender maid came out and hurried to her service cart, which was standing near the elevator. I pretended to be talking on my phone, and she went back into the room carrying shampoo bottles, leaving the door wide open. I knew that farther down the corridor, in another room, another woman was doing the same thing: changing towels, fluffing pillows, emptying trash cans. There was a sudden loud noise that went quickly quieter. A moment passed before I understood—the slender maid had turned on the TV. *"Bebé, baila conmigo,"* I heard her singing along with the singer on the screen.

I walked quietly toward the room Jamal's mother had gone into and stood outside it. Something in me hoped to hear music here as well, but the silence was absolute, so thick that for a moment, I wondered if she could have left the room without my seeing her.

Through the half-open door, I saw the mess left by the guests who had slept there. Towels tossed on the floor, candy wrappers from the minibar scattered on the large bed, bedclothes jumbled. And there she sat, Jamal's mother, in her gray maid's uniform. She wasn't fluffing pillows. She wasn't changing sheets. She wasn't dusting furniture. She was simply sitting on the king-size bed, staring at the wall in front of her, almost motionless, limbs as heavy as the mahogany nightstand near the window. Her fingers were the only things moving in the room. On her lap, they seemed to be moving of their own accord, lightly, gently.

Suddenly, I was frightened—of the silence in the room, of the song being played on her lap, of myself. I turned around and walked quickly to the elevator and didn't look back even once. Because Lot's wife, when she looked back, turned into a pillar of salt. And I didn't have time to turn into salt. I had a dinner to cook and a son, a living son, to pick up.

On the way home from school, I asked Adam about his meeting with Detective Peterson. "It was a short conversation," he said without looking at me, his left hand squeezing his right forearm. The detective had asked him if he'd seen Jamal take anything during the party at Josh's house and if he knew of kids at school who sold drugs. "And she also wanted to know if I took drugs." I was surprised by the last question. My nerdy son was so far from the image of the drug-addicted, problem teenager that I was sure Detective Peterson couldn't have thought otherwise.

"Did you ever see anyone with drugs in school?" I asked.

"I don't think anyone is stupid enough to bring drugs into school," Adam said.

"And after school, at parties?"

He looked out the window. "I'm not usually invited to parties."


## 25

I WENT TO her house. There was a smell of burned rubber on the street, and the wail of a fire engine came from the adjoining alley. I looked around. There was no smoke in the sky, only that irritating smell. I'd reached the address I had looked up online. The slip of paper in my hand was damp from the touch of my fingers, but even though I already knew the address by heart, I didn't throw it away. I crumpled it over and over again in my hand. I stopped in front of number 124. The door was very white. I waited for my hand to be steady enough to knock. Jamal's mother opened the door. She was wearing an enormous bathrobe that was dark blue, almost black.

"Hi, I'm Lilach Shuster. We spoke on the phone."

She looked down at my face, examining it from her greater height, and frowned as if she were trying to remember something. *You've already seen me once,* I wanted to tell her, *on the Hart lawn when they led you to the police car and Adam and I were right next to you, and maybe a bit earlier, through the living-room window, when they took you to identify the body. Some people say that at such moments, everything becomes fuzzy, but there are others who claim they remember every detail. Perhaps that's how you remember it, not only his tortured face on the carpet, but also my face at the window, peering inside.*

Mrs. Jones took a few steps back and opened the door wider. "Hello, Leela, come in. Please call me Annabella."

The living room was small and clean. On a table was a large picture of Jamal in a gold frame.

"You're the first parent to come this week," she said as she placed a tray with a bottle of Coke, two glasses, and a plate of cookies on the table. "His friends come almost every day, and I keep the Oreos and Coke for them, but the parents are busy working." She sat down in a wicker armchair that squeaked lightly whenever she moved. She gestured for me to sit in a similar armchair, bolstered by a pillow.

His friends, I thought—they must be the other boys who bullied Adam. Since Uri's visit, I'd been thinking about them quite a bit. The longer Adam kept silent, the wilder my guesses became. I imagined them loud and violent, an amalgam of the mean kids in all the American high-school movies I'd ever seen. I had a hard time making the image I had of teenage bullies jibe with the image of boys who came every day to console Annabella Jones, drink Coke, and eat cookies. And it was even harder to make that image jibe with the bright, open face of the boy in the gold frame.

"You're whose mother?" Annabella looked at me, waiting.

"I'm Adam's mother," I said quickly. "I'm sorry, I should have told you that before."

"Adam," she said, frowning. "I don't think he was here." She immediately added, "But Jamal had so many friends, maybe I forgot. When we first moved here from Chicago, I was afraid he'd have a tough time in high school. You know, most of the kids...come from a different background. But he fit in beautifully. Only now do I understand how happy he was here. The kids don't stop coming."

A brief, embarrassing thought buzzed in my head: *If Adam died, how many kids would come to our house?*

"You want to see his room?"

I said yes, I did. But when I stood up, my legs shook. I stole a glance at the picture. The boy in the frame looked out the open window at the street where the smell of burned rubber hung heavy in the air.

Jamal's mother disappeared into the dark, narrow hallway. I walked behind her. The walls gave off a moldy smell that lemon spray had tried in vain to mask. We walked past two closed doors (the doors of living children, children who would get angry at you if you opened them without permission) to a room with a wide-open door.

We walked in. I was surprised by the mess. The clutter in the room was the complete antithesis of the order of the rest of the house.

"This is how he left it," she said in a vaguely apologetic tone. "This is how he left it and now I can't bring myself to clean it." And without warning, she burst into tears. Not the aristocratic, controlled tears she had wept at the funeral, but wild sobbing that aroused my pity and frightened me in equal measure. I hugged her, trying to encircle her large, shaking body with my arms. At first it was a reserved, American hug, but it turned into a strong, unrestrained hug that surprised me and seemed to soothe her. I don't know how long the hug lasted, but finally her sobs subsided and the apologies began. "I'm sorry, I don't know what got into me. I'm sorry."

I thought she would take us out of Jamal's bedroom and back to the living room. I longed to return to the wicker armchairs and the cookies, even to Jamal looking out the window, but Annabella sat down on the bed, trying to catch her breath, looking around as if she were there for the first time. I hesitated, but she gestured for me to sit down beside her. The mattress sank slightly under the weight of our bodies. This was where he had slept.

"I have to get his things together," she said, "give them to charity. The police gave me the clothes he was wearing at the party, but I had no idea what to do with them. I just put them down there, on the chair."

I said nothing. She smiled to herself. "He dressed like a peacock. I told him he shouldn't waste money on name brands and all that junk, but he never listened to me."

I looked around the room, so different from Adam's and at the same time so similar. Puma sweatshirts on the chair, identical to those I'd put into the washing machine that morning. A messy pile of jeans in the corner. And, just like in Adam's room, a laptop on a desk opposite the window.

"What a good boy he was. You know, he insisted on going to the supermarket for me so I wouldn't have to carry heavy bags later, because he knew that after work, my legs hurt and it's hard for me to stand. Did you ever see such a good boy?"

"No," I said honestly. Adam never offered to go to the supermarket for me.

"Now the police say he did drugs. Does that make sense to you, that a boy who looks after his mother like that would do drugs?" Her eyes were two pools of black despair.

"Maybe he just wanted to experiment," I said gently. "They say all kids that age try something at some time."

She shook her head resolutely. "Not my boy. I told the police, 'Jamal knows what that shit does to your body. He saw enough of it when we were in Chicago. He doesn't touch that garbage.' I asked his friends. They swear he never took anything the night of the party. I told the police that."

"And what did the police say?"

Annabella Jones smiled bitterly. "Excuse me for saying it, Leela, but when a Black kid from the east side dies of an overdose, not too many eyebrows get raised. The police are investigating just because they want to know if there are any other kids in the high school who use or deal. But I'm telling you, my boy wouldn't touch drugs of his own free will. Someone put something in his drink."

"Why would anyone do that?" I asked.

"Maybe they thought it was funny," Annabella said. "Maybe they wanted to get him in trouble. Who knows what kind of reasons kids have at that crazy age."

She tried to catch my eye, but I dropped my gaze. "The police don't believe me," she said quietly, "and neither do you. But I'm telling you, if they don't investigate it, I'll hire a private detective to find out what happened. I have money! I have savings!"

I was surprised how quickly she had switched from speaking quietly to shouting. I think she was surprised as well. Annabella bent forward and buried her head in her hands. After a moment's hesitation, I put a hand on her shoulder. She took a deep breath. We heard the wail of a siren in the distance.

We stayed that way for a while, sitting side by side on Jamal's bed, Annabella with her face in her hands, and I with my hand on her shoulder, my gaze wandering along the walls. Suddenly, words in Arabic shouted out at me from a poster on the far wall. I leaned forward to make sure I was seeing correctly.

I thought I'd forgotten the Arabic I'd learned in high school long ago. But here, in the darkness of the room, the words glittering on the wall came back to me. *There is no God but Allah and Muhammad is His messenger.* Next to them was a large black-and-white picture of Louis Farrakhan. Now she saw what I was looking at, and her expression darkened.

"It was his father and his older brother, in Chicago, that got him into that crap about the Nation of Islam. You have no idea how many times we fought about it—Farrakhan, of all people!—but it gave him pride. You know how it is with kids. He was the representative of the Nation of Islam in the Bay Area high schools. He talked about it all the time. Like a peacock he was. You understand?"

Yes. I understood. It was one thing to be the son of a maid at the InterContinental who lived on the east side, and something else to be the representative of the Nation of Islam in the Bay Area high schools. And we both laughed silently at that title, *representative*, the laughter of mothers who know how much their children love those kinds of titles and positions—Vegan Club representative, student council president, Scout troop leader.

I looked at the poster of Farrakhan and wondered if anyone had told Annabella about the graffiti on the school walls. Maybe someone had sent her a picture of the bleeding Star of David next to Jamal's name. I asked myself whether Jamal's friends, his brothers, maybe the person who sprayed the graffiti at the high school had sat in this room, on the dead boy's bed.

Annabella straightened the sheet with her right hand. Her left hand remained on her lap. I looked at her, her long fingers moving in that familiar, hypnotic rhythm. *What are you playing?* I wanted to ask her, and I might even have done so if I hadn't noticed them there, in a corner of the room.

The shoes were identical to Adam's, just as I'd thought at the party. Adam kept losing things. He'd go out with a new schoolbag and forget it in the schoolyard. He'd take off his shoes at the pool and come home barefoot. I started writing his name on his things, the way they did in the laundry on Mikhael's kibbutz. I wrote ADAM in permanent red marker on the tag of his jacket, on the inside of his schoolbag, on the soles of his shoes. He was furious with me for marking up the shoes—"Nobody does that, Mom," he said—but after that, he really did lose fewer things. But a month ago, he lost those very expensive Jordans at the pool.

And here they were, those shoes. The word ADAM stood out in

black on the red soles. Suddenly I understood what I should have understood earlier. He hadn't lost anything. He hadn't forgotten anything. His things were taken from him.

From minute to minute, more and more of Jamal's things looked familiar to me. The sweatshirt with the yellow stripe that Adam said he had torn was lying, half inside out, on the back of a chair, as if it had been taken off in a hurry, and I recognized my handwriting inside the collar. An Indiana Jones hat that we bought at Disneyland was hanging on a hook over the bed. My pulse pounded in my temples. My eyes darted around the room like mice. Nike sweatshirts. A Gap jacket.

I wanted to run over to the closet and go through the jackets, shirts, and pants. *What did you snatch from my son? What did you take from him?* A burning sense of humiliation filled my throat. I left the room, trembling, refused everything Annabella offered ("You sure you don't want any Coke? Maybe coffee?" "No, thanks, I'm in a hurry"), stormed through the living room (a package of Oreos, Jamal smiling in the gold frame), and went out the door, leaving behind the lemon-scented moldy walls, Jamal's room full of Adam's things. Like a person fleeing a haunted house, I ran straight into the street, where the smell of burning rubber still hung in the air.

## 26

I DIDN'T WANT to drive home. I was afraid of the moment I'd have to stand in front of the washing machine I'd turned on that morning and take out Adam's shirts, wondering how many items of my son's clothing were now sitting in Annabella Jones's washing machine. I called Mikhael from the car and asked if he could leave work and meet me. It was just after noon and I knew that he'd just started his lunch break, that he was surrounded by programmers and would soon be eating his organic food and drinking his fruit smoothie as he had done since the company announced a nutritional revolution in the executive dining room.

"Just for an hour," I said. I thought I heard Berman's baritone and Jane's ringing laughter in the background. I pictured him pressing the phone to his ear, making sure that my alarmed voice stayed between us and didn't slip out and zip across the stainless-steel trays to other ears.

We went to a small Mexican restaurant not far from his office. Mikhael gave me a worried look and asked if everything was all right.

"I went to visit Jamal's mother," I said, "a sort of condolence call."

"That was nice of you," he said, somewhat surprised, "very nice of you." And before he could tell me again how nice it was of me, I told him what I'd seen in Jamal's room.

A waitress came to our table with menus but retreated when she saw Mikhael's face.

"Are you sure?"

"Absolutely sure, Mikhael. Adam's name was there. I saw it."

He paused for a moment, then said quietly, "You'll be angry with me, but I'm almost glad that boy's dead. I know it's a terrible thing to say, and of course I'm not really glad, but the thought of him doing things like that to Adam makes my blood boil."

"I don't understand why he didn't tell us anything," I said, my voice cracking. "You really think he was too embarrassed? I'm his mother. Why would he be embarrassed to tell me?"

"I'm not surprised he didn't tell us. He didn't want us to see him humiliated. And I'm still not sure we should bring it up with him. The bullying is over. He doesn't want to share it with us, and I think we should respect that."

His voice was calm and cool, and something about that coolness made me angry. "How am I supposed to go on as usual when I know he's capable of suffering like that and not saying a word to us? Can you let him go to school tomorrow when you know that if they hit him and steal from him, he won't tell us?"

"It's terrible," Mikhael agreed, "but I'm not sure we have any other choice."

He waited for me to calm down and signaled to the waitress. He ordered drinks. Neither of us felt like eating. When they were delivered, I didn't touch my club soda. I watched him sip his juice. I told him about the Nation of Islam poster on Jamal's wall. I said that maybe Jamal's bullying had something to do with the fact that Adam was Jewish. Mikhael shook his head firmly. "Kids hit each other all the time. That doesn't make it a pogrom."

"Do you really think Jamal could just as easily have hit another Black kid?"

Mikhael thought for a moment. "If they don't harass you for being Jewish, then they'll hassle you for wearing glasses or being fat or because your father looks weird."

I'd hoped he would say that. When we decided to stay in the States, I told my mother that I wanted to raise Adam in a place that had no wars. Now I was afraid we'd been wrong. We'd thought we were protecting Adam from the Israeli insanity, but maybe we were actually exposing him to a different kind of insanity.

Mikhael finished his juice and glanced at his vibrating phone. His secretary Jane's name flashed on the screen. In the office they were clearly wondering where he'd disappeared to. He turned the phone over on the table and put his hand on mine.

"Look, Leelo, what happened to Adam is terrible, but it'll pass. Most kids get hit at school at some point." He'd said *most kids,* not *all kids,* and we both knew it was because he, Mikhael, the strong kid on the kibbutz, had never been hit.

"And I'll tell you something else—I'm pretty much convinced it won't happen to him now that he's in Uri's class. It's giving him the confidence to beat off shits like that." He asked the waitress for the check and said quietly, "It doesn't matter if you live in Kiryat Ono or California, every high school in the world has a kid who smacks other kids around and does drugs."

"Annabella Jones is positive that Jamal didn't take drugs," I said.

Mikhael raised an eyebrow. "In the newspaper it says that he accidentally overdosed on a homemade drug."

I told him that Jamal's mother planned to go to the police or hire a private investigator. "She's sure that someone at the party put something in his drink as a joke or to hurt him."

There was something else. Something I couldn't make myself say. A vague, formless thought. A sentence that still had no words, only white spaces and a question mark at the end. We paid the check. When we stood up to go, I said I'd walk Mikhael to his office. Only when I was walking beside him, when he wasn't facing me and my eyes wandered over the passing cars, did I say, "That boy bullied Adam so badly that our son wished him dead. And now his mother says that someone put something in his drink."

Mikhael stopped. He wasn't the type to raise his voice, certainly not in the street. And he didn't raise his voice now, but I sensed that he'd never been as close to it as he was at that moment.

"I don't believe you can even think such a thing. Listen, that Jamal wasn't a victim. He bullied our son, he did drugs, and in the end, he got fucked up by an overdose. His mother should take responsibility for the way she raised her son instead of accusing the whole world and its brother."

## 27

I WALKED MIKHAEL to the door of his office. He gave me a half-hearted kiss goodbye, and I went slowly back to my car. I still didn't want to go home to an empty house, so I decided to go to the retirement home, even though I wasn't scheduled to work there today.

I looked for Martha in the lobby. Most of the residents were in the lounge watching sports on TV. When I asked Armando if he'd seen her, he was so focused on the football players moving around on the field that he didn't reply at first. "They're in the garden," he finally said impatiently. Although he was more than forty years older than me, for a moment I felt like a mother interrupting her son watching TV.

*The garden* was nothing more than a no-man's-land of nearly bare earth surrounded by buildings. In winter, the rain graced the soil with a covering of green, but in the summer, the grass turned into yellow weeds the superintendent was quick to mow. I spotted Martha sitting on a chair in the far corner. When I opened the glass door, I heard the sound of a man's voice, and only then did I see that another person was sitting opposite Martha, his back to me.

"Monday. Today is Monday." Today was Thursday, but Dwayne repeated, "When the doctor asks you, 'What day is today?' tell him, 'Monday.' Okay, darlin'? Repeat after me: 'Monday.'"

I was surprised. Lucia hadn't told me that the cognitive evaluation was scheduled for the following week.

"Now," Dwayne said, "when the doctor asks you about bathing, what do you tell him?"

Martha stared into space. The sparse grass in the garden moved in the wind. "Darlin', what did we say about bathing?" Dwayne turned around and saw me, then turned back. "Martha, darlin', what's the answer about bathing?"

"That I have no problem bathing by myself," Martha said after what seemed like an eternity, then added, "Hello, Leela. It's nice to see you. Today is Monday."

Her white hair was braided in a coil on the back of her head. Two typed pages lay on Dwayne's lap, a list of standard cognitive-evaluation questions. Lucia would be furious if she saw it. Dwayne folded the pages and put them in his coat pocket. Another gust of wind shook the grass as well as Martha's thin shoulders. "Maybe we should go inside," I said.

The sound of cheering came from the lounge. "I think I'll go see the game," Martha said when we were standing in the lobby, and she suggested we join her. I refused politely. I knew that the minute I sat down in front of the TV, images from Jamal's room would come back to haunt me. In the time that had passed since I left Annabella Jones's home, her claims had shriveled, seeming bizarre and far-fetched now, but my burning humiliation at seeing the things stolen from Adam had continued to grow.

Dwayne helped Martha walk into the lounge, then turned to me and said, with the broad smile his son had bought for him before taking off for Maryland, "Leela, darlin', don't be insulted, but you look awful."

I wasn't insulted. I really did look awful.

"You want some tea?" Dwayne asked. "Ever since my daughter married that crazy shaman of hers, she's been sending me all kinds of healthy teas." Dwayne's daughter was a yoga teacher, a woman of more than sixty. She visited once every six months, yelled at the medical staff for neglecting her father, and disappeared.

I didn't want tea, but I didn't want to offend him either. Dwayne wasn't one of the residents who usually invited you to their rooms. Despite his broad smile and openness, he always maintained a safe distance from the staff. I knew that when he was young, he'd been wrongfully sent to prison. He was later acquitted and given a small sum as compensation. I assumed that the experience had left him deeply suspicious of authority figures. I thanked him for his offer and followed him.

His room was small and plain, like the others. His grandchildren smiled at me from silver frames that hung on the walls: adorable little girls with ponytails, older girls with cornrows. And a boy who looked so much like Dwayne that I was momentarily stunned.

"So what happened?" he asked as he filled the kettle. His movements were smooth and limber, as if someone had forgotten to tell his body that its owner had just turned ninety. I told him about finding Adam's things in Jamal's room. While I listed the lost items I'd seen in the room, his large fingers reached out for the jar of tea leaves but hesitated for a moment before opening it. When I was through, he said gravely, "That's not the kind of thing a mother wants to know." The cups he took out of the cupboard clinked slightly in his hands, but I knew him well enough not to offer help.

"Bullying stinks," he said. "It's a shame that your son had to go through that."

"And what upsets me the most is that he didn't tell me anything. Not a single word about what he was going through."

"I'm not surprised," Dwayne said. "My wife always said that being a mother or a father means always being anxious. You know, I once thought that the greatest mystery in our lives was our parents. Today I think that maybe the greatest mystery in people's lives is their children."

He handed me the tea, which was exceptionally bitter, and took out a tangerine that he peeled with practiced hands.

"I think that maybe they bullied him because he's Jewish," I said. "My husband doesn't agree with me."

"You know what Chan told me once when I asked him about

China? He said there wasn't any racism in China at all. Because there are no Black people there." Dwayne burst out laughing and handed me half the tangerine. "I grew up in Oakland," he said. "My friends and I mostly beat on the Mexicans who lived down the block, and sometimes we beat on each other. When I was a kid, there were no Jews in my neighborhood, but if there had been, I'm pretty sure I would have beat on them too."

"I thought bullying stinks," I said.

"So does shitting," he said, "but everyone still does it."

The tangerine I was holding left a damp orange stain on the tips of my fingers. I couldn't eat it. And I didn't know where to put it.

"I'm sorry," he said suddenly. "I apologize if I offended you. But that's how we're built, Leela, all of us."

I thanked him for the tea. I couldn't stay another minute. I needed to see my son.

## 28

I DROVE STRAIGHT there without hesitating for a second. But when I finally parked, right in front of the rec center, I didn't hurry to get out of the car. The building was large and run-down, and a few bicycles were locked up by the door. I recognized Adam's. I felt a flash of pain when I thought of the skateboard we'd bought Adam at the beginning of the year, the one that had disappeared a short time afterward. It broke, he'd told us; he'd slammed it into a railing and it broke. At the time, I had even suggested calling the manufacturer to complain and get a replacement.

How stupid can a mother be.

They weren't there. The door was open, but the place was

empty. I looked around and was horrified to see two rats run across the floor in the darkness and vanish under a large poster board. When my eyes adjusted to the dimness, I could read the words hand-painted on the board: IF SOMEONE COMES TO KILL YOU, RISE UP AND KILL HIM FIRST. Hanging on the wall not far from it was a large picture in a glass frame, a group photo of the members of the class, sweaty after practice, camouflage paint on their foreheads and cheeks. How young their faces were, how artificial their tough expressions.

I examined the picture more closely. A short, chubby boy stood next to a lanky, pimply-faced boy, and beside him, a robust, curly-haired boy with broad shoulders and eyes filled with confidence. Next was a redhaired freckled boy wearing a kippah, and beside him, a handsome boy with enormous eyes and sculpted lips shaped into a half smile. I lingered on his face, trying to figure out where I knew him from. Adam stood next to him, and it seemed that he had absorbed some of the power radiating from that boy because I had never seen my son stand as tall as he did in that photo.

But where were these boys now? The empty space suddenly made me uneasy, as if I had invaded an off-limits area. I turned and peered outside. If they had left the place open, they had to be nearby. The natural light illuminating the parking lot was dimming. The streetlamps had not yet gone on. The sky was filled with pregnant, purple clouds. There was no sign of Uri and the boys. I went outside and walked around the building. Stretching out below it was a large overgrown lot bordered by a grove of oak trees.

At first, I didn't even realize I was seeing them. Dark, motionless spots buried in the grass. One of the spots began to move, but so slowly that I wasn't at all sure it was really moving. A moment later I saw the other spots, which I had thought were rocks, also begin to move toward the trees at the far side. I leaned forward, straining my eyes. In the twilight, I couldn't see their faces. The boys were crawling doggedly away from me up the rocky slope. They didn't make a sound. I looked around. The ground was blanketed with small, sharp rocks, nettles, and thorns. When they got home, their arms would be covered with bloody cuts, scratches, and bruises. It would drive their parents crazy. (I realized that their parents didn't know, and I thought about how Adam had been strangely insistent, these past few weeks, on wearing long-sleeved shirts at home, even though he usually walked around in boxers and nothing else.)

I was trying to pick out my son from among the crawling kids when I saw two boys I hadn't been watching creep away from a tall bush, dragging something behind them. A large sack. Or maybe a stretcher. Something heavy. A third boy hurried over to them—it was Adam, I realized—holding a penknife that glittered in the last of the daylight. With a single thrust, he cut open the sack. I stifled a cry.

Someone was in there, a person. He was lying on his back, his limbs limp. Adam and the two boys extricated him from the sack and began to drag him toward the trees. *It's an exercise,* I told myself, *just an exercise. A member of the class pretending to be wounded or posing as a terrorist the patrol has abducted deep in enemy territory.* But the unconscious man wasn't pretending—he was totally and utterly helpless. They dragged him, and I was horrified to hear the sound of his body thudding along the rocky ground. None of the students in the class could pretend that well.

The boys continued to drag the unconscious man. He was barefoot, I noticed, and I stared wide-eyed at the soles of his feet as the boys supported his arms and strained with his weight. I wanted to shout, but my throat was too dry and my mouth was paralyzed, like I was in a bad dream. The other boys who had been crawling arrived one by one at the edge of the grove and crouched there, motionless.

The last light turned purple, then darkened, and finally disappeared. And right then, in the light of a sudden red flame, I saw Uri.

He was standing beside a pile of twigs that had just been lit. His handsome, chiseled face glowed in the light of the campfire. The boys who had arrived gathered in front of him, eager to hear what he would say. A slight movement of his head was enough for them to understand, and they hurried to clear the way for the last three boys. They approached him, barely able to drag the body, and placed it in front of Uri. I could see it in the light of the campfire.

Expressionless face. Closed eyes. No lashes. No eyebrows. A straight, assembly-line nose. Mouth open, ready to breathe. It was a golem. A training doll. And I felt my heart once again start to beat normally. *Everything's okay, you nervous wreck, it's just a class for teenagers that takes itself a bit too seriously.* But I still didn't step out of the shadows, where I stood watching. I didn't introduce myself to them—*Hi, I'm Lilach, Adam's mother. I came to see your class.* Because even though the training doll no longer looked menacing, just grotesque, I still felt shaky inside. In the grove, Uri spoke.

Although I didn't hear the words, it was impossible to miss their effect—the boys were electrified. Here and there I saw a vigorous nod of agreement, a fist in the air. It took a moment to find Adam among them again—his eyes were fixed on Uri, glowing with the same fire that burned in the other boys' eyes.

I approached quietly. I had to hear. The wind changed direction and carried Uri's voice to me over the crackling of the campfire.

"This week's outstanding student is Adam Shuster. I always tell you that a fighter must know how to defeat his demons. Adam has done that. He fought his demon, and he won." Quiet nods from the boys. Fists raised in appreciation. "I gave Adam my Leatherman when we started this exercise, and he'll keep it until our next class." My son's face turned fiery orange. His eyes were luminous. He was holding Uri's knife, and I knew that, right then, it was the most important thing in the world to him.

"Training exercise over," Uri said, and before I could understand what was happening, the boys had formed a circle. The tall, curly-haired boy turned to the short boy beside him and punched him in the stomach as hard as he could. The short boy didn't utter a sound, suffering the blow in silence. He took a deep breath, turned to the boy on his other side—and punched him in the stomach with all the power of the pain the first boy had apparently caused him. I choked. The boy crumpled with the force of the blow but didn't say a word. A moment later, he stood up. He turned to the boy on his other side—Adam, I saw—and hit him as hard as he could. I couldn't watch. I fled.

## 29

I WENT BACK to the car and got in. A knock on the window made me jump. I turned my head, expecting to see Adam, but on the other side of the glass was Einat Greenbaum.

"I always come early by mistake and wait here," she said, lighting a cigarette. I got out of the car and stood next to her. Though I hadn't smoked since the army, I took the cigarette she offered me. The smoke we exhaled hung in the freezing night air for a moment before dissipating. I could feel how the threads of smoke bound us together in the solidarity of motherhood.

"I have to tell you something," I said, and I described what I'd seen in the grove, stealing glances at the building as I spoke.

Einat Greenbaum nodded. "Boaz told me. He's doing about a hundred sit-ups a day now so he can take the punches quietly."

"But why exactly does he have to take punches quietly?"

She took a relaxed drag of her cigarette. "It's like asking why boys need motorcycles. To prove to themselves that they're boys." She glanced over at the door of the building. "Look," she said in a conciliatory tone, "obviously there has to be limits. When Boaz wanted to get a tattoo of the motto Uri taught them, I told him no way."

"What motto?" I asked.

"'If someone comes to kill you, rise up and kill him first.' Can you believe it?"

She smiled, but I didn't smile back. "And what if some kid takes it too far?" I asked.

Einat waved her hand in dismissal. "Let's not get carried away," she said. "It's not like the kids will create an ultraright underground here."

I didn't say anything. She put her hand on my shoulder. "Lilach, as a mother, you have to admit that with everything that's going on now, the Krav Maga class helps you sleep better. There's a kind of war going on out there."

"I'm not sure there's a war going on out there," I said. "I think that we've all gotten a little paranoid."

Einat looked at me in surprise. "After Paul Reed and that awful graffiti, you still doubt that they're out to get us?"

"Let's put things in perspective: Reed acted alone. The graffiti at the school could have been done by some overzealous kids."

"Look, Lilach," Einat said decisively, "you and Mikhael are not active in the community, so maybe you don't understand the full extent of what we're facing." Her beautiful fair skin reddened slightly into the flush women have when they're angry or making love. "Even before Paul Reed, the number of antisemitic incidents in California schools doubled since the last operation in the Gaza Strip. I think it's great that the kids are learning to fight back."

I wanted to argue with her, and at the same time something inside me whispered that maybe she was right. Maybe Uri was giving Adam exactly what he needed, the thing that would have kept Jamal from bullying him from the start.

That night, Adam was distant and I stuck to him like glue. I had never chased after boys—a combination of pride and shyness, I think—but I'd always chased after my son; did I ever. I took up his hobbies. When he showed an interest in dinosaurs, I learned to recite the names in Latin. Dinosaurs were replaced by superheroes, superheroes by model airplanes. I was a diligent pupil but always a step behind, noticing his loss of interest a moment too late. I ordered a new model plane to build, and he told me he was done with that. As your kids get older, Noga once said to me on the phone, you begin to choose activities that don't require talking: going to the movies, taking a bike ride, something to hide the fact that you no longer know how to speak to your children. We signed up for a deep-sea-diving course. We went camping in Yosemite. We did things. We took pictures of ourselves doing things. If anyone asked, "Where were you when your son was growing up?" I could show them. I had an alibi.

I asked him so many questions when I came home from my visit to Annabella Jones: What did he feel like eating? Did he have any homework? Where did he want to go on vacation? But at no stage did I manage to ask the one crucial question: *Why didn't you tell me they were hurting you?*

After dinner, I called Einat. If we were living in Israel, I probably wouldn't have bothered, but if you've relocated, you're very careful not to fight with anyone. That was the first law I learned when we arrived here. Yael Golan told me about it when she explained the difference between friendships in captivity and friendships in nature.

"Friendships in nature are what you have in Israel: You meet a girl in high school or in the army or in college, and you fall in love with her the way girls fall in love with each other—completely but without the sex—and everything is great. And then there are friendships in captivity. Imagine," she said, "that you and the women here had to eject from your planes and were captured by the Egyptians, like the pilots who were prisoners of war together. I'm sure those pilots, who couldn't stand each other before, joined together in order to survive. Like us, the relocated women in our American captivity."

I knew right away that Yael Golan was going to be a friend in nature. What I didn't know was that six months later, she would move to the East Coast. So whenever I met new women, I learned to feel them out—*How long have you come for, really? Are you temporary or permanent?*

Einat Greenbaum was permanent. When Adam and Boaz started high school, we signed up to be each other's emergency contact. And as much as she had annoyed me in the parking lot, I knew you shouldn't be quick to break off friendships in captivity.

"It's so great you called," she said with what sounded like genuine relief. "I was just planning to call you. I want to invite you to a meeting of our task force."

"Task force?"

"To fight against antisemitism," Einat said. "I coordinate collecting negative comments about Jews."

Most of the women here coordinated something. I coordinated cultural activities in the retirement home. Living in my neighborhood were the coordinator for the Enrichment of Jewish Children's Day Care Centers in San Mateo and the executive coordinator of the Jewish Community Centers. The women who weren't lucky enough to coordinate anything—even coordinating has limits—were forced to move to a less prestigious category: consultants. There were sleep consultants and breastfeeding consultants and toilet-training consultants. There were also couples therapists and art therapists. But the people who provided real care were the Hispanic women who came to our houses every day by public transportation. They took care of the art therapists' children while the art therapists were taking care of the couples therapists' children.

In addition to the coordinators, the consultants, and the therapists, there were the artists.

Every other garage had been converted into a studio of some kind: Pottery. Restoration of vintage furniture. Silk-screen printing. Like adults who let their little girls host imaginary tea parties, encouraging them to act as if the plastic dolls were real guests, the men nurtured the Silicon Valley women's belief that we had real jobs. We stayed at home, but not as housewives. We invented words that would hide us from ourselves.

"Thanks for the invitation," I said to Einat. "I'll really try to make it to your meeting." Because, in spite of everything, I had learned a thing or two in America about how to say no.

## 30

MARTHA'S COGNITIVE EVALUATION was scheduled for nine o'clock Monday morning. Lucia told me that after apologizing—not very genuinely, I thought—for not having updated me. In order to get to the home in time, I had to race to drop off Adam at school and, from there, rush to Daly City. But when I reached the home after dashing from the parking lot, a sour-faced Lucia told me that the doctor had called to say he wouldn't arrive until noon.

I caught my breath and went into the lobby. Martha was sitting there, wearing her best dress, light purple in color. Her white hair was curled nicely, and I thought I could see Armando's touch—he had been an expert women's hairdresser; according to him, he had blow-dried Rita Moreno's hair on the set of *West Side Story*. Martha was sitting inside the dress and the hairdo, looking tense. She fingered the string of fake pearls she wore around her neck as if to check that they were really round and were still there. When I sat down beside her, she stopped touching her pearls and put her hand on my back. A few moments passed before she said she wanted to go up to her room and rest. I walked her to the elevator and then went into my office and closed the door. I had intended to pre-pare the Friday-morning workshop, but my hands went to my computer.

*The Nation of Islam is an African American religious organization founded in 1930. Its current leader is Louis Farrakhan.* The web entry was long and detailed. I didn't skip a word. I read about Abdul Alim Muhammad, who accused Jewish doctors of deliberately injecting Black people with the AIDS virus, and about Jeffrey Muhammad, who preached that Jews sucked the blood of the Black race. I moved from one link to another as if, if I only searched enough, I'd finally reach the entry that showed Jamal Jones's room, and there, in the precise language the internet excels in, I would find an explanation of what the hell had happened between the dead boy, who had a picture of Louis Farrakhan hanging on his wall, and my son.

I left my office to wash my face, then headed to the lounge to calm myself down with some tea. Dwayne, who was sitting alone on a tattered armchair, was surprised to see me.

"Today's not your day here."

"I wanted to be at Martha's cognitive evaluation," I said. He studied me. "And maybe I'd rather be here than alone at home," I added as an afterthought. I expected that would make him happy, but his face twitched slightly, almost invisibly, as if I'd confirmed an idea he'd been undecided about.

"You look worried," he finally said. "Were you at that dead boy's house again?"

"The boy's mother doesn't know much," I said with an unintended tinge of criticism in my tone. "Her son bullied my son, and she doesn't know anything about it."

Dwayne's eyes darkened. "Maybe you need to move to a safer place," he said dryly. "Maybe put him in a private school. I'm sure no Black kid would bully your son there."

His sarcasm surprised me. "What's up, Dwayne?"

He leaned back in his armchair.

"I can't understand exactly what you're complaining about," I said.

The old man smiled, showing all his teeth. "No, darlin', I'm not complaining. We're the residents. We can take our complaints to Lucia, because that's her job. They pay her for that. But you're practically a volunteer, so we all ought to be grateful you're here, right?"

I was shocked. He looked at me steadily. "Listen, Leela, maybe a Black kid can beat up your son after school, but when school is over for real, it'll be your son who acts as if this country is his parents' backyard. The dead boy's mother, she was born in America and she'll die here, but I'm telling you, you're more a part of this place than she'll ever be."

A moment later—although it seemed like an eternity—Lucia

opened the door of the lounge. Dwayne gave her the bright smile of a ninety-year-old and left. She looked at my face for a fraction of a second, was surprised at what she saw, then said matter-of-factly, "The doctor's here, if you still insist on being at the evaluation."

The doctor was a balding, middle-aged man with worn shoes and a tired look. I wondered how many retirement homes he'd already visited that day. Lucia shook his hand and asked him to inform the office of the results. I walked to the lobby with them. Martha was already there with her hairdo and her purple dress. When Dr. Ng asked her where she wanted to talk, she thought for a moment and said, "My apartment. I'll feel more comfortable there." But when we reached her apartment, Martha didn't look comfortable at all. When we sat down in the narrow living room, she hurried to pour us some cold water, almost spilling it when she put the pitcher on the table.

The doctor asked her what day it was, and Martha said, "Monday." She repeated it three times, even though he didn't ask again. He asked her the address of the home. Martha shot me a pleading look. The doctor said, "It's okay, take the time to think." The ornate clock on the wall ticked off the seconds. I stared at it intently, at the small birds on the moving hands. I couldn't bring myself to look at Martha's face. I continued to focus on the hands of the clock when she didn't answer or gave only partial replies to the following questions: What month is it? Can you list the names of your living relatives? How do you manage in the shower?

"And how do you manage with day-to-day chores?"

"I help her." Dwayne came out of Martha's bedroom wearing a flannel bathrobe and looking like a permanent fixture in the apartment.

"Excuse me," the doctor said, examining the man standing in

front of him. "I had the impression that the lady lived alone." He turned to me. "This will greatly change my evaluation of her safety here in the apartment."

"The lady and I share a household," Dwayne said before I could open my mouth, "and I know what our address is and how to walk back here from the supermarket, and I make sure that this sweetheart doesn't go walking outside without me."

Dr. Ng shifted his gaze back and forth between Martha and Dwayne, then turned to me. "Is that a fact the staff will corroborate?"

Martha's wall clock dinged faintly, announcing the hour. I looked away from the small bird on the hand. "Yes," I said.

Ten minutes later, I walked the doctor out. As we waited for the elevator, he took off his glasses and cleaned them with the edge of his shirt. For some reason, he didn't look so tired anymore. "I'm not sure about those two," he said. I couldn't tell if there was a rebuke in his voice. The cheery sounds of a harmonica came from behind the door of Martha's apartment.

## 31

THE LAST BELL echoed in the schoolyard. Teenagers came running out. I tried to locate Adam among them. Blond heads passed me, buried in phones or in conversations with each other. I looked for the black curls, eager to catch sight of his distinctive walk. I guessed it would take a few minutes before he came out. He was almost always like that, dawdling, putting his books in his bag with the slowness of the end of a school day. I wasn't waiting impatiently, but with pleasant anticipation. I liked to play that game when I came to get him—the yard full of kids and I have to pick out my son as quickly as I can.

At that hour of the afternoon, the parking lot was half empty. When I drove him to school in the morning, the asphalt was covered with cars, fathers and mothers dropping off their kids before they went to work. But now, only a few mothers were waiting with me. The children of working parents would go home on their own. I looked again at the gravel path that led from the main building to the parking lot, waiting for Adam to come out.

When I saw her, she had her back to me. Her black hair was pulled into a loose ponytail. I thought she must have come straight from her job at the InterContinental because she was still wearing her maid's uniform and flat shoes. Standing there looking at the path, she could have been any mother who had come to pick up her son from school. It was as if she believed that, if she stood there long enough, Jamal would emerge from the main building and walk toward her in the crowd of teenagers.

A group of boys and girls came out and headed to the parking lot. They blinked as they tried to adjust to the strong sunlight in the yard. I recognized Josh Hart among them, his arm lying casually over the shoulder of a girl with large breasts and a sweet face. She said something to him. He laughed. He threw his head back and his teeth glowed white.

"Excuse me—"

Annabella Jones walked across the yard to the group. They watched her with those closed expressions young people have when they look at older people. But Josh's face changed instantly. He pulled his arm off his girlfriend's shoulder as if there were something inappropriate about his fingers being so close to the girl's skin, a few centimeters from her breasts, in front of the dead boy's mother. The smile on his face vanished, replaced by an expression that resembled panic.

"I'm Jamal's mother," Annabella said. The kids nodded. They

knew who she was. The boy standing next to Josh cleared his throat and said, in an embarrassed voice, what Americans say in such cases: "I'm sorry for your—"

But before he could complete the sentence, Annabella asked, "Do you know who does drugs in the school? Who sells?"

The boys looked at her in surprise. Her speech was blunter than anything they were used to.

"The cops say it was something he tried to make himself, but Jamal would never try to make drugs. Do you know who could have given it to him? Maybe mixed it in his drink?"

Now it was the pretty girl's turn to speak. "I'm sorry, Mrs. Jones, we don't know anything."

"How can none of you know anything?" Her voice was loud and desperate. She grabbed the girl's hand, and though the girl flinched, she didn't dare pull away. "My boy is dead and none of you know anything!" The boys exchanged anxious looks.

"You're all lying," she said. Everyone in the schoolyard was silent now. Parents in the parking lot next to the path. Boys on the grass. They were all looking at Annabella Jones and they all heard her say loudly, "You're lying. You're all lying. Tell me the truth. Who gave meth to my boy?"

A security guard left his post at the entrance and walked toward the yard. "Excuse me," he said, and his official, metallic voice made it clear to me that he knew nothing about the circumstances that had brought this distraught woman there, or perhaps he did and he was still determined to restore public order.

"Ma'am, if you could please leave school property and wait outside the yard. We don't encourage parents to enter the grounds when they come to pick up their children."

Those were the rules. We all knew them. The yard was reserved for the students and school staff. Parents waited for their kids in the adjoining parking lot. But Annabella Jones hadn't come there to wait for her son. Annabella Jones wasn't interested in rules. She dropped the girl's hand and spoke to the guard.

"They know what happened there, don't you see? They know, and they aren't telling me." She shook her head, and her eyes darted feverishly around the schoolyard. Suddenly, she shouted at a pair of girls walking down the steps: "Hey, you two, do you know who was dealing drugs at that party? Tell me!"

They looked at her in confusion. The mother of one of the girls, who was waiting by her car in the lot, waved at her daughter to come to the car quickly. Josh Hart and his friends also moved away from the woman who had been driven mad by sorrow. "Help me," she said to the security guard. "Maybe they'll tell you."

"If you'll just walk back to the parking lot with me," he said.

Tears began to run down Annabella's face.

"You don't believe me. You think he's just a kid who got high. I'm telling you, it's not true!" Her voice rose to a scream. Her hands crushed her uniform apron. The guard was still speaking politely, but his voice was now tight and angry as he asked her again to leave.

"I have to talk to the kids," she said. "Don't stop me talking to the kids."

I was afraid that the guard would remove her forcibly. I hurried over to them and put my hand on her shoulder. "Annabella."

She recognized me immediately. "Leela, thank God you're here! He wants to chase me away, but I have to talk to the kids. Can you tell him it's okay? He'll listen to you."

I looked at the guard. I knew what he was afraid of. That the kids would complain to their parents that a weird lady had accosted them. The administration would reprimand him. I opened my mouth, planning to say something levelheaded and responsible that would prevent the guard from dragging

Annabella out of the yard and keep her from embarrassing herself in front of the entire school. That's when I saw him appear
behind them, coming out of the door of the main building,
alone. I gave him a warning look telling him to stay where he
was and wait for me. He understood right away and remained on
the top step.

"Annabella," I said gently, "there's no point arguing with the
guard. Come with me, I'll call an Uber to take you home."

She refused weakly. Adam looked at her from where he was
standing. She didn't notice him. I took her arm. This time she
didn't object. She let me lead her away, as soft as a rag doll, while
the students and parents watched.

## 32

**WHEN ADAM AND** I got into the car, neither of us said
a word. Annabella Jones had been picked up by a polite Uber
driver several minutes earlier, and the students had gone on their
way. The guard had thanked me and wished me a great day. All
that time, Adam had stood on the top step as motionless as one of
the statues the art students sometimes placed around the school.
Finally, he'd jogged down the steps, crossed the lawn, walking
around the spot where Jamal's mother had stood a moment ago,
and joined me.

We'd walked to the car and he waited quietly while I rummaged
around in my bag. When I finally found the keys, the car made its
usual strident chirp and the doors opened. Everything sounded
too loud to me—the bleeps as I pressed the buttons of the alarm,
the noise of the doors opening and slamming shut, the sound of
the safety belts snapping into place. I turned the wheel and took
us away from there.

The first traffic light, which was always red, was red this time too. Adam and I didn't look at each other. "Poor woman," I said. I thought he nodded, but I wasn't sure. "You think there's something to what she says, that someone put drugs in Jamal's drink?" My eyes were fixed on the road and I didn't know if Adam shrugged or just responded to my question with silence.

When I glanced in his direction, I saw that his eyes were tightly shut and his lips were pale and bitten. "Adam, what happened?"

"I have a headache."

I pulled over to the side of the road. He opened his eyes and looked at me, puzzled.

"Is it because of what just happened with Annabella?" I asked.

"No, I've had it since this morning."

He was waiting for me to start the car and drive us home.

"You can talk to me," I said. And when he didn't reply, I added, "That Jamal, I heard he was a problem kid."

Adam closed his eyes again. "Mom, my head is exploding. I don't feel like talking about Jamal."

"But if you ever want—"

"Then I'll tell you."

I took a bottle of water out of my bag and handed it to him. "Take it, maybe you're dehydrated." I watched him as he drank small sips, his eyes still closed. "His mother is a maid at the InterContinental," I said a moment later and immediately cursed myself for saying it, because what difference did it make where Annabella worked? Why, of all the things in the world, did that have to come out of my mouth?

Adam kept his eyes closed. I drove home along the same route I'd driven two hundred times, but today it felt four times as long. When I glanced over at him, I saw that he'd opened his eyes. I insisted on taking it as a sign. Even if he didn't feel like talking about Jamal or about Annabella's awful visit to the school, talking about something—anything—was better than that silence.

"So how's the self-defense class going?" I asked.

"Don't call it a class," he said. "That makes it sound stupid."

"So what should I call it?"

"Uri."

"Uri?"

"Yes, that's what we call it."

"That's what you say?" I asked, puzzled. "That you're going to Uri today?"

"Yes. What's so weird about that?" He sounded annoyed. I didn't understand why.

"I didn't say it was weird," I said. A moment later, I added hesitantly, "So how's Uri going?"

When we got home, Adam went upstairs and I made us a snack, which I ate alone because when I knocked on his door, he said he wasn't hungry. Two hours later, he came down and took the dog out without being asked, and when he came back, he poured himself a glass of water and went upstairs to his room again. I sat in the living room, jumping at every sound, not actually knowing why I was so jittery, why I was charting in my mind every single one of his movements, keeping a chronology of doors opening and closing, noting every time he appeared in the hallway, the sound of his footsteps on the stairs.

A phone call from Lucia rescued me. She wanted to know if I could change my work schedule the following week. Two staff members were ill, and it would really help her. I prolonged the conversation as much as I could, and when it was over, I went upstairs. The bathroom next to Adam's room was filled with steam. He must have showered while I was on the phone. I went inside, stepping carefully across the wet floor, asking myself what the hell I had to do to get him to clean up after himself. I swept

away the water with a squeegee and opened the window. I was
about to leave when I saw the blood on the rim of the tub.

Not a lot. Definitely not. A single smear. Nonetheless, I tensed,
because why should there be blood on the tub? Even if he'd cut
himself shaving again, he shaved in the morning, at the sink. And
shaving cuts bleed very little, but this was a stain, not large, but
still a bloodstain. *There's a bloodstain on Adam's bathtub.*

I left the squeegee and went into his room, not hysterical,
just to ask what was happening, so nothing prepared me for the
angry shout he greeted me with. "Mom, you could knock!" he
yelled, still in his towel, and even though other children yelled at
their mothers a hundred times a day, in our home, it had never
happened, Adam wasn't one of those kids who shouted, just as
Mikhael wasn't one of those men who shouted. They showed
their anger in an accumulation of silences. I was so astonished
that at first, I didn't feel the hurt, only the shock.

"Why are you yelling at me?" I said.

"I asked you a hundred times to knock first." Then he added,
"Sorry," in an angry voice, his left hand clutching his right forearm, and behind him, on his desk, was the Leatherman Uri had
lent him, the knife with the serrated blade.

"Show me your arm."

That caught him completely unawares. His hand tightened
slightly around his forearm. "What? Why?"

"Because I want to see your arm."

"What's going on, Mom?"

(*I want to know if you've cut yourself. I want to know if, when
you hurt too much inside, you choose to drain the pain out of you in
drops of blood. I want to know if it's inherited. I was once sixteen,
Adam. But I grew up. My emotional wounds scarred over, and I made
you. I won't let you hurt yourself, won't let you raise a hand against
yourself. No Leatherman, no box cutter will touch your forearm. You*

*were perfect when you came out of me, and perfect you will remain.*) "Because there's blood on the bathtub and I want to see if you're hurt."

I decided that if he didn't take his hand off his forearm right then and there, I'd go over and move it forcibly so I could see. (After all, it was only ten years ago that I still had full possession of his body; I dressed him, undressed him, took his temperature. *Open your mouth wide, I want to see if there's a hole in your tooth. Lie here and don't move, I want to see if you have lice.*)

He took his hand away from his forearm.

The skin was untouched, slightly pink from the shower. "Now can you please leave my room, or do I have to take my towel off so you can examine me?"

Embarrassment flooded me like a pailful of cold water, but something inside me wouldn't let me stop. "So where's the blood from?"

"I was trying to carve an avocado pit and cut my thumb." And before I could ask, he pointed to the half-carved avocado pit he'd put down next to his laptop, eyes and nose visible on it, and showed me a superficial cut on the inside of his thumb. I sat down on his bed even though he hadn't invited me to.

"I feel like we've forgotten how to talk to each other," I said. "I can see that you've been going through something since what happened to Jamal, and I want you to know that you can talk to me." I stammered out a few more similar remarks, and they all sounded equally hollow. There had to be another way to talk, I thought, a way that would be ours alone, like the private, babbling language we had when he was a year old, a language imbued with the essence of who we were, not like the words I was saying now, words that sounded as if they'd been taken from the frozen-food section of the supermarket, ready to be defrosted in the microwave.

"Mom, I know you don't mean to, but you're bothering me. I want to be alone now, okay?"

I should have respected that, I know. I should have picked myself up and left his room right then. But I could see his eyebrow twitch slightly, that small tic, and thought that maybe, even though his mouth was saying I should go, his body was trying to say something else.

"You're sure you don't want to try and tell me what happened with Jam—"

He was aiming for the wall, I'm certain of that. He meant to hit the wall. His fist was aimed at the wall and should have hit the wall, but because he wasn't looking, his fist shot out in the wrong direction and smashed into the window, opening a hole in the glass and emerging on the other side. I swallowed a scream and hurried over to Adam, who was looking at his hand in surprise, as if it were alien to him. Dozens of shards were stuck in his closed fist, making it look like a glass porcupine.

"I'll call an ambulance," I said.

"I don't need an ambulance." Adam moaned. He opened his fist gently and straightened his fingers, checking that nothing was broken. Blood began to pool around the shards, but the bleeding on the back of his hand and his fingers wasn't serious. What upset me more was the bleeding from his wrist, which had been cut by the broken glass when he'd pulled his hand back in through the window. He groaned in pain. I ran to get the first aid kit and bandages from the bathroom. I put a pressure bandage on his wrist, checking the veins to see if they were still bleeding. New blood stained the white cloth, but the bleeding was weaker now, and a few moments later, it seemed to stop.

"Are you okay?" I asked. Adam nodded. He looked at the broken window, stunned. We were both stunned. I put his hand under running water to wash away the shards, then disinfected the superficial scratches on his fingers and the back of his hand with iodine. I checked again to make sure the bandage on his wrist was tight enough. When I heard the front door open, I let Adam go downstairs to greet Mikhael and closed myself in the bathroom, guilty and horrified.

*He lost control.* That's what I'd tell Mikhael later. *Ever since Uri's Krav Maga class, he's been completely off-kilter. He hasn't raised his voice to us since his terrible-two tantrums, and all of a sudden, he yells at me for no reason, makes a fist, and accidentally smashes a window.* And Mikhael would say, *It's a tricky time, we have to be patient,* and he'd suggest gently that maybe I'd gotten a little carried away with all my questions. *The boy feels like he's being interrogated and that upsets him. You have to ease up, Leelo, for both your sakes.*

## 33

**OVER THE NEXT** few days, I discovered that you can miss a child who's sitting next to you at the table. You can miss him even as he sits beside you and drinks the cocoa you made for him. I saw him swallow, and I wanted to be swallowed by him too, to slide down his throat, go to his stomach, to his circulatory system. *What do you have there, Adam, under your skin?*

When I drove him to school in the mornings, I watched him carefully, looking for residue. I tried to remember when that eyebrow tic had first started. I asked myself if it had begun after Jamal died or before, during the time he was being bullied in school. And the nail-biting, which Mikhael was constantly after him about and, according to the internet, could be a sign of stress. And the stooped way he walked. "It'll pass," Mikhael repeated every time I raised the subject. "With time, it'll pass."

"If only he was willing to share with us what happened," I said to Mikhael one night, and, shrugging, he replied that kids don't usually share their feelings with their parents.

"If Ofri were here, he might have been able to talk to her," I said.

Mikhael was silent. He didn't like to hear me talk about her. That's why I mentioned her so infrequently. But I kept talking to her. When she was in my womb, I'd talked to her so much that it became a habit, and when she came out, it was hard for me to stop. Two months after she was born, I told Noga that I still spoke to her and asked her if that was normal. Yes, she'd said, it's a way of coping. Her brother had died of cancer ten years earlier, and sometimes she went to the cemetery and sat next to his grave and spoke to him. Ofri didn't have a grave, I told her. It's as if, as far as the world, the country, were concerned, she'd never really existed. Only in my head. In my womb.

Labor had taken eleven hours. I asked them to do a C-section, I wanted to get it over with as fast as possible, but the doctor said it would be better not to because it increased the risk of complications in future pregnancies. It took a long time for her to come out of my womb, and for weeks after she did, I bled out the lining my uterus had prepared for her. But she never left my mind. The lullabies I would sing to her, the clothes I would dress her in, the games we would play—all those things were still in my mind after the birth as if in a completely furnished room, and I had no idea where I was supposed to put them.

At first I kept talking to Noga about her, but when Noga became pregnant, I didn't want to frighten her. I didn't even speak to Mikhael about her very much. I didn't want to worry him. In the months that followed, I learned to turn aside whenever I saw babies, and there were babies everywhere.

"These things happen," the doctor had said when I went for a follow-up examination. "And we don't always know why they happen. Sometimes women blame themselves, think they did something wrong during their pregnancies. But that's nonsense. Intrauterine deaths have many causes, and the great majority of them are not under the mother's control." That was nice of her, saying that, and the part of me that was capable of thinking straight definitely believed her. But there was another part of me—primal, almost supernatural—that wondered if we had done something bad, and after Adam was born and the doctors said I couldn't have any more children, I already knew that it was because we'd had it too good before. We'd been so sure of our happiness that we didn't know it was arrogance, and we would be punished for it.

## 34

THE SECOND CALL from Uri came about a week later. Adam was in his room, Mikhael and I were sitting in front of the TV in our Sunday-night languor. Earlier that day, Adam had gone to his class, and Mikhael and I ate French toast, read the papers, and went back to bed for an afternoon nap. A moment before I dozed off, my head on Mikhael's chest, I thought that maybe it would really be all right. Maybe the muscle that had been contracting inside me since that meeting with Annabella Jones would gradually relax. When I woke up, Adam had returned home and was sitting at the table, letting Kelev eat from his plate despite my objections. He hadn't changed his shirt after practice, and the smell of his sweat filled the room, powerful and aggressive.

In the evening, we sat down to watch TV, and Mikhael put his hand on my thigh. That's how we were sitting when the phone rang. Uri asked if he could come the next morning to talk to us briefly. And the next morning, the black coffee again, the cookies again, the fingers skipping the bell and knocking on the door again.

"I know you're in a hurry to get to work," he said to Mikhael as soon as we sat down, "but I didn't want to wait and I didn't want to talk on the phone." With a brief, matter-of-fact movement of his hand, Mikhael made it clear that he understood Uri's reasons. Uri's body filled the armchair. He hadn't removed his coat when he arrived, even though I'd offered to take it.

The day before, in class, he'd heard the boys talking about Jamal. It was during the break between exercises when he'd gone to get water and they probably hadn't realized he was within earshot. One of the boys said it must have been meth, the drug that killed him. Adam told them he'd looked online and found out how easy it was to make methamphetamine at home and he promised that after class, he'd show them a video that explained how to do it.

"Look, I bet there's no kid in Adam's high school who didn't look up meth online after the party to try and understand what happened to Jamal," Uri said. "But I still told Adam after class that he had to erase his search history and be more careful in the future."

To my surprise, Mikhael nodded in agreement.

"But why should he erase his search history?" I asked. "After all, you said yourself that all the kids must have Googled it." My voice was more aggressive than I had intended.

Mikhael flashed me a warning look, the same one he gave Kelev whenever he started growling for no reason. "Leelo, you know I'm not worried about Adam, but it might look bad to someone on the outside. They're investigating drugs in the school and the police can confiscate the students' devices at any time. What would they think if they found that kind of search on the phone or computer of an outstanding chemistry student who'd been on bad terms with Jamal?"

"They would see that he searched after Jamal was dead," I said.

Uri cleared his throat and turned to me. "I think we have to consider the possibility that Adam did a search on how to make meth even before the party." He immediately added that he didn't think Adam had really tried to make drugs—he was too smart to do something like that—but a Google search was something else. "It's true that there's a huge difference between reading about how to make it and actually doing it, and if the tragedy at the party hadn't happened, no one would be interested in Adam's internet searches. But the tragedy did happen. A boy is dead. And from what they say, Jamal's mother is looking for someone to blame."

I didn't say anything. I remembered the nagging doubt I'd felt when I left Annabella Jones's house, a feeling of distress that I could barely put into words and that, with the distance of time, now seemed totally implausible.

"I appreciate your concern," Mikhael said a moment later to Uri. "I'd like to think that there's no need, but you're right. A detective coming across that search might think that Adam tried to make meth, even just as a challenge, then took it to the party. And it would be better if he didn't have to go to the police station and explain to them that they're wrong."

Silence in the living room. Finally, I broke it, saying, "If that's the case, we have to speak to Adam. Tell him to erase his search history." Uri said that the decision, of course, was Mikhael's and mine, but he thought our conversation should remain between the three of us. He himself could talk to Adam and make sure there were no other searches to worry about.

"I'm his mother, I'm the one who should talk to him."

But Uri insisted. He said that if Adam knew he had come to

speak to us, Adam might close himself off from all of us. "I don't want to lose his trust. Especially now, with all he's going through, it's important for him to have someone he can talk to." He was right, of course, but the way he said it infuriated me. That man had come into our lives a few months ago, and now he knew more than we did about our son.

It seemed to me that Uri felt my resentment. His green eyes looked hesitantly at me. He couldn't make up his mind about whether to say something, and he finally decided to speak. "When Jamal died the night of the party, I was the first person Adam called." After a beat, he added softly, "I told him to call you."

Uri sought my eyes again. To my surprise, I saw an almost apologetic expression on his face. "Look," he finally said, "Adam is a good kid. That internet search of his—I'm sure it was just a coincidence. But with the atmosphere in town now, all the tension between communities since Paul Reed...we don't need to start a rumor mill here."

I froze. Mikhael nodded in agreement. He and Uri spoke some more, something about the harebrained things kids do and about the cyber world and the problems it brings. Uri stood up and said, "I won't keep you," and Mikhael said, "Don't be silly, you're not keeping us," and spoke to him for a few more long minutes before walking him to the door, stopping in the foyer. "Thanks, *akhi*, really," he said. Through the cold, liquid matter that had been floating in my brain for the last few minutes, I could still recognize that word—*akhi*—a word Mikhael had not used since his days in the army.

I forced myself to get up and join them in the foyer. There was another of those pat-on-the-back-hug things that men do, longer than the previous one. Then, skipping the handshake of his last visit, Uri leaned over, hugged me briefly, gave me a quick kiss on the cheek, and said, "Thanks, Lilach, bye. Everything will be fine."

My legs were like lead weights. I plopped down on a kitchen chair. After a moment's hesitation, I picked up my phone and texted Lucia that, unfortunately, I couldn't come in today. I knew she didn't like last-minute cancellations, but I couldn't bring myself to get up out of the chair. Mikhael, however, was bouncy and full of energy, as if the news that had dragged me down had actually decreased the pull of gravity on him.

"It's a lucky thing he's here," he said as he went up the stairs to get his laptop. "Just imagine how much trouble Adam could get into with that nonsense of his. Kids today search for the craziest things on the internet and don't understand how it could mess up their lives." A minute later, he came downstairs and bent over the shoe holder near the door.

"Mikhael?" My voice shook slightly. He looked at me in surprise. "Should we be worried about what he told us, about what Adam searched for?"

He shook his head. "Who doesn't dream about killing the kid who bullies him in high school? Remember how you used to daydream that your doctoral adviser would die in an accident?"

"Then why are we afraid that the police might find his search history?"

"Because they don't know him. I know my son."

His voice was so firm that I thought twice before I said, tentatively, that maybe we didn't totally know our son. That stopped him. He sat down beside me and asked what I meant.

"Look," I said, "I know Adam's Social Security number by heart, I know his height, his weight, the curl on the back of his neck, I know that he likes red peppers better than yellow ones, that he eats his cucumbers peeled, that he loves ice cream but hates milkshakes. I know that he listens to Kendrick Lamar and David Bowie and the Beatles, that he thinks *Lord of the Flies* is the best book in the world because it's the only book he ever read on his own, that he loves chemistry and us and Kelev, and that he admires Uri and Tamir and Aviv. But it's a fact that we didn't know anything about what was going on in school."

"I know," Mikhael said quietly and added that from the time Adam was in day care, he knew the possibility existed that he might be bullied. He thought I felt it too, which was why we were so eager for Adam to go to the Krav Maga class after the synagogue attack—not only because of Paul Reed, but because we knew in our hearts that Adam was that kind of kid, the kind people do things to. He had always seen that vulnerability in him, Mikhael said, and he was just as sure now that Adam was not capable of hurting Jamal or putting something in his drink, even as a joke.

## 35

THE NEXT EVENING, we sat on Fisherman's Wharf, not far from the raft of sea lions. Our weekly date night was Tuesday. After the conversation with Uri, I was sure we'd cancel this time. I didn't feel like going out, but Mikhael insisted. Maybe he felt that canceling lent too much importance to what had been said, and he even reserved a table at an especially expensive restaurant. Nothing suited my mood less than the elegant dress code, but I didn't have the strength to argue. I took my Ralph Lauren dress out of the closet. I'd bought it after I saw Jane wearing a similar one at a company party, but Jane was twenty-nine and I was forty-four, and the dress knew it. I changed into something more conservative and, feeling defeated, went downstairs to join Mikhael.

We drove to the city. The restaurant was lovely and expensive, with candles along the shoreline and a view of Alcatraz. We drank white wine. A plate piled with oysters sat in front of us on the table. Mikhael was in a strange mood. "Did I ever tell you about Omer Shapiro?" he asked.

A quick survey of the database. My brain held the most comprehensive, updated research on Mikhael Shuster. Everything was cataloged—memories of childhood, memories of adolescence, memories of the army. I ran a rapid search of past experiences. Present insights. Future ambitions. No, there was no Omer Shapiro there.

"He was from a different kibbutz, Mishmar HaYarden. He came to the first day of middle school on a quad bike."

I leaned forward. I didn't know who Omer Shapiro was. For a moment, I was surprised that there even were such things—memories that Mikhael still hadn't told me about.

"He made my life miserable, Omer Shapiro. From the minute we met, he couldn't stand me. Maybe because we both had the same reputation—I was the high achiever from my kibbutz grade school; he was the high achiever from his. We met when grade school had just ended and middle school was just beginning, and he wanted to make sure I didn't dethrone him. Someone had told him I was adopted, and he wouldn't let it go. 'How come you're brown and your parents are white?' 'How come your eyes are black and theirs are blue?' Stuff like that.

"We were having a swimming lesson in the pool. That morning, the kibbutz clothing storeroom had given me red trunks, and that made him laugh even more. I don't remember exactly what he said, only that he kept putting me down until at some point, I pulled him underwater. Dunking each other was a game boys played back then—they did it to each other all the time. But I stayed under too long. I mean, I held Omer Shapiro underwater too long. His hair swung back and forth under the surface. He had long hair, we all had long hair then, and when it was wet, it looked like a bunch of water snakes. All of a sudden, I couldn't feel him struggling anymore.

"I let go of him immediately. I was terrified. Everybody else was busy doing their own thing, and with all the noise and commotion, no one noticed. I started yelling. I pulled him out of the water to the edge of the pool. I tried giving him mouth-to-mouth resuscitation like I saw them do in movies. A minute later, they moved me away. The lifeguard and medic were working on him, and the gym teacher grabbed my hand and pulled me aside so I wouldn't be in their way. All the kids at the pool were hysterical—Omer Shapiro was drowning and Mikhael Shuster had saved him. And every time someone arrived and asked what happened, they repeated it: 'Omer Shapiro was drowning and Mikhael Shuster saved him!' That's how I realized that they thought I was some kind of hero and that, because of me, Omer Shapiro wasn't underwater but on the edge of the pool.

"Those seconds beside the pool were the scariest in my life. Long after Omer Shapiro coughed, turned onto his side, and vomited, long after they took him away from there, my legs kept trembling.

"I didn't go to class for a whole week. I was afraid the police would come and arrest me. I was sure he'd tell them. When I finally went back to school, he gave me a strange look in the hallway. I waited for him to say something, but he didn't. I once read that people who lose consciousness sometimes report that the minutes before they pass out are obliterated, a kind of short-term memory loss. Or maybe he did remember and didn't want to say. In any case, he kept his distance from me after that. We didn't speak to each other until the end of high school."

Mikhael drank his wine. I drank my wine. A group of tourists were standing in front of the raft of sea lions, snapping pictures of them. Mikhael looked out across the bay at the land on the other side. Route 1 crosses the bridge there. If you keep driving on it, you reach Alaska.

"I haven't thought about him for years, and yesterday, after talking to Uri, I thought about him. And I also thought that Adam would never do such a thing, would never drown a kid like that. Not even as a joke. Yes, he dreamed about getting back at the kids who bullied him, and yes, he Googled how to make meth so he could feel strong and cool. But he doesn't have the killer instinct. I'm sure of it."

I put my hand on his thigh. He pressed it with his own, but he still looked distant. "What you said about Uri was right, Leelo. What he did, making sure Adam erased that idiotic search history, and the care he showed coming to talk to us about it, no one else would have done that for us. I'm going to talk to Berman, ask him to offer Uri a job."

## 36

BERMAN HIRED URI that same week. It didn't surprise me—in all the years Mikhael had worked there, he had never recommended anyone. Here and there, in rare cases, he passed on a CV, but always by e-mail and at a calculated distance so as not to undermine, even a little, the sanctity of the company's professionalism. But this time, he himself went into Berman's office to say he vouched for the guy. And when someone like Mikhael—impressive, businesslike, professional—knocks on the CEO's door and says something like that, the result is predictable.

"This was really perfect timing," Mikhael told me a few days after Uri was fast-tracked into the company. Orion had folded three and a half months ago, so there was no large gap in Uri's

CV. Anyone skimming it would see the same calendar year and not realize that the guy had been at home for almost four months. In Silicon Valley's competitive job market, an unemployed programmer smells like a corpse rotting in the sun.

"Why couldn't he find a job by himself?" I asked.

"I know that he and his wife split up and she went back to Israel not long after the company closed. Maybe he couldn't decide whether to go back or stay here for a while."

"His kids went back to Israel and he decided to stay here? How can he live like that?"

"There's some kind of money problem," Mikhael said. "They bought a house here before Orion closed down, and they couldn't sell it. I'm not sure he can afford to go back to Israel in the near future. Just try to pay a mortgage in dollars when you're earning shekels."

The next day, even though I didn't bring up the subject, he said, "The thing that's great about Uri is that, instead of just sitting home in front of the computer, he started that class. You were right about him, he really is a good guy."

I kept my misgivings to myself. I could have told Mikhael that I hadn't liked the look on Uri's face that night in the grove when he told the boys to hit each other. I could have talked about his knife, which the boys passed around with such reverence and safeguarded with almost religious adoration. I could have claimed that there was something odd about a person who chooses the motto "If someone comes to kill you, rise up and kill him first" as motivation for a class of teenage boys. But deep inside, I was angry at Uri for a different, simpler reason: my son had a new love.

It was actually Adam's chess teacher from middle school who helped me tone down my anger. I met him standing in line at the pharmacy. Jacob asked if Adam still played chess, and I said no, he'd gotten hooked on a new self-defense course. To my surprise, he asked if the instructor was Uri Ziv. He knew Uri well because he'd taught Uri's son chess a year earlier and also because he'd advised him about chessboards for the visually impaired.

"But Uri isn't visually impaired," I said in surprise.

"He plays with Leah Weinstein's father now," Jacob said. "You know, that's the only thing Peter Weinstein does these days."

Jacob and his husband, Matthew, were members of the Reform synagogue. They'd been there the night of the attack.

"We function normally during the day," he said, "but we still can't sleep at night, so we take this natural shit," he said, waving around the homeopathic medication the pharmacist had given him. "I'm not sure it works, but at least it's not addictive, like tranquilizers." Tranquilizers were Susan and Peter Weinstein's mistake. Someone gave them a bottle right after the funeral, and Jacob said that now they couldn't stop. Leah's mother sat on the couch in a fog, and Peter almost never left the house. The community was helpless. And then Uri had shown up—his daughter did a Torah reading in the synagogue—and he stayed in touch. He'd asked Peter Weinstein if he wanted to play chess with him. They played every Saturday in the club now. "So you can see," Jacob said, "I have a lot of respect for Uri Ziv. Even if it means that the chess world has lost a player to his self-defense class."

And Uri really was wonderful. He picked Mikhael up in the mornings so they could drive to work together. He got tickets for Mikhael and Adam to see a Golden State Warriors game. One Sunday, Mikhael joined Adam at Uri's class and came back rhapsodic. "It's incredible what goes on there," he said that night. "It's no wonder they adore him. He listens to those kids, really listens—doesn't just pretend to listen while waiting for them to stop talking so he can tell them what he'd planned to tell them in the first place." And he demanded things from them that no one had ever demanded—not only to train in the pouring rain but also to stop putting each other down. He helped them with their math. He talked to them about movies they liked. He really listened to the rap lyrics they sang and tried to understand why they moved the boys so much.

And he was so completely natural, so comfortable with who he was. Like when he asked for my recipe for tahini cookies, then tried to bake them himself and brought over a tray of half-burned cookies that made us all laugh. "After Tali and I split, I learned to cook really well," he insisted, "but baking is another story."

That night, I found her on Facebook. Tali Ziv looked like everything any Israeli man could ever want. Tall. Slim. Wearing a shapeless sweater that only a beautiful woman could carry off. Her status said that she was in a relationship. I wondered whether that was from before she'd given up on her previous man, the one who'd been in our house earlier that night, or if she had a new man. I scrolled down the page looking for another picture, but apparently Tali Ziv wasn't the picture-taking type. Instead, I saw a chubby teenage girl and a gorgeous little boy with blond hair and bright eyes doing a handstand on Frishman Beach in Tel Aviv—I recognized the Dan Hotel in the background—and wearing a Batman costume on Purim. *How much that boy resembles Uri,* I thought. *What a handsome man he'll be when he grows up.*

After that night, something in me changed. No more polite friendliness but the budding of genuine affection for that man, whose wife and kids had gone back to Israel soon after he lost his job. When Mikhael suggested a family trip to Lake Tahoe for our vacation, I was the one—not him, not Adam—who said, "Let's ask Uri to come along so he won't be alone over the holidays."

PART TWO

# MEXICO

## 37

**ON THE MORNING** of our trip, Adam was so excited that I thought he'd suggest running to Tahoe. All the way up there, he chattered enthusiastically in a mishmash of Hebrew and English, asking when we'd finally meet up with Uri and planning which trails he'd ski with him the next day. The cabin we rented had two floors and three bedrooms. We agreed that Adam would sleep on the top floor with his hip-hop and the TV, and Mikhael and I and Uri would have the two downstairs bedrooms.

When Uri arrived—he'd exchanged his padded jacket for an expensive snow jacket—I thought for a moment that we'd made a mistake. It took a while for the conversation to get going. We talked about the weather, about snow equipment, about the traffic jams on the way. There were long silences. I suddenly felt stressed by the possibility that we'd spend the next three days engaging in forced small talk. *Maybe it's too soon,* I told myself. *You're not actually friends; you don't even really know him.*

But very quickly, I realized that I was worrying for no reason. The initial awkwardness was like a cork stuck in a wine bottle. On the days that followed, we cooked, drank, and talked endlessly. Uri had the strange ability to bring out the traits in each of us that didn't usually come to the fore, that were buried behind our day-to-day lives. I realized it on our first night in Tahoe when Uri got Mikhael to cook. In the afternoon, they'd come back from skiing and Uri suggested that they drive to the supermarket and buy the ingredients to cook a sumptuous dinner together. I figured that Mikhael would say anything to keep from going into the kitchen, but to my surprise, he said, *"Yalla,"* and pulled out his phone to Google interesting dishes. Only five minutes later, they left for the supermarket with Adam and when they came back, they spent the rest of the evening in the kitchen preparing crab pie with Roquefort.

"I can't believe it," I said to Mikhael. "You hate cooking." I immediately regretted saying it, because why did I always have to take on the role of gatekeeper, the one who watched over him so he wouldn't go beyond the familiar Mikhael to other Mikhaels?

During our previous visits to Tahoe, Adam and Mikhael would come back exhausted from skiing, and we all went to sleep early. But this time, we stayed up late. We laughed a lot. I couldn't even say exactly what we were laughing at. I felt interesting. All of us, I think, felt more interesting and better-looking than we actually were. We started conversations and didn't know when they would end. We said things that were different from what we usually said. We were different at an age when people no longer become different. Uri's presence woke us up. He got me skiing. In all the years we'd gone there, I had skied maybe three times. I knew the technique, but the speed scared me, and the few occasions I'd joined Mikhael and Adam during previous winters, I'd spent most of my time on the slopes calling out "Careful!" and "Slower!"

On the second morning of our vacation, after we finished eating, Uri said to me, "So, are you coming?"

Adam laughed. "No way," my son said. "My mom doesn't ski."

"Lilach? Is that true? You don't ski?" The disappointment in his voice pleased me but not enough for me to go out into the snow.

"Only in emergencies," I said with a smile and cleared the table.

"Today your mom will ski with me on the beginners' slope," Uri said to Adam loudly, so I would hear. "And by tomorrow, she'll come up to the black diamonds with us."

I didn't go up to the black diamonds the next day, but I did ski with Uri all that morning, slipping and falling and rolling. "I can't believe you talked me into coming," I told him when we were back at the bottom of the hill after a long day of skiing on the easy slopes, the blue lake alternately glittering and disappearing. Uri smiled. "You got Mikhael to cook and Adam to do sports and me to ski—you're really good at getting people to do things."

My words seemed to embarrass him. "Everyone has something he's good at and something he's bad at," he said. "Maybe that's what I'm good at, like you say—getting people to do things."

I smiled. "Mikhael tells me that in the army, they said you would be chief of the general staff."

I thought that would make him happy, but my words had the opposite effect. The light in Uri's eyes dimmed at once. "The worst thing that can happen to an eighteen-year-old kid is to be told that he can do anything he wants."

Embarrassed, I didn't reply. But at the same time, I admired his frankness. Where we lived, people told each other everything except the truth. The cakes I brought to dinners at friends' houses were always amazing, even if I'd mistakenly put salt in it instead of sugar. And your children were always wonderful, even if they hadn't spoken to you for a month. And so, when we walked toward the lift that would take us up again, Uri's refusal to act as if everything was terrific made me draw back a bit and, at the same time, like him more.

"So what exactly happened?" I asked while we waited for the lift. "With your family."

When he responded with silence, I was afraid that my question had been inappropriate. But a moment later, when the gondola lift arrived, Uri sat down beside me on the bench and said, "The relocation finished us." He looked out the window. "I put every last cent I had into Orion. Tali said from the beginning that it was a bad idea. I had a good job at Wix, so she didn't understand why I gave up the bonuses and stock shares for a start-up that might take off or might just as easily crash. But I was sure I could do it."

Mikhael and I had had this same conversation ten years ago. Mikhael couldn't decide whether to leave his secure job in the company to develop his own start-up. I refused to take a position. I didn't want to be the one who prevented him from going where his passion took him. I told him that whatever he decided was okay with me. I don't think he regretted that, in the end, he chose to stay. He climbed the corporate ladder, and with the bonuses and shares, he earned as much as the Israelis who had made exits. But sometimes I could see the way he looked at men who had taken the leap, the ones who had fought tooth and nail for their ideas, had invested their savings, and now walked around Silicon Valley glowing like the corona of a comet.

"At first it seemed like the right decision," Uri said as the gondola hovered above the mountain slope. "I raised a lot of money from investors. I had a good turnover. But I went public too quickly. It isn't enough to go all out, to move people. You have to know where you're running to. And I ran us straight into the abyss."

Uri's green eyes wandered over the snowy, fir-tree-dotted mountain that spread far below us. I thought he'd finished speaking, but as the gondola approached the top station, he suddenly said quietly, "I miss the kids. That's why I volunteered to teach the class. I couldn't stand the quiet in my house anymore."

"And you never thought of going back to Israel?"

He took off a glove, exposing his large hand, red with cold. "We bought a big house here before my company went under.

We were in a bit of a financial mess, so we thought I should stay and try to resolve it."

He put his glove back on. His reply was as clean and open as the snow around us, something white and frozen offered up just as it was.

"And you," Uri said, his green eyes fixed on mine, "have you ever thought what would happen if you went back to Israel?"

I smiled and said that that was the sort of question people shouldn't ask because it led to bad places.

"Why bad?"

"Because it's followed very quickly by the question of what would have become of me if we'd stayed in Israel."

"And?"

"Maybe I would have continued my research and found a position in some college. Maybe I would have gotten my doctorate published, with a pretty cover and a launch in Jaffa." I hesitated before continuing. "But that's why you have to attack life with everything you have, and I was never the attacking type. I didn't find a position, never mind tenure. When Mikhael's company offered us relocation a second time, I was almost happy to get out of the race."

I didn't tell him that I had begun to envy the women I'd once found repellent, the ones who didn't do anything. When I quit my postdoc, my mother warned me that I'd regret it, but after my defeat in the academic world, and especially after what happened with Ofri, I just wanted to go far away. I was silent about that with Uri, but I think he managed to hear at least part of it.

We got out of the gondola near the empty restaurant. Uri ordered us hot cider. "I think I can understand what you're saying," he said. "Maybe that's part of what bothered Tali. At first, she wanted the change as much as I did, but at some point along the way, even before what happened with Orion, she began to be angry with me for taking her so far from everything."

"I'm not angry with Mikhael," I said quickly. "Absolutely not. I like my work and I like our family, the three of us."

Uri sipped his cider and said gently that it wouldn't always be the three of us. In a few years, Adam would go to college. Only now that he was far away from his children did he begin to understand how difficult it would be when they grew up and went off on their own.

In the afternoon, I stayed in the cabin to cook, and Uri went skiing with Adam and Mikhael. When everything was ready, I turned off the flames under the pots and went upstairs to shower. The mirror in the bathroom was huge and ruthless. I undressed without looking in it. Then, making a quick decision, I turned around and stood in front of it.

I'd forgotten when I'd last looked at myself that way, in the light. My breasts were still okay, I thought, and my ass too, but my stomach was disgusting, and the sight of my skin saddened me, because I knew that if I were a peach in the market, I wouldn't pick myself up. And thinking of myself as a tired peach in the market—no matter how I tried to break it down into power structures and gender theories, the thought remained, simple and sharp: I had turned from a beautiful woman into a woman who looked good for her age.

The others came back cheerful and noisy and very hungry. At dinner, I looked with amazement at Adam—how much this trip with Uri had boosted his spirits, how involved he suddenly was in our conversations. The following day, after we skied, we Skyped with Mikhael's parents, and Dina told us about a knife attack in the territories. To my surprise, Adam said, "Israel has to take retaliatory action." I argued with him. I was annoyed. But I was also pleased that he had left his laptop and was saying what he thought, that he was looking around, thinking.

On the last night, Mikhael, Uri, and I sat in front of the fireplace and drank hot wine with cinnamon. Adam was watching TV upstairs, and when I went to see how he was, I found him asleep. I covered him and went back down to Mikhael. I told him that no matter how much I disagreed with Adam—"Retaliatory action, can you imagine?"—it was nice to see him taking an interest in politics.

Mikhael added more wood to the fire. "I don't understand why you get so excited about politics, Leelo. That's what's jamming up the Middle East. If people would forget ideology and focus on their personal welfare, everything would be different."

Uri appeared from behind us and sat down on the couch. He'd brought a blanket with him and handed it to me. I spread it on my lap so that only my bare feet were exposed to the heat of the fireplace. I thought he'd change the subject, but he turned to Mikhael and said pensively, "So you think we have to give up ideology? What does that actually mean?"

"Look at what's happening here in America: People come to Silicon Valley to get rich. The nation, politics—they put everything aside in order to make money. And the world moves forward because of that. Look at Sundar Pichai. The guy was born in India and became CEO of Google. Capitalism conquered racism. Think about how the world would look if instead of Israeli and Arab, there were simply Amazon engineers, Apple programmers, people who weren't defined by color or gender, only by their performance rating."

Uri sipped his wine quietly. Then he said, "That scares me. Money is the most dangerous ideology there is. It holds nothing sacred and allows you to do anything."

We drank our wine. Stared at the fire. In the end, we went to bed, Uri in his room adjoining the living room, and Mikhael and I in the room down the hall. Mikhael climbed into bed, sleepy. It was late. The next morning, we had to drive all the way back. But something in me was aroused. A pleasant tingling between my thighs. I took off my clothes, and instead of putting on my pajamas, I slipped naked under the covers and pressed up against his back. I stroked him until he turned to me, awake and hard. I climbed on top of him, wet, hungry, and slipped him smoothly inside me. The bed squeaked a little, and Mikhael, maybe afraid that Uri might hear us from the next room, shifted me slightly in an attempt to stop the noise. He touched me there and I focused, stopped moving, let him do it, and when I felt I was getting close, I moved again quickly, faster, forgetting the squeaking bed. Or perhaps the opposite was true; I enjoyed it. Because when Mikhael put his hand over my mouth and whispered, "Shh, so Uri doesn't hear," it was the "Uri" spoken between us, in the dark, that suddenly made me shudder so powerfully that I could barely restrain my cries. And the clear knowledge that he was there, down the hall, hearing us, made me come even harder.

## 38

WHEN ADAM TURNED six, Mikhael said that maybe we should go back to Israel. At the time, we lived near the company headquarters in Texas, and we were counting the days until the move to his next post. If we went back in the next couple of years, Mikhael said, Adam would still be an Israeli kid.

We both knew that if we stayed here, a boundary line would be drawn between him and us. Because Mikhael and I were Israelis who also spoke English, and Adam would grow up to be an American who also spoke Hebrew. There were things he knew that we didn't understand, such as jokes about baseball that we didn't get, even after years, and social situations we navigated hesitantly. And I had reconciled myself to that. Because our job was to be a bridge, our feet planted in Israel, our bodies stretched over the ocean, and our hands reaching out, stuck in the good earth of the new continent. It was on our backs, on that bridge, that Adam could cross.

One morning, Adam asked me and Mikhael to stop speaking Hebrew to him outside the house. We were living in Seattle then. We walked to school together every morning, and Adam would point to cars on the street and ask Mikhael how much horsepower each one had or ask me to tell him about great white sharks. One day, he said, "Sharks, Mom, not *krishim*," when I used the Hebrew word. He switched to English and refused to answer until I had switched as well.

I called his teacher to sound her out about any unusual incidents in class, wondering if perhaps American children smelled foreignness the way great white sharks smell blood. Maybe someone had made fun of him, I suggested. Miss Johnson sounded horrified. "I don't believe such a thing could happen here, Mrs. Shuster. Our school is very proud of its cultural diversity." And the cultural diversity was indeed displayed on the walls in bright colors—images of a Chinese boy holding the hand of a Black boy who was holding the hand of an Indian girl.

The next day I asked Adam about it and received an identical answer: No one had laughed at him; he just didn't feel like speaking Hebrew outside the house. But Miss Johnson didn't give up her cultural diversity easily—twice we were invited to appear in front of the class and present the Hebrew alphabet (from right to left! Amazing!), and, devoting myself to the forced labor of parenthood, I cut out twenty-seven identical pieces of construction paper with the word *shalom* written on them in Hebrew letters that all the kids in the class could color. But even after the word *shalom* in Hebrew adorned the walls of the class-room, Adam persisted in his refusal to speak the language outside the house. He didn't want to be part of the school's cultural diversity. He wanted to be like everyone else. My son wanted to be swallowed up in English as if it were the protective stomach of an enormous whale.

"I told you this would happen," my mother gloated on the phone. "Be thankful he's still willing to speak Hebrew at home."

"It'll pass," I answered with much more conviction than I actually felt.

"What are you talking about? It'll only get worse," she rejoiced. "Just like I didn't want your grandparents to speak Yiddish around me—that's how much you'll embarrass him."

But my grandparents had been refugees, I wanted to tell her, survivors who hoarded canned food. Mikhael and I weren't like that. We knew the monologues from *Pulp Fiction* by heart. We recited scenes from *Seinfeld*. When we were in high school, we closed the door and, with the volume all the way up, listened to songs written in America, and when we made love for the first time, we called it *sex,* in English. We were loyal citizens of the empire.

"Wait and see," my mother said, "an immigrant is an im-migrant."

But after refusing to speak Hebrew outside the house when he was six, my son suddenly changed his mind when he was sixteen. The Israeli-ness that had lain dormant in him awoke all at once. He didn't want to be an American teenager who ran away when a terrorist charged into a synagogue. He wanted to be a fighter, with a gun, who took retaliatory action.

"Can you imagine him as a soldier?" I asked Mikhael on the drive back from Tahoe.

Adam was asleep, his mouth slightly open, his legs folded under him. Mikhael studied him in the rearview mirror as if trying to decide what unit he would put him in.

"You've never thought of him that way?" he asked.

"No. I don't even want to try to think of him in uniform. It gives me the chills."

He slowed down before a curve in the road, and I said, "But you know what's weird? I actually did think about how Ofri would look in uniform." I waited for a reply, but Mikhael said nothing. The snow outside froze by one more degree.

## 39

THE POLICE ARRIVED in the afternoon. I was peeling a pumpkin for soup, the Mashina playlist on in the background, and perhaps that's why it took a few moments for me to realize that someone was ringing the front doorbell. I put the pumpkin in a bowl and went to the door. Standing on the other side of it was a uniformed policeman, and beside him, a man in civilian clothes who said, "Mrs. Shuster?"

"What happened to Adam?" I asked in alarm. An infinite number of horrendous images had already formed in my mind: an accident, a shooting in school, a terrorist attack. They looked at me, confused, and of the two of them, it was the uniformed policeman who understood first and quickly assured me, "Everything's okay, we didn't come to inform you of anything."

*Breathe, Lilach, breathe. Nothing happened. Calm down, it's just a knock on the door and a police officer on the other side. Could it be that only in Israel, this sounds like the beginning of a tragedy?* The guy in civilian clothes—a detective, I suddenly realized—looked at me inquisitively.

"Why was your first thought that something had happened to him?"

I shrugged. "I'm a mother. When I see the police at the door, that's the first thing that crosses my mind."

He nodded, but I wasn't sure he really understood.

"Do you have children?" I asked. He shook his head. "And you?" I asked the uniformed policeman, and I guessed he would nod before he actually did. That's why he'd been so quick to jump in.

Detective O'Malley and Officer Barry introduced themselves and asked if they could come in. I led them to the living room, which was still filled with the voices of Mashina.

They certainly heard the music, but they didn't say anything about it. They didn't ask about the foreign language. Maybe they were being polite. Maybe they didn't care.

"Mrs. Shuster, I understand that your son isn't home now. Can you tell me where he is?" As the detective spoke, I remembered that I had seen him before. He was the man who had been leaning on the patrol car beside Detective Peterson.

"He's at his self-defense class. Why?"

"We'd like to talk to you about the death of his classmate Jamal Jones. I assume you know the details."

"Yes, he died at Josh Hart's party." The police officer nodded and looked at me, waiting for me to continue. "At the funeral they said it was cardiac arrest... later on, they talked about a meth overdose, and you were looking for drugs in the school."

"You were at the funeral?"

"Yes, all the parents went."

"And Adam?"

*I don't want to go, Mom.* "Yes. Of course Adam went."

"Did you notice anything different about his behavior on the days following the death?"

"He was upset. You know, a boy in his high school died right in front of him."

Detective O'Malley leaned forward, and I thought of Uri, of the way he had sat on this very couch when he came here the first time, his bearlike hand wrapped around the small coffee cup.

"Would you like something to drink?" I asked.

"No, thank you. What do you know about the nature of Adam's relationship with Jamal?"

"They weren't friends, if that's what you're asking." (*What, in fact, are you asking?*)

Detective O'Malley nodded. He knew that. The uniformed policeman said, in a voice that sounded gentler, "The kids at school say that Jamal bullied Adam on a regular basis, online bullying and physical altercations."

"Yes," I said, "I heard that." I knew they both assumed that Adam had told me, maybe had cried in my arms. And I was ashamed at the way I had really found out about it—a red marker on the soles of his shoes in a stranger's house, inanimate objects that screamed out at me what my son had never said.

Detective O'Malley looked around our living room, his eyes lingering on the photo of Adam next to the window. "Did Adam ever speak to you about wanting to hurt Jamal?"

"I assume that every child dreams of someday getting back at the person who's bullying him." (*Good for you,* Mikhael applauded me in my mind. *Those morons should leave you alone and go deal with real problems.*)

"But he never talked to you about a plan like that?"

"Plan? What do you mean?" Because, yes, Uri had told us that Adam's phone or computer had weird and troubling searches on it, but that was no different from porn videos that kids looked up on-line. *You watch on the screen everything you dream will happen and know never will. That's not a "plan," Mr. Detective, that's digital daydreaming.*

He turned to look again at the photo of Adam, and even though I knew every detail in that photo by heart—I was the one who'd taken it on the beach in Cabo—I stared at it as if it might have changed without my noticing.

"We received a report that your son planned to kill Jamal Jones."

"What! Are you crazy? He's a sixteen-year-old kid!"

"He talked to another kid about it a few times."

"Do you have any idea what kind of nonsense kids tell their friends? How much kids brag about things that have absolutely no basis in reality?" And when he didn't reply: "And who is that kid, anyway? Why is he remembering only now?" And when he still didn't reply: "You're completely out of your minds."

Detective O'Malley remained calm during my outburst, as if it was exactly what he had expected. Then he asked, in the same kind but businesslike tone, "Maybe you could tell us a little bit about Adam?"

When I finally spoke, my voice shook with indignation. "He's a good boy. He loves animals."

"Is there a girlfriend?" I pictured the girl from the cemetery. Clearly defined lips. Huge eyes. A resounding slap. "Not that I know of."

"Special interests?"

"TV, hip-hop, the after-school class he goes to."

"What class is that?"

"It's a class that started after the attack on the synagogue. They learn self-defense. Krav Maga. Boys' things."

"Do you mind if we take a look at his room?"

They followed me upstairs. There was mud on Officer Barry's shoes. I promised myself that the minute they left, I'd clean the entire house.

"Here," I said as I opened the door widely, defiantly, an I-have-nothing-to-hide-and-you-should-be-ashamed-for-even-thinking-it movement. "This is his room."

The blanket on the bed was jumbled, the sign of a late, hurried awakening. There was a pile of textbooks beside his laptop. A shirt and a pair of pants were lying on the floor. (*His,* I thought, *everything here is his. He didn't take any of it from anyone.*)

Detective O'Malley pointed to the poster on the wall next to the picture of Kendrick Lamar. "The periodic table?"

"Because of that series *Breaking Bad*. After he saw it, he started loving chemistry. He's in the Stanford junior chemistry club, and now he's taking more chemistry classes at school." *And in our garage, there's a small lab set for kids, the Young Chemist, it's called, but I won't tell you that, Detective O'Malley, because I don't like your expression, the way you're looking at my son's things. You have no sons, so you don't know how much they're attracted to things like that: weapons, pirates, poisons. Officer Barry here, standing next to you, is a father, and he does understand. Take Mikhael, for example. When he was thirteen, he made gunpowder from leftover fertilizer on the kibbutz, and Moshe, his father, still keeps the gun he confiscated on the West Bank, even though in Israel, unlike in America, we are not allowed to have guns at home. He still keeps it, because boys, whether they're eight or eighty, like to feel that they have a deadly weapon close at hand. That doesn't mean they'll do something with it, Mr. Detective, they just enjoy knowing it's there.*

I waited for them to finally leave Adam's room, but O'Malley was in no hurry to go. He pointed again at the poster of the periodic table. "That club in Stanford, did they teach them how to make solutions? Or distill?"

"He learned how to make a stink bomb."

I followed O'Malley and Barry downstairs. I heard their shoes squeak on the gray wood planks and imagined the pail of water, the foaming floor detergent. Maria was scheduled to come clean the next day, but I knew that as soon as they were gone, I would change my clothes and wash everything.

I walked them to the front door. Kelev came out of his dog-house in the yard to welcome the visitors. He wagged his tail, suspicious but friendly. Since Adam had begun spending most of his time in the self-defense class, Kelev missed the company of people. O'Malley bent down to pet him and I thought that was to his credit, because most people recoiled from petting Kelev. He ran his hand along the dog's back, gently bypassing the scar.

"Who did that to him?"

"A gang of boys. Adam saved him from them. They beat him up too."

O'Malley averted his eyes. Maybe he felt the implied accusation in my voice: The boy who was willing to be beaten up in order to save a dog—that boy couldn't hurt anyone.

## 40

AS SOON AS the police left, I called Mikhael. He didn't answer. I hadn't expected him to. The night before, he'd flown to New York for a series of important meetings. The time difference worked against me. I left a message with his secretary asking him to call me back. But I didn't say *urgently*. I didn't say, *Jane, tell him my legs are shaking and my insides are frozen*. I just asked for him to call me back, please, when he was free.

I decided to drive to the self-defense class and talk to Uri. Detective O'Malley's serious voice played in a loop in my mind. *We received a report that your son planned to kill Jamal Jones. He talked to another kid about it.* Kids made stuff up—how could they not get that? Adam was making stuff up. If Jamal Jones died of a meth overdose, it was because the California police didn't do enough to solve the drug problem among young people. They should leave my son alone.

But the doubt was there in the sharp way I turned the wheel. In my angry honking at polite American drivers who gave me horrified looks in their rearview mirrors.

He'd talked about hurting Jamal to impress the other boys, to protest against the humiliation. And yet, in my mind, the wordless thought. A white space. I wasn't even able to say it to myself.

I parked outside the building. Since Uri had begun to work in Mikhael's company, the class had been pushed to an hour later, and when I got to the parking lot, it was already dark. I expected to find them inside—who sends kids out to do orienteering exercises in total darkness?—but the rec center was empty, though the lights were on.

As I entered, I remembered the rats I'd seen there on my last visit and hoped that Uri had managed to deal with them. A can of rat repellent stood near the wall, and I saw it as a sign that the area was clean. I decided to wait inside for the class to come back. It was cold and dark outside, and I didn't want to be closed up alone with my thoughts in the narrow space of the car. The center imbued me with a kind of calm.

I sat quietly on a bench. The minutes passed and no one came. My gaze wandered over the wall, skipping the poster and lingering on the group picture of the students. *We received a report that your son planned to kill Jamal Jones. He talked to another kid about it.*

I got up from the bench and walked over to the opposite wall. There was the redhead with the kippah. He had a closed, slightly dull expression, which made it clear to me that he wasn't the one Adam had spoken to. There was the robust, broad-shouldered kid, just the type Adam usually kept his distance from. There was that handsome kid wearing a too-large King's School shirt, his enormous eyes looking straight at the camera, and I knew instantly that he was the kid Adam had spoken to. Even in the picture, he had something that made you want to get close to him, to grab his attention. I looked at him. Large eyes. Well-defined lips. And suddenly, as if I'd been slapped, I jumped back.

I recognized the girl with the short hair from the cemetery.

## 41

THEY CAME BACK fifteen minutes later, sweaty and panting. When they saw me, they quieted down all at once and suddenly got that secretive look I remembered from the circle of punches in the grove. But this time I barely gave it a thought. I studied them quickly as they came in and decided she wasn't there. Adam was one of the last to arrive. He was angry when he saw me, as I'd expected. He came over to me and asked in a whisper, "Mom, what's with you? Why did you come in the middle of Uri?" But his anger didn't bother me at that moment. Uri came in after everyone, wearing his short-sleeved training shirt despite the cold, and I went over to him and asked if we could talk outside for a minute.

"What happened?" he asked as soon as we were outside. "You look worried." I told him about the police visit, and, to my surprise, he looked completely unruffled.

"Some kid blabbed something, so they have to check it out. The important thing is that you gave them all the right answers. They'll understand on their own that what Adam said is just nonsense, the stupid boasts of a teenager."

"So you're not worried?"

"Definitely not. If they thought Adam had something to do with making meth, they would have brought the drug squad to your house along with a search warrant. The fact that they sent a patrolman and a low-ranking detective shows that even they know it's nonsense."

I bit my lip. I could feel tears fill my eyes against my will. He touched my shoulder. "That's it, it's over," he said, and with his fingers, he wiped away the tears running down my cheeks.

"You think I should tell Adam that they came?"

He shook his head. "It'll only upset him. He's finally starting to get over that whole business with Jamal. And I really don't think they'll come back."

"And what about the boy they say reported him?" I don't know why I didn't ask about her directly. Maybe I was embarrassed by the intrusive way I'd looked at the photo of the kids.

"I assume they didn't tell you his name."

"No. They only said that some kid made a report to them—but *kid* can be a boy or a girl."

A spark flashed in Uri's green eyes, then died. I noticed that almost invisible stiffening of his shoulders. I expected him to mention the girl with the short hair now, to say that yes, there was one girl in the class whom Adam was in contact with—maybe she was the one who'd talked to the police. But Uri didn't say anything like that. "Forget it, Lilach. Let's be happy it's behind us."

I stayed silent and looked at him, still waiting for him to say something about the girl.

He looked around, shifted his weight from foot to foot. Finally, he opened his mouth and said, "I have to get back to the boys."

## 42

**A THUNDERSTORM AND** the flu. The only two times Mikhael—not I—was the one to take Adam to school. Last year, an unusually powerful thunderstorm struck the Bay Area. The news reported five deaths in road accidents because of the flooding. I was afraid to drive. Six months later, I caught a murderous flu that kept me bedridden. Since then, though, Adam and I had been in the car every weekday morning. But the morning after the conversation with Uri, I didn't take Adam to school. I had a different school to visit.

I woke Adam earlier than usual. I drove him two blocks to where the Fuchs family lived. Ashley was sitting next to her mother in the front seat of the car, staring straight ahead and looking bored. Adam got in the back, withdrawn and angry. I waved goodbye and drove away. I didn't want to be late.

King's School was a public high school fifteen minutes away. When I reached it, the parking lot was filled with cars, fathers and mothers saying goodbye to their kids. I parked not too far away and watched them, waiting for her to arrive. Finally, the bell rang. The last of the kids hurried inside and she still hadn't come. Maybe she was sick, I thought. After all, she hadn't been at the self-defense class either. I started the car, planning to leave. And that's when I saw her walking down the street wearing torn jeans and a gray hoodie. Her bangs fell into her eyes, and she didn't bother to push them aside.

Another bell, short and admonishing, startled the schoolyard. I expected the girl to hurry, but she kept walking at exactly the same pace. Or perhaps even slower, as if, instead of urging her on, the bell had actually set off a rebellion.

I turned off the engine, got out of the car, and came up behind her as she turned into the schoolyard. "Excuse me?"

She kept walking. I had never come up against such blatant disregard. Only a moment later did I see the cable of her headphones sticking out from under her mane of short hair and disappearing into her hoodie.

"Excuse me?" This time I touched her shoulder.

I was afraid the touch would startle her, but she merely stopped, unconcerned, removed her earbuds, and said, "Yes?"

"I'm Adam Shuster's mother," I said in Hebrew.

"Okay."

"And you?"

"Netta."

I didn't really know where to go from there. "What are you listening to?"

"The Pixies."

"Kids your age listen to the Pixies?"

"I love oldies," she said.

I didn't say anything. She didn't say anything. I didn't know if she was standing there out of politeness or if it didn't make any difference to her whether she went to class or stayed there with me.

"You're in the self-defense class with Adam, right?"

She shook her head firmly. "I stopped going."

"Why?"

Netta hugged herself, her face unreadable. "The drive there—it was too far for me."

I saw her look over at the school entrance. She didn't like my questions. In another minute, she'd leave me and go inside.

"I don't want Adam to attend the class either," I suddenly said, urgently. "At first I thought it was a good idea, but now I don't know." A small crack of curiosity appeared in her expression. I charged at it. "Was there someone there who caused you to leave? I saw the way the boys punch each other. Does that have anything to do with it?"

"I can take a punch as well as the boys can," Netta said in a proud, hurt voice. "That's not the reason I left."

"So what was the reason?"

Her lovely face froze for a fraction of a second, after which she straightened her bag on her shoulder and started walking toward the school. "I really need to get going. I have class."

"I promise you I won't tell anyone about it. I just need to know." The pleading in my voice stopped her. Netta looked at the now empty schoolyard. She reached up and ran her fingers through her hair nervously.

"We had rats in the rec center," she finally said. "At first Uri said he'd call an exterminator, but then he changed his mind. He wanted us to take care of it together. He said we had to learn to do things ourselves. He bought traps and spread them around."

She hesitated a moment before going on. "A week later, I was late for class. When I went inside, they were all standing around something in the corner. When I went closer, I saw that three rats were still alive. Uri asked who could kill them with their bare hands. He made a whole ritual out of it."

With a tinge of insolence in her eyes, she scrutinized me to see the effect of what she'd said.

"There's no way Adam took part in something like that," I said. My conviction seemed to surprise her.

"Adam was the first one to volunteer," she said. "The other boys stood there and cheered him on."

"That can't be," I said. "Maybe you didn't see clearly."

The blue of her eyes darkened. "Are you calling me a liar?"

Something inside me warned me to stop before I offended her. I could imagine how the other boys must have responded when she dared to stand up to Uri, to all of them. A moment later, I said cautiously, "Is that what you and Adam were arguing about at the cemetery?"

Her fingers with their black nail polish tightened their grip on her bag.

"What were you fighting about, Netta?" I asked gently. "What happened between you?"

"Nothing happened."

"Something happened. Otherwise you wouldn't have slapped him."

"Just don't make it sound like I attacked your fucked-up kid or something."

She said the words with such hatred that for a moment, I forgot she was a sixteen-year-old girl.

"He's not fucked up. He's a good boy. And you have no right to talk about him like that, and you definitely have no right to slap him."

Her lovely strawberry lips pulled back into a smile full of bitterness. "Well, I'm telling you that in Uri's class, your good boy couldn't stop talking to me about how much he wanted to get back at the kids who were bullying him. And when Jamal died, I was worried and went to the funeral and asked him if everything was okay, and he told me that he was overjoyed it had happened. O-ver-joyed."

"He was in shock," I mumbled. "He was confused."

Netta shook her head. Her short hair danced on her forehead and neck.

"Your son, lady, is a total nutcase, just like that Uri he admires so much. Can you believe that lunatic teaches them to kill animals with their bare hands?"

I didn't know what to say, so I stood there, defeated by a sixteen-year-old girl. Finally, I stammered, "E-even if you don't like the way Uri runs the class or Adam's insensitivity, you could have talked to him about it instead of going to the police."

Netta looked at me, shocked. "What police?"

I couldn't decide if her surprise was genuine. "You think I would go to the police?" she said, offended. "I'm no snitch."

## 43

NETTA TURNED AND walked into the schoolyard. Classes had already begun, but she still didn't hurry. Her bookbag on one shoulder, her gait defiant, she walked up the wide steps. I waited until her figure, tall and slender, disappeared inside. When I turned around to leave, I saw the guard looking at me, an unknown woman harassing a young girl with questions in front of her school. I walked away quickly.

I got into the car and turned on the radio. I didn't start the engine. I let the music play.

*What were you doing at the party that night, Uri? What were you talking to the police about at the Hart home?* In the army, everyone thought Uri would be chief of the general staff, Mikhael had told me, and I definitely understood why. That Pied Piper of Hamelin voice—you had no choice but to follow him.

I closed my eyes in the parked car. I pressed my temples with my hands. My head was exploding. Colored spots flashed behind my lids, orange circles in the dark, Einat Greenbaum's cigarette that night in the parking lot. *I think it's great that the kids are learning to fight back,* she'd said. And when I asked Uri at Lake Tahoe whether he was thinking about cutting classes down to once a week, he'd said, *Of course not. With all the antisemitism these days, it's important for the kids to know how to fight back.* Kids' nonsense, that's what it was. Children playing soldiers, subduing the enemy in a grove in California as if they were deep in Lebanon. They even had a commander in chief, General Uri Ziv, commando, Mossad agent, programmer in a military-industry company in the Silicon Valley.

And suddenly I was angry at myself, suspecting the man who had been so good to us, who had put himself at risk for us when he told Adam to delete his search history. How could I doubt someone who finally took my son out of his shell of loneliness? My son had friends now, a real group of friends, and it was only because of Uri's class.

When I finally started the car, it was already nearly nine thirty in the morning. Mikhael was supposed to land at ten thirty. I decided to pick him up at the airport. I didn't want to wait until he got home to talk. Last night, when he'd finally called me back from a bar, cheery and slightly drunk, I told him we'd talk when he got home. I knew that he was surrounded by work colleagues, that the social occasion was for making business contacts. I knew he wouldn't really be able to hear me in the middle of a bar in Manhattan.

The automatic doors in the terminal opened and closed, giving birth to a new face each time: a man with a briefcase, a couple with their arms around each other, a woman with a backpack. Excited children ran to hug their father, back from a trip. A man handed a heart-shaped balloon to a smiling young girl carrying a large suitcase. The arrivals board showed that the flight from New York had just landed. I stared at the doors impatiently, waiting for the moment they would open and my man would finally emerge. When it happened, ten minutes later, I hurried over to him. He wasn't expecting me, so he hadn't scanned the arrivals hall, had simply begun to walk toward the exit, passing a woman in a sari who was lifting her daughter in the air and crying, "I missed you!"

"Mikhael," I called. "Mikhael!" He didn't hear me. There was too much noise. I was making my way to him when I saw him stop. But not because of me, because of Uri, who stood in front of him and gave him a warm, manly hug.

Mikhael saw me then and exclaimed, "I always go home alone from the airport, and today, two people have come to pick me up!"

We walked toward the exit, Mikhael's arm around my shoulders, a tired but gratified smile on his face.

"In this case, I think it would have been better if only Lilach were here," Uri said, "because the bad news is that I've come to abduct you to the office."

"Really?" Mikhael said in surprise.

Uri smiled in apology. "Berman wants us to meet about the MCJ in an hour. I'm supposed to bring you up to speed now, on the way there. The Washington guys made their presentation earlier than expected."

Mikhael's eyes widened in appreciation. "The MCJ? He put you on that team? *Akhi,* that's more top secret than the unit!"

I didn't ask them what the MCJ was. I knew they couldn't answer. While other companies in Silicon Valley developed apps for internet shopping, the company Mikhael worked for developed security products, which was a nice way of saying "weapons." That's why Mikhael's phone was sometimes turned off for entire workdays, locked in compartments the company supplied to their employees to keep them from taking cell phones into the labs.

That's why his answer to the question "How was your day at work?" was usually a monosyllable: "Good."

"Can we have two minutes to talk?" I asked Uri.

Uri blushed slightly, embarrassed, and said, "Sure, of course, I'm sorry," and stepped back, leaving us some private space.

"The police came yesterday," I said, and I saw Mikhael's face suddenly turn serious. "They said Adam talked to another kid about wanting to kill Jamal Jones."

"And . . . what happened?"

"I told them it was nothing, just a kid making stuff up."

Mikhael nodded in approval. "Did they ask to talk to Adam?"

"No. I think their conversation with me was enough." I knew that if I wanted to say something about Netta, about Uri, I should do it now, but I didn't know exactly how to begin, and Uri was too close. "Come home as soon as you can," I said. "We'll talk tonight."

I drove home alone. Mikhael went to the office with Uri. He'd said goodbye to me with a big hug and a kiss on the lips. Uri gave me a small hug and a kiss on the cheek, and they both got into Uri's car and waved.

I called Shir. Over the past few weeks, we'd met once for coffee and once for dinner, but mostly we texted. When I called, I wanted to tell her everything, or at least part of it, but when she answered, I found myself talking about nothing, asking how she was, sticking to trivialities.

"You sound a little strange," she said after a few minutes.

I didn't deny it. "Want to come out for a spontaneous lunch? I'm close to the city."

"If only," she said. "But I can't leave the office for quite a while. Maybe drop by here for coffee?"

Shir's company offices in the financial district had been designed with clear simplicity. Like Shir herself, there wasn't a drop of pretentiousness about them. I counted twenty employees walking around, most of them younger than us. Shir hugged me and led me to the patio.

"I can't believe you're the owner of all this," I said.

"Sometimes I can't believe it either," she said, smiling, and I knew that she meant it.

She didn't ask what had happened but left small spaces between her sentences so I could fill them if I wanted to. I asked what was going on with Zach. Her face clouded over.

"I offered to put money into his start-up," she said. "I thought it would make him happy, but apparently that was a mistake."

We had coffee and ate granola and fruit. I thanked her silently for every minute we spent together. Adam's additional chemistry classes would keep him in school until late. If I went home now, it would be just me and Kelev. And yes, I had things to do. I had a workshop to plan and laundry to fold and schnitzels to fry. But I didn't want to go home, and I hoped that, maybe, I'd manage to talk.

"I have to go into a meeting," Shir said apologetically an hour later. She walked me to the elevator and leaned down to kiss me from the height of her high heels. I felt like an abandoned little girl. I felt like grabbing her arms and begging her to stay a little longer. I stumbled my way to the car. On the drive back, I thought anxiously about walking into the empty house, which was why I was so surprised when I found it noisy and bustling: policemen and dogs and narcotics agents, and Detective O'Malley, who was kinder than usual when he showed me the search warrant.

## 44

**IT HAD RAINED** at noon, and the smell of the grass was fresh and good. The sniffer dogs ran around inside the house, poking their noses in every corner. Kelev and I stood in the foyer and watched them, our hair bristling. They trotted from one side to another, their noses twitching and their muscles quivering under their black fur. Fifteen minutes later, they came out with tails raised, peed next to the cypress tree, and jumped into the police van. I heard footsteps behind me and saw Maria, still wearing her cleaning gloves, looking guilty and scared.

"Señora, I'm sorry for letting them in. I didn't know what to do, señora. I tried to call you but you didn't answer." The submissiveness in her voice embarrassed me. As if she were afraid I'd do something bad to her.

"I was with a friend," I said. "Everything's okay. Of course you let them in. When there are policemen at the door, we have to let them in."

She nodded, but her eyes continued to search my face to see where I was hiding my anger so it wouldn't catch her unawares. Suddenly I realized that she wasn't apologizing only for letting the policemen in but also for talking to them about us when they'd asked her questions about her bosses.

O'Malley walked past us and Maria averted her gaze, as if simply daring to look directly into the eyes of a representative of American law might cost her dearly. A bald policeman came down the steps from the top floor carrying Adam's laptop. He promised me it would be returned to us undamaged after it had been checked. "Sorry for the inconvenience, Mrs. Shuster."

I nodded limply. Across the street, I could see the curious faces of our neighbors.

Another policeman came out of the house carrying a few of Adam's notebooks and crossed the lawn to the squad car. O'Malley came over and stood beside me. "We tried not to make too much of a mess," he said. I didn't say anything.

The policeman with the notebooks got into the squad car that was parked next to our fence. O'Malley said, "We'd like to take a look in the garage too."

"Just a minute," I said. "I'll open it." I did so feeling slightly tense but also relieved, because I didn't like hiding anything. On the contrary. *Look and see—my son has a small chemistry set in the garage. It's nerdy and sweet, and you'd have to be crazy to think of it any other way.*

The white garage door squeaked mechanically as it rose. Kelev dashed inside, and O'Malley and I followed. His barking echoed in the dark space, loud and piercing.

"What? What happened?" O'Malley asked and bent down

beside him, petting his brown fur, careful not to touch the scar. "What's here that's making you bark like that?"

I knew that it wasn't something there that was making him bark. It was something that wasn't there: the garage was empty. Of course, the three bicycles, ski equipment, toolbox, and lawn mower were there. But Adam's chemistry lab, the one that used to take up almost all the space—the table and kit and small cabinet—had all vanished without a trace.

O'Malley left the garage and came back a moment later with the dogs, who sniffed around and ran out. Kelev sat at the garage door and kept barking, maybe at the other dogs, maybe at the empty garage. O'Malley bent down and petted his back. He examined the garage walls. Finally, he stood up and began walking toward the yard. "We'll be in touch in the next few days," he said as we stood on the path. "We'll want to talk to Adam too."

The van on the other side of the street pulled away from the curb. The bald policeman drove a few feet and stopped in front of us. The detective nodded his head in farewell and didn't look surprised when I declined to return the gesture. He got into the car. Kelev raced after the van for quite a distance before he came running back to me. I petted him. My shaking hands stroked the scar on his back. The feel of the pink flesh, which usually repulsed me, didn't bother me at all now. And Kelev, who usually didn't let anyone but Adam touch his scar, let me pet him there this time.

I went into the house and called Maria over. "I'm not angry," I assured her. "I just want to know what they asked you." She nodded eagerly, said she would tell me everything. At first the detective wanted to know if the señora had asked her to clean anything special this week. I could imagine O'Malley waiting tensely for her answer, leaning forward the way Kelev did when

I took a can of dog food out of the pantry and waved it in front of him.

"I told him that you asked me to clean the vegetable bin in the fridge," Maria said.

"And that's all?"

"They asked me about Adam too—if he wanted me to clean anything lately."

"And did he?"

"At first I didn't remember, señora. I said no, and then they told me I should think back about the last few weeks and try to remember if there was any special request. And that's how I remembered that, a while ago, he wanted me to clean the garage."

"And what did they say when you told them that?"

"The detective wrote it down. He was very interested. He asked what I saw when I cleaned."

"And what did you see, Maria?"

She shrugged. "Except for a dirty floor, there was nothing there."

I thanked her and waited for her to go back to cleaning. I took out my phone and called Mikhael's number. It went to voice mail. I called the office, Jane's extension. "Mr. Shuster is in an important meeting," his beautiful secretary said in the syrupy voice I hated so much. I didn't tell her that the police had searched our house. I only said, "Can you ask him to get back to me the minute he's free?"

"Of course," she replied, "I'll tell Mr. Shuster," saying his name in that cloying way I found so revolting. It suddenly occurred to me that, despite my request, she wouldn't tell Mikhael. My next thought, even worse, was that she'd tell him and he still wouldn't be in any hurry to call me back.

The call was about to end, and I tried to prolong it. "Is Uri Ziv available, by chance?"

"Uri?" she asked.

"Yes. Uri Ziv. He started working there not too long ago."

I waited while Jane checked. I looked around at the grass trampled by strangers' shoes, at the neighbors peering through the gate.

"He's in the meeting too," she said in her syrupy voice. "I'll tell both of them that you called."

## 45

WE DIDN'T MAKE the six p.m. flight. We were fifteen minutes late. The woman at the airline counter suggested that I fill out a form to get a partial refund, but I only wanted to know the time of the next direct flight. She checked the computer for me. I watched as her fingers, the nails covered with bright red polish, tripped over the keyboard. Seven thirty the next morning. I didn't want to wait. I decided it would be easier to fly an hour to Los Angeles or San Diego and drive from there. The clerk found me a flight to San Diego. Half an hour from the border. All that time, Adam sat in the last chair in a row in the waiting area, buried in his iPad, searching for scuba diving in Mexico. We did this every once in a while, spontaneous family trips across the border, and maybe that's why he didn't think it was strange when I picked him up from school, suitcases in the trunk, two passports in my bag. He was really excited.

The flight was terrible. Turbulence and wind. Everything shook. I clung to the cheerful voices of the flight attendants, who were sitting in the back chatting away, enjoying the unexpected freedom, because the service carts couldn't be used in that kind of weather. Apparently, everything was all right. If the situation had been really serious, they wouldn't be laughing that way. Even Adam didn't seem bothered by the lurching. He dozed for most of the flight.

When we got off the plane, I bent over to vomit, and I wasn't the only one. In San Diego, a thunderstorm had darkened the sky. Adam asked if we shouldn't reconsider and was surprised when I barked, "No way." The man at the car-rental counter assured us that tomorrow's forecast for Mexico was sunny. Maybe it was true. Or maybe he was afraid we'd cancel.

When we got into the car, I switched my phone from airplane mode to normal. I left it on in case Mikhael came out of his meeting and called while we were driving. I pulled onto the main road. Torrential rain pounded the windshield. I could imagine Mikhael in the warmth of the meeting room, totally unaware of how far away from home we were.

The border crossing in Tijuana was almost empty. That made sense: evening, lousy weather. Two or three groups of college kids dying to get their hands on cheap alcohol; that was it. Right before the border, Adam suddenly asked if it wouldn't be better to postpone. Why cross the Mexican border if the weather was so awful?

"It's supposed to get better," I said as I changed lanes.

"Mom, is everything okay?" Adam asked.

"Yes," I said, then stepped on the gas pedal hard and turned on the radio, full volume.

When we reached Ensenada, I decided it was time to stop. I found a good hotel on my app. The reception clerk, a round-faced Mexican kid with the sparse beginnings of a mustache, looked to be Adam's age. I tipped another kid, also Adam's age, who carried our suitcases for us and said, "Here's your suite, señora. Enjoy."

Two queen-size beds. A balcony overlooking the sea. Under

other circumstances, it definitely would have been a lovely place. When I came out of the shower, I saw three unanswered calls from Mikhael on my phone. Adam was already lying on the bed near the window. He was wearing his earbuds, so he hadn't heard the phone ring. He didn't hear me either until I stood over him and gestured for him to remove them.

"Adam," I said, "I want us to talk."

He looked at the clock on the nightstand. It was already eleven p.m. I hadn't realized how late it was.

"I'm tired," he said. "Can't it wait until tomorrow?"

"No." He was surprised at how firmly I spoke. For the first time since I'd picked him up from school in the afternoon, he really looked at me. I'd had long hours to plan this conversation, but I still wasn't ready.

"I want you to tell me what happened between you and Jamal."

"What?" He sat up on the bed. "What's that got to do with anything now?"

"The police were at the house today. They searched it."

The sound of the restless murmuring of the sea came through the window. Adam looked at me in surprise. "What did they want?"

I sat down beside him on the bed. I spoke cautiously. "The detectives said that they received a report that you wanted to hurt Jamal. They said he bullied you in school." When I mentioned the bullying, he looked away. He kneaded the bedspread, which was the same greenish color as the rugs and wallpaper. Now came the hard part. I had run the words through my mind during the entire trip. I knew I had to say them.

"They took your laptop to be checked." A deep breath. "Was there anything on it that could get you into trouble?"

He thought, then said, "A few weeks ago, I read a lot about meth."

Someone in a neighboring room turned on a radio. Music came through the walls, and then the volume was suddenly lowered.

"Why did you read about meth?"

He shifted on the bed. "I like to read about stuff that interests me. I also read about homemade bombs. I hope the police won't think I was planning a terror attack or something."

"It's not funny, Adam."

"And this week I did a search on genetic engineering and cloning. You think they'll accuse me of cloning the cashier in the cafeteria?"

"Adam!" I shouted. "It's not funny! There were policemen in our home and they want to question you!"

Someone turned the music off completely. Maybe they were afraid that my shouting in Hebrew was about the noise coming from their room. Adam looked horrified. I had never shouted at him that way before. I was afraid he'd burst into tears, but he didn't cry. He only asked in English, in a different, slightly suspicious voice, "When is Dad coming?"

"Dad had to stay late at work. He'll probably catch a flight tomorrow."

Adam gave me a worried look. "But he knows we're here, right?"

"Of course he knows." And quickly, before he could ask any more questions, I said, "The policemen who were in the house checked out the garage too. I saw that you took out the Young Chemist lab."

"Yeah, I got sick of it. I thought of putting in some exercise machines and weights and other stuff like that instead."

"But on the night of the party, the lab was still in the garage. I saw you doing something there with the cabinet." He froze. "Adam, what was in the cabinet?"

"I can't believe it. Are you stalking me?" He got up angrily and shoved open the glass door to the balcony. The murmur of the sea sounded like a roar now. The man behind the car-rental counter in San Diego had lied; the storm was battering Mexico too. You couldn't distinguish between the sea and the sky. I followed Adam out to the balcony, where a small roof protected it from the rain. "Answer me, please."

He turned his back to me. Part of me was wary of asking more questions. I remembered what had happened last time, a fist covered with shards of glass, and who could say that it wouldn't be worse this time? But I also knew that I had to find out once and for all.

"Adam, what was in the cabinet?"

"Ritalin."

"Ritalin? Since when do you take Ritalin?"

"I don't take it. Yochai does and he agreed to give me some."

"But your grades are great."

He turned around to face me and smiled bitterly, as if he had anticipated my total inability to understand.

"You sniff it, Mom. You crush it into a powder and sniff it. Dad wanted me to go to Josh's fucking party. So I thought I'd try it."

It kept on raining, but it wasn't cold. The rain in Mexico can be like a lukewarm shower. I remembered that from our previous trips.

"I can't believe you sniffed Ritalin."

"In the end, I didn't. I gave it to another kid at the party."

"Jamal?"

"Don't be crazy. I gave it to Jason, Josh's friend. He's one of the popular kids, but he's pretty nice to me."

"And what happened to Jason?"

"Either he sniffed it at the party or he gave it to someone else."

I was silent. Trying to take it in. A moment later, I asked, "You're sure it didn't somehow get to Jamal?"

He waved his hand impatiently. "Ritalin doesn't kill anyone, Mom. Half the class takes it in pill form during exam time, and half sniffs it for the high. Besides, Jamal died of a meth overdose. That's a totally different drug."

"Is it possible that the police will find something like meth at our place? Is it a substance that resembles Ritalin in any way?"

He looked at me as if I were an idiot.

"Come on, Adam, I didn't study chemistry. Explain it to me."

"I told you, they're two different things. Ritalin is methylphenidate and meth is methamphetamine. But the thing is that when you make meth at home, you sometimes use a small quantity of rat poison to create a chemical reaction, and that's what I think killed Jamal, because when people make the stuff at home, they sometimes mess up the quantity. The users think they're sniffing meth, but they're actually sniffing rat poison."

The rain was letting up now. You could distinguish between the sky and the sea again.

I was exhausted, so exhausted that I could barely stand. "Come inside," I said. "Let's go to sleep."


When he came out of the bathroom, his hair wet, he looked younger than his sixteen years. He got into bed without saying good night. But a moment later, lying with his back to me, he said in the darkness, "Mom?"

"Yes."

"What we just talked about—is that what the police asked you when they came to the house, or are those your questions?"

I didn't say anything. He turned around on the mattress. I couldn't see his face in the darkness of the room, but I thought he was looking at me.

"It's the police, the fucking police," I said, trying to choke back my sobs.

"Don't cry, Mom, please don't cry," he said, frightened by my weeping. I forced myself to stop and bit my lips in the darkness.

When he fell asleep, I went out to the balcony. I called Mikhael. He answered immediately. "Where are you?"

"In Ensenada."

*"Mexico?"*

"The police came and searched the house this afternoon. They want to talk to Adam. So I thought it would do us good to get away for the weekend."

He was silent a moment, absorbing my words. "Searched?"

"Yes. With a warrant and sniffer dogs and everything. I asked Maria to straighten up the mess, but I didn't want Adam to come home from school and see the house upside down."

"So you just up and took him to Mexico?"

"I knew it would take you hours to get home. I thought you'd join us tomorrow for the weekend."

"Leelo, is everything okay?"

"Yes, why wouldn't it be?"

I spoke quietly, my tone reasonable and calm, and that confused him.

"Because it sounds pretty hysterical, taking off for Mexico like that."

"We've done it many times. Remember that spur-of-the-moment Thanksgiving trip to Cabo?"

"Yes, but that wasn't like this. It's as if you're on the run with him or something."

"What's so terrible about going to Ensenada? A kid died right in front of him. Now the police are harassing him. We wanted to take a break."

"Yes, but it doesn't look good. I mean, it seems a little crazy."

"So now I'm crazy because I wanted to spend a weekend in Mexico?"

"Is it because you were scared?"

"Of course I was scared. I'm telling you there were policemen in our house. And sniffer dogs. They took Adam's laptop. It was horrible, and I couldn't reach you—you were in your meetings—so I had to make a decision by myself. Stop acting like I kidnapped him or something!"

"Okay, calm down, it's okay." He hesitated on the other end of the line, then finally said, "Look, I can't come tomorrow, I'm loaded down with work. You can stay there for the weekend if you feel like it or come back on Saturday, whatever's best for you. But right after that, first thing Monday morning, I want to take Adam to the police station, on our own initiative, and talk to them. We'll explain that it's all nonsense. If it'll calm you down, we'll take a lawyer with us, even though I think that would only show panic when it's obvious that there's no reason to panic and that everything's fine. Okay, honey?"

The waves roared in front of me. Everything was amazingly logical. "Okay," I whispered. Fifteen minutes later, Mikhael called again. He was on his way to us. He'd probably be here in the early hours of the morning.

The next day, the sky was blue. Not a trace of the storm. Mikhael arrived just in time for breakfast. After we ate, he went upstairs to nap, and Adam and I went scuba diving at the site adjoining the hotel. Afterward, we had a nice time sitting together on the beach, eating empanadas and drinking pineapple juice. At noon, Mikhael joined us. We rented a boat and sailed around the inlets.

"Look at how beautiful it is here," I said. "I'm glad we had the chance to unwind." They both agreed that, yes, it was really beautiful. None of us mentioned last night or the fact that both Adam and Mikhael secretly wondered whether I'd lost it.

When we finished with the boat, we went upstairs to rest. Mikhael looked at the suitcase I'd packed hurriedly the day before and didn't say anything, but when I came out of the shower, he put down his phone and said, "I asked Jane to book us the first flight back Sunday morning. Adam wants to get back in time for Uri."

In the evening, we ordered a seafood dinner at the restaurant on the beach. Adam told Mikhael about our morning dive. Mikhael listened, asked what kind of fish we'd seen, and kept looking at me with a strange expression on his face, the expression of a diver who's come across a deep-sea creature and is trying to decide if it could be dangerous.

## 46

ON MONDAY MORNING, they went to the police station. Mikhael waited outside the room while Adam told the detectives about Jamal's bullying. He told them he'd dreamed about killing him and talked to other kids about it, but without any real intention, the way the guys in his class who were virgins boasted about how they'd fucked the brains out of some girl and she'd begged for more.

The policemen asked him questions, but not too many. The search of our house hadn't turned up anything and there was no trace of drugs in the garage. In Jamal's room, however, they'd found traces of weed. There was an item about it in the newspaper. It quoted Annabella Jones. ("All the kids sometimes smoke a joint," she said in the article. "It doesn't mean that he did meth. Addicts do meth, and my son wasn't an addict.") After an hour's interrogation and a cursory examination of Adam's phone, the police said he could go. He'd given logical answers for everything. They had no real reason to suspect him. That evening, at home, Mikhael told me he was glad they'd gone to the station. "It would have looked bad if Adam hadn't gone in to explain on his own initiative. A person doesn't run away if he's got nothing to fear."

Mikhael looked at the closed door on the second floor and said in a low voice, "You know what makes me crazy? How easily they twist things in this country. Our son is the victim in this whole story—Jamal bullied him. How could the police have even thought of him as a murderer?"

Nobody but the three of us knew about the trip to Mexico, but everyone knew about the search of our house and Adam's inter-rogation at the police station. The people who lived on our block and saw the squad car come and go greeted us coolly over the next few days. Ashley's mother stopped me in the school parking lot and said it was outrageous, snooping around in a kid's home like that, what did they think they would find there? Even if Ja-mal had bullied Adam, that was no motive for murder. When she said the word *murder*, her eyes widened with emotion that looked almost sexual. I mumbled something quickly and walked away. In the afternoon, I got a call from the guidance counselor for Adam's grade, a small woman with a big mouth, who asked the three of us to come in for a talk. I barked at her that my son had suffered enough from those false accusations and she should leave us alone.

I was worried about my son. I pictured him walking down the high-school corridors, surrounded by whispers. That evening, I told Mikhael that I was still worried. "You know how closed off he is. Maybe he's just not showing us how much those rumors upset him."

The next day, I tried to feel him out, asked whether he wanted to change schools. He rejected that idea out of hand. "My friends are here," he said, "the kids from Uri."

That night, Mikhael and I sat in the living room. Adam hadn't come back from his run yet. It felt as if we were delaying going upstairs to our bedroom. Since my impulsive trip to Mexico, a coldness had developed between us, and perhaps that's what made me put off telling Mikhael about that conversation with Netta. I was afraid of how he would react when he found out I'd ambushed a girl I didn't know at the entrance to her school. But in the end, I told him. He listened, his expression serious. When I finished, he said, "I don't see what the problem is."

"You don't see what the problem is when a person encourages children to kill animals with their bare hands?"

Mikhael shrugged. "People use rat traps all the time. You're just used to the exterminator doing the job for you."

"But it's not that Uri set a trap, the way normal people do. He leaves the rats alive so the kids can learn how to kill them."

I searched his eyes, but Mikhael was looking out the window at the night outside, which enveloped the house and stopped at the threshold of our illuminated door.

"It's as if he wanted them to experience killing," I said.

Mikhael returned his gaze to me, but his eyes were distant. "Maybe that's how the girl understood it. But think about it this way: Let's say they put out twenty, maybe thirty traps. That's a reasonable number if there's a serious rat problem and you want to make sure the place is clean. And let's say that most of the traps kill the rats as soon as they're caught, but three of them have broken operating mechanisms. The rat is injured, but not dead. What happens then?"

"I don't understand the question."

"What do you do with those three rats? You don't want to

set them free, because then you'll have a rat problem again, and in any case, they're so badly injured that it would be cruel to let them live. And you don't want to drown them—which, by the way, is what they do in Israel—because here it's considered inhumane and illegal to kill pests that way. You have to kill those rats yourself with a single blow to the head. And that's exactly what Uri asked the kids to do. To take responsibility and kill the rats that survived in the traps."

"Even if you're right, doesn't it bother you that Adam volunteered to do it? He was such a sensitive child, and now he's the first to kill an animal with his bare hands in a kind of sick coming-of-age ritual."

"I don't think it's sick."

"So why did Netta describe it like that?"

"Because she's a girl who loves being onstage. Really, Lilach, don't you see she's disturbed? The slap she gave Adam in the cemetery and the chutzpah of the way she spoke to you, that's the behavior of a classic attention-seeker."

We sat in silence for a few moments. Finally, Mikhael stood up from the couch and said he was tired. I remained alone in the living room, waiting for Adam to come home.

## 47

WHEN I REACHED the lounge, most of the residents were already sitting down. I said hello and apologized again for my sudden absence because of my trip to Mexico. Martha wasn't in her regular place. The first sounds of *Breakfast at Tiffany's* came from the screen, and Audrey Hepburn walked down Fifth Avenue. *When the film ends,* I thought, *I'll talk to them about romance and capitalism.* I sat down next to Chan. I was glad to see that Dwayne was in the audience. The residents leaned back in their chairs, the music coming from the screen enveloping them, and that's why it took me a moment to realize that the shift supervisor was shouting.

Martha had fallen out of bed. At first they thought that was the problem, a fall from bed. But when the ambulance arrived, a paramedic said, "I think it was a stroke." From that moment on, the medics didn't smile or chat with us but moved quickly and seriously. Lucia wasn't there. The supervisor said, "I'll ride in the ambulance with her," but it was clear that he was offering only because that was the protocol. He was new and didn't really know Martha.

"I'll go with her," I told him. "You call her family." He forgot to hide the relief on his face when he nodded.

I wanted to ask Dwayne to come along with us, but when I saw him sitting on the couch, withered and frail, I thought that might not be such a good idea. I got into the ambulance with Martha. She was still wearing her pajamas, which smelled lightly of mothballs. The stroke had made her speech a bit muddled, but her eyes were open and she moved her hand down my back in the same familiar way. The ambulance driver turned on the siren and sped off.

Martha's skin was now almost as white as her hair, and she'd closed her eyes. The driver reported to the hospital that they were on the way with an elderly woman suffering from a possible stroke. I held Martha's hand and tried to remember where her children lived, if they'd get here in time.

*America is so big,* she'd once said to me. *The children rolled all over the continent, in all directions, and like marbles, they landed in the farthest-away places.*

Martha opened her eyes and spoke now, but not in English. A foreign language—Polish, maybe. I hadn't even known she wasn't from here. Perhaps she immigrated before I was born. When we drove onto the highway, she stopped talking for a moment, then spoke again in her strange language, this time loudly, firmly. The paramedic leaning over her peered at me, possibly to see whether I spoke that language. At the end of Martha's words, a question mark rang out clearly, demanding. She waited for a reply.

"Martha, I'm here with you," I said in English, pronouncing the words loudly and distinctly so my English would be a lighthouse she could navigate her way by. But she repeated the incomprehensible sentence she had spoken earlier—at least I thought it was the same sentence.

"Martha, everything's all right," I whispered, and she held my hand tightly and answered me in her strange language, loudly, with a passion I'd never known she was capable of. She stopped speaking and looked at me. I nodded. She smiled in satisfaction and kept speaking. As we drove on, she spoke and spoke and I listened carefully and nodded so she wouldn't know that her final words were falling on uncomprehending ears.

Perhaps I should have recorded her so that someone could decipher what she said, maybe her son, who would fly in the next night and come to the home with dark shadows under his brown, slightly slanted eyes. But at that moment, it didn't occur to me, and when we entered the emergency room, it was already too late. Only when it was all over did I remember that I'd left my coat in the ambulance. When I went down to the ambulance bay, I saw that the paramedic who had treated her was still there.

"Is she gone?" he asked.

I nodded.

"When she started speaking in her language, I knew she would go," he said and added that people on their deathbeds almost always spoke the language they'd been born into. Elderly Mexicans who had lived sixty years in the States suddenly reverted to

Spanish in his ambulance. Others, whose accents were so light that you couldn't even tell they had immigrated, suddenly spoke Hungarian or Turkish. He'd even heard Hebrew once.

I took a Lyft back to the home. The driver was from Senegal. His visa, he told me, although I hadn't asked, would expire at the end of the month. But he'd try to extend it and stay. He'd appreciate it if I gave him a good rating on the app—it would bring him other passengers. *If there was an accident now,* I thought, *he'd leave this life in Senegalese and no one would understand him, and I'd leave it in Hebrew and no one would understand me.* But of course, there wouldn't be an accident; I'd get out of the Lyft in front of the home, give him a high rating on the app, and add a tip. He would say, *Have a nice day,* and I would reply, *You too.*

## 48

I DIDN'T RECOGNIZE her voice when she called. It was very hoarse and old, as if it were coming out of the throat of a ninety-year-old woman.

"Leela? This is Annabella Jones. Could we meet today?"

It took a minute for me to understand what she was saying, and when I did, my heart skipped a beat. I said yes. I suggested her home or maybe the neighborhood where she worked, but she rejected my suggestions politely and said, "If it's okay, I'd like to come to your place. I get off work at two."

She knocked at the door a few hours later. She was wearing a tight black dress. I couldn't tell if she just happened to be wearing black or if it was a mourning dress. Her voice could barely push its way out of the depths of her body. "I lost my voice two weeks ago, and it hasn't come back." She wore a golden locket around her neck, and there was no need for me to open it to know that Jamal's picture lay against her heart. I invited her to sit. She perched on the white armchair in an uncomfortable position, her hands on her lap. She glanced around our spacious living room, looked through the bay window at the well-kept garden. I went into the kitchen to get us tea and jam cookies. My hand shook a little when I put the teacup down in front of her. Annabella pushed a lock of her hair behind her ears, and I suddenly thought that I had never hosted a Black woman in my living room.

"There are brownies too, if you don't like jelly cookies."

She made a small gesture with her right hand—those long pianist's fingers—signaling to me that there was no need.

We sat there. Annabella didn't touch her tea or the cookies. My throat was dry. I took a sip of my tea and warmed my frozen hands on the hot cup. Annabella noticed the photo of Adam beside the window, the same one that had caught Detective O'Malley's attention, and examined it intently.

"That's Adam?"

"Yes."

She leaned forward to see the image better. "He looks like a happy kid."

And yes, in that photo taken on the beach in Cabo, Adam did look like a happy kid. That's why I'd framed it and hung it on the wall.

"You have other kids?"

"No," I replied.

"I have three. My husband wanted more, but I told him to find work first, and then we got divorced. Now I'm sorry I didn't have ten."

I hugged my cup with my hands. I breathed slowly. Annabella said, "The kids in school are saying things."

"I know."

She looked away from the picture of Adam and directly at me now. "They said that the police were here."

"They didn't find anything."

Her glance moved away from me, back to the photo. "Do you know your son, Leela?"

"Yes," I said. "He's a good boy. Maybe he said things. Kids spout a lot of nonsense, but he's a good boy."

She was silent. The sun flickering on the bay window threw dancing shadows on the opposite wall. On the corner table was a large bouquet of flowers that Maria had arranged the day before yesterday. Annabella was looking at it as she said, "Jamal was a happy kid. Open like a book, that's what I always said. He loved hip-hop, like all the kids do. Those clips on TV with the girls dancing half naked. That's why I didn't understand when I looked at his laptop and found the pictures."

Before I realized what was happening, Annabella's eyes filled with tears. I stayed where I was for a moment, frozen, then jumped up from the couch to take a tissue out of my bag. But my hands remained hanging in the air when I tried to give it to her. Annabella opened the small, speckled black bag that lay at her feet and rummaged around inside it for a long time, searching for her own tissue, and when she didn't find it, she wiped her eyes with her sleeve. She wouldn't take anything from here, I suddenly realized, not cookies or tea or a tissue.

The tears subsided. She spoke again. "Even after the pictures I found on Jamal's computer, I still couldn't believe it. I thought it was a joke. A mother is supposed to know her kids, right? But then I found the texts on the phone and the account he opened under another name on a dating site."

I looked at her, confused. I didn't understand what she was telling me. And she apparently saw my confusion. She gave me a broken smile and said, "My son was gay, Leela. He liked boys. His brothers and I didn't know about it. He always had girlfriends."

She wiped her eyes with her sleeve again. "And I don't know what's sadder—that I didn't really know him or that he didn't know me at all. Because if my son had known how much I love him, he would have understood that he didn't have to hide anything from me."

I sat there, paralyzed. Annabella pointed around the living room. "I thought that if I saw your house, I'd feel something, that somehow I'd know. But I'm sitting here and I realize that I don't know anything."

She leaned forward on the white armchair, her entire body tilted toward me. Her eyes were as dark as velvet, like Jamal's. "So before I go, Leela, I want to ask you again: Do you know your son? Because I'm burning inside my skin from not knowing what happened to my boy. I don't sleep. I don't work. His brothers make their own meals because I don't have the strength for anything. It's killing me, these unanswered questions. It's torture to live like this. If you know anything, you have to tell me. Promise you'll tell me. I don't know if I can go on like this much longer."

## 49

I DROVE TO pick him up at school. It was only two o'clock, but after my conversation with Annabella, I wanted him home with me. The clouds were low in the sky, white and enormous, like an animal about to give birth. The first drops of rain fell on the windshield during the drive. When I parked in the lot adjoining the school, the drizzle had already stopped, and a jagged winter sun blinded me. I walked straight to the gate, shading my eyes with my hands, blinking angrily against the glaring whiteness. The guard smiled at me and asked how we were today. I smiled and said, "Great, how are you," and didn't stop walking.

I went to the office. I knew that the secretary didn't like parents picking up their children before the end of the school day.

"He has a doctor's appointment," I told her.

The secretary nodded and said, "I'll call him."

I waited. The office walls were decorated with trophies and certificates. Basketball champions. Football champions. And even a certificate that Adam could be proud of: chemistry champions the previous year. A few moments later, I could hear the secretary's heels clacking in the hallway. Surprisingly, there were no other footsteps approaching. When she opened the door, she looked embarrassed.

"Adam's not here," she said. "The math teacher said she saw him in the morning, but he apparently left without permission after the lunch break. Unfortunately, we have to make a note of it in his personal file. This is the second time this year."

"The second time?"

The secretary gave me an admonishing look. She was a woman of almost sixty who had helped shepherd generations of students in accordance with strict rules rigorously observed, and she believed that it was only thanks to those rules that the percentage of the school's graduates who attended Ivy League schools was so high.

"The second time," she said grimly. "At the beginning of the year, he was caught off school grounds with Jamal Jones. It appears in his file. We e-mailed you the notification, and you returned it with your signature."

I didn't tell her that I had never signed such a notification. Instead, I asked warily, "Are you sure it was with Jamal Jones?"

The secretary said she was positive. They kept meticulous records. She checked both Adam's and Jamal's files on her computer, then nodded and said, "Yes, they both have notations about it in their files. The gym teacher saw them in the park off school grounds during school hours." Seeing my confused expression, she softened her tone. "Look, children that age can fight and make up so quickly that you and I can't even imagine it. One day they're best friends and suddenly, something flares up between them and they stop speaking."

The park stretched out along the other side of the school. Shade trees. Hidden corners. Squirrels ran from me as I walked on the damp ground. A girl in jeans and a sweatshirt smoked a cigarette on a bench. She was listening to music on her phone and didn't glance in my direction. I kept walking, passing a juniper hedge, and when I reached an isolated spot, I heard a rustling in the bushes. I focused on where the noise was coming from, thinking for a moment that I might see Adam there, but instead, I saw two pairs of eyes. A girl and a boy were lying on the ground, his hand under her shirt, her hand on his pants. I hurried away. I took out my phone and called Adam. When he answered, I cried, almost shouted, "Where are you?"

"We went shopping."

"*What?*"

"We saw that Decathlon was having a twenty-four-hour sale, so we drove over."

"Who's 'we,' Adam? Who are you with now?"

And I didn't need his response to know.

How is it possible that I haven't Googled you until now, Uri Ziv? What kind of mother doesn't Google her son's guru? The English search yielded no results except for a few ads about Orion with information I already knew. The Hebrew search generated many entries, far too many: Uri Ziv, a vet in Kfar Saba; Uri Ziv, social worker in the Petah Tikva welfare department. Four lawyers, an occupational therapist in Nof HaGalil. It took a lot of time, but I was a woman with time to spare. Time dripped from my hands. Finally, I saw his picture: First Lieutenant Uri Ziv receiving an outstanding reserve officer medal from the chief of the general staff in a formal ceremony at the end of the Second Lebanon War. The description of the operation that led to the award was so vague that it was impossible to learn anything from it.

All it said was that, with great presence of mind, First Lieutenant Ziv had launched an attack under difficult conditions and demonstrated determination, persistence, and operational creativity during a complex military action, never losing sight of the objective: to engage the enemy. I assumed that behind the nebulous words was a considerable number of wounded soldiers, perhaps dead ones as well, on our side and at least one dead terrorist on the other. I wondered if Uri hadn't hesitated to use his hands to complete the job in Lebanon, as he did here with the rats. I looked at the picture of the young man he had been, eyes shining with controlled emotion as the commander in chief leaned over to pin the medal on him, wondered how he must have imagined the continuation of his life in the light of that moment, bathed in glory. And what must have happened to him when he realized that the most significant thing he would ever do was already behind him, carried out by the twenty-four-year-old Uri Ziv.

An hour and a half later, I heard the front door lock click. Adam and Uri had come home. "Look, Mom," Adam said and showed me an ornate leather case that held a new Leatherman. "Uri bought it for me so I would have it on trips." His smell of teenage sweat, especially pungent after long hours spent outside, entered the house along with him. I felt like pushing him into the bathtub and scrubbing that nauseating, adolescent-boy stench off him.

"Did I give you permission to cut school?"

He glanced quickly at Uri, who was standing at the door. I saw how much he wanted me to delay the rebuke, not to tell him off in front of Uri. "Go upstairs and put that in your room," I said. He went upstairs, the new Leatherman in his hand. Uri and I remained standing in the entryway. He pushed his hand through his hair and began speaking hesitantly.

"Sorry, Lilach. I should have asked you. It's just that a meeting was canceled and I knew Adam was feeling down about what's been going on lately. That whole business with the police. I wanted to cheer him up."

"Does it seem reasonable to you, asking a kid to cut school without his parents' permission?"

Uri looked at me, stunned. He had prepared himself for a friendly scolding. Not this. "I talked to Mikhael about it, but I should have talked to you. I see that now. Not for a minute did I want to worry you."

I didn't reply. I was embarrassed by my outburst but I couldn't bring myself to apologize. I couldn't even look at him. He waited a beat, cleared his throat, and finally said in a different, hurt tone, "So I'll take off now."

Before I could say anything, he was outside. Kelev walked him to the gate, barking cheerfully. When I turned around, Adam was standing at the top of the stairs, his face red. "Mom, what's wrong with you? How could you let him leave like that?"

And before I could reply, he went into his room and slammed the door.

## 50

ADAM DIDN'T COME out of his room that entire afternoon. When I knocked on his door and asked if he wanted to have dinner with me, he opened it and snarled, "I'm not hungry."

I ate alone. Mikhael arrived late, smelling faintly of alcohol and complaining about a boring dinner with the reps who'd come in from New York.

"Why didn't you tell me that Uri was going to pick up Adam in the middle of the school day?" I said the minute we walked into the bedroom. "I was worried sick."

Mikhael hung his jacket on a hanger. "I knew Adam didn't finish school until late today. I had no way of knowing you'd pick him up early."

"So you decided to let him cut school behind my back?"

"Adam is an excellent student. I didn't think it would matter if he missed classes once. And I thought it was good that Uri wanted to cheer him up."

"I'm not so sure anymore that Uri is a good influence on Adam."

He had just taken off his pants, and, standing there in his underpants and button-down shirt, he gave me a tired look.

"You knew he was taking him out to buy a knife?"

"Oh, that," Mikhael said, his hands moving slowly down the row of shirt buttons, his fingers undoing them one by one.

"The guy always tells the kids in his class that they have to fight back, and now we find out that he bought our son a knife as a present."

Mikhael looked at me with the relaxed smile of someone who has drunk at least three glasses of wine. "Next you'll turn him into a serial killer. Leelo, all the guy did was buy our son something you take on camping trips, to make him happy."

"But why does our son need a knife? It's not a toy, Mikhael. I think it's even a criminal offense to walk around the streets with something like that."

Mikhael sat down on the bed. "Listen, Lilach, Uri meant to do something good. If you don't like it, I'll explain that to Adam and return the gift."

He took off his shirt and pressed the remote for the blinds. The room grew dark, and the light from the streetlamps remained outside. "Now, are you ready to come to bed, or are we mad at each other?"

"I have dishes to do."

I went down to the kitchen. When I finished the dishes, I attacked the electric kettle with my descaler. I cleaned the counter, scrubbing off layers of grease, but despite all my efforts, I couldn't remove the hurt. Or the alcohol I'd smelled on his breath when he came into the house, or the question I didn't ask—*Was it only the reps from New York at the dinner you went to, or did Jane join you?*—or the weariness in his voice when he spoke to me and in his eyes when he looked at me.

## 51

THAT NIGHT, ADAM cried in his sleep. Mikhael was sound asleep. He didn't hear, but I did. Even when he was a baby and cried in his bed, I was the one who heard and went to him. But when he was a baby, I leaped off the mattress the instant I heard him crying. And now I stayed in bed, undecided about whether I should go to him or not.

In the end, I got up and tiptoed down the hallway. I opened his door and hesitated at the threshold. His eyes were tightly shut. He moaned in his sleep. I went in and sat down on the edge of his bed. "Adam?"

He startled awake. I put my hand on his shoulder. A moment later, he seemed a bit calmer and pulled the blanket over his head. I reached out to move it from where it covered his face. But he pulled it back. I heard him sniff under the blanket. And all at once, I began to cry as well. How deceptive he was, this child. I had almost believed his tough facade, the "Everything's fine" he reeled off every time I asked about school. But in fact, nothing was fine. Since the search of our house and the police interrogation, Jamal's friends looked at him as if he were some kind of murderer. Teachers gossiped about him. Parents whispered about him.

He turned over. Maybe he was embarrassed about the way his dream had fallen apart. His pain was alive and intense, and the bed was saturated with it, just as, when he was a toddler, he used to wake in the middle of the night with his bed and pajamas saturated with urine. I wanted to ask about him and Netta, about him and Jamal, but I could tell that he was beginning to calm down and I knew he would let me stay only if I didn't speak. I ran my hand down his back. Even through the blanket, I could feel how thin he was. I waited beside him until he fell asleep.

In the days that followed, I observed him carefully. He went to school with his head held high. His face showed no sign of the pain he'd suffered that night. I waited for the whole story to end, the way I had once when a huge wave caught me on the Santa Monica beach and flipped me over and over—I'd stopped breathing and let my body be slammed against the sand on the ocean bottom. I closed my eyes tightly, careful not to inhale salt water, and waited for it to be over so I could lift my head out of the water and breathe. *Only another few days. Another few weeks.* That's what I said to myself, that's what I whispered to Adam in my mind. I never imagined that the current wave was nothing but a ripple. The real wave was still making its way to us.

The morning it happened, when the real wave broke over us with all its power, we got into the car two minutes early. Mikhael was scheduled to fly to Washington later that day, and he walked us to the front door and waved goodbye as we pulled out of the driveway.

"What do you want to listen to?" I asked Adam and was surprised when he chose Bob Dylan for us. As we drove to school, he looked out the window and mimicked Dylan's singing in a slightly nasal voice, which made us both laugh. My son's laugh hovered in the air of the car like a rare butterfly. I didn't ask anything. I didn't say anything, trying not to destroy the moment.

While we waited for the light to change at the intersection, he began to talk about the training they had done this week—carrying someone wounded on a stretcher for a long distance.

"Usually, in the army, they relieve the people holding the stretcher every fifteen minutes, because it's really heavy, but Boaz and I decided we wouldn't hand the stretcher over to anyone else until the whole exercise was done—the way they do it in the general staff. And we did it!" How much pride there was in his voice. "It's a matter of physical endurance," he explained seriously. "The important thing is not to use all your energy right at the beginning, because then you get tired."

I considered telling him that the important thing was not to get yourself into a situation where you had to run up a hill while you were being shot at from every direction and carrying a wounded buddy on your back, but I kept quiet.

"I'm making it louder, okay? This is the best part."

I was glad, because I also thought that Bob Dylan's opening to "Mr. Tambourine Man" was the best part, even if it was a little hackneyed, and how great it was for Adam that it wasn't hackneyed for him yet because he'd only just started listening to Dylan.

I stopped at the gates to the school. Bob Dylan played his

harmonica. Adam and I listened quietly. He didn't hurry to get out and I didn't push him. *Sit with me for another minute. School will wait.*

"*Yalla,*" I finally said, "you have to get to class." And later, how much I regretted urging him, how sorry I was that I'd been the one to tell him to get out of the warm, protective car. He opened the door and a gust of cold air blew inside. "Put on your coat," I said, because at that moment, I still believed that the greatest danger awaiting him outside the car was the cold. "Have a great—"

I didn't finish that sentence. My eyes were drawn to the spray-painted words. I stared at the red letters screaming at me from the wall surrounding the school: JEWS ARE THE DEVIL. SHUSTER IS A MURDERER. POLICE COVER-UP.

I got out of the car and walked over to the high concrete wall. The words were written on the upper part by the strong hand of a large boy, someone whose muscles wouldn't quiver when they stretched to that height and carefully sprayed letter after letter. Someone like Jamal.

A Black boy who was standing not far from me also stared at the words. I turned and studied him. He looked back at me, straight into my face, without fear and without blinking. *Grab him, someone stop that boy!* The shout rose up to my mouth but never passed my lips.

Of course I couldn't say it. Of course I couldn't shout hysterically at an African American boy who hadn't done anything but stare. Which is what most of the people there were doing.

Parents, children, teachers standing in the school parking lot and looking at the red, screaming letters.

While everyone was staring at the graffiti, I looked down at the grass, at the red drops that spotted it. I followed them, walking cautiously, the damp leaves drenching my canvas shoes. I didn't know what I expected to find, but I nonetheless followed the drops of paint along the wall, to the corner. Now I could no longer see the parking lot, the parents, the students. I could no longer hear the whispers and the talking. Awaiting me on the other side was an absolute, ominous silence. Broken glass bottles lay on the ground. I took large steps over them and then stopped. Why had I even come here? I had to go back. Adam was waiting for me. I'd already turned around when a red stain on the wall caught my attention. I moved forward again, squeezed between the wall and a row of hedges. Why would someone take the trouble to spray graffiti here, where no one would see it? It was as if he enjoyed toying with me, forcing me to dirty my shoes with mud and my body with leaves. I pushed farther and farther onward between the hedges and the mossy wall until I could clearly see the message: REVENGE IS COMING.

I hurried back. I didn't care about the dirt anymore. I just wanted to get to the lot. I stepped on the broken glass bottles, and there was a clear picture in my mind: When I reached the parking lot, I wouldn't find him. Adam would have vanished. They would have taken my son.

But when I peered past the corner to the parking lot, my son was exactly where I'd left him: beside the car, looking at the graffiti.

"Do you know who did that?" I asked.

He shook his head. He tried to look unconcerned, but the tic in his eyebrow gave him away.

"Get into the car. We're going to file a complaint with the police."

"Mom, it's just words."

"Whoever wrote them can do more."

"If he had the courage to do more, he wouldn't have come

here in the middle of the night like a coward to write crap on the walls."

The boy who had cried in his bed earlier that week was gone. Adam zipped up his jacket decisively. It was a matter of physical endurance. He had lifted the stretcher and walked with it until the exercise ended. His lack of emotion, his cold, sober analysis of his situation, was no less frightening than the graffiti. His demeanor as he stood beside me was that of a stranger, cold and detached. And only a moment earlier, we'd been sitting together in the car, enveloped by the sound of a harmonica, and my son had laughed.

"Did you see it?" Einat Greenbaum intercepted me a few minutes later, zipping over to me in the parking lot like a launched rocket. Adam had just disappeared into the school—"You're sure you want to go?" "Yes, I'm sure"—and I was standing beside the car waiting for my hands to stop shaking so I could drive. In addition to the graffiti on the front wall and near the hedges, there were two more graffiti messages—CORRUPT POLICE and SHUSTER OUT—sprayed in red near the parking lot.

"It must be the Nation of Islam," Einat said, her hands playing with the gold chain around her neck. "All they want to do is accuse a Jew."

Moran, Yochai's mother, joined us. "The principal promised me they would remove it by noon."

"They expect the kids to learn in a building that has *Jews are the devil* written on it? This persecution has to stop," Einat said. "The chutzpah of those Nazis."

Although I didn't say a word, their eyes were drawn to me. I was the undisputed focus of this social encounter. Other parents approached us, pointed to the graffiti, and expressed their horror in Hebrew and English.

"First the attack in the synagogue, and now this," Zach Cohen said.

"We have to increase security," Moran said. "Someone who writes this could easily slip into violence." Then she waited for me to speak.

Behind the women standing before me, I saw the words sprayed on the wall and was devastated. They must have sensed how upset I was because Einat Greenbaum suddenly gave me a hug that had the scent of recently shampooed hair. I didn't want to cry, but I did. Einat nodded her approval. Her hug was like a mother's whose son, ignoring her warnings, runs and falls. She kisses his wounds and comforts him, but deep inside, she's kind of happy about his fall, because it brought him back into her arms.

## 52

AS SOON AS I was alone in the car, I called Mikhael. I cried hysterically. He was sure it was one of Jamal's friends, maybe even one of his brothers. He said I should pick him up and we'd go to the police station together. "They'll catch that chickenshit."

I'd hoped to see Natasha Peterson, but instead of the detective with the braid, it was O'Malley who came out. He apologized for keeping us waiting so long. We followed him to the small interrogation room at the far end of the corridor. He pointed to the chairs and asked how he could help us. We told him about the graffiti. To my surprise, he knew the details. It turned out that the school administration had already filed its own complaint.

"If that's the case, do we need to file a complaint too?"

O'Malley shook his head and said that the matter was being handled.

"How is it being handled?" Mikhael asked.

"According to procedure," O'Malley replied.

I told him I was afraid that my son was in danger. "They wrote that revenge was coming, and that sounds like a threat to me."

O'Malley leaned back in his chair. "I understand your concern," he said, "but I don't share it. If you knew how much graffiti is sprayed in schools in this country every day—the insults, the threats, the sexual insinuations—but I've never seen it go beyond the wall it was written on."

"This is not exactly a normal situation," I said. "A few months ago, there was a terror attack against the Jewish community. Now there's antisemitic graffiti directly targeting my son. You can surely understand why I'm concerned."

O'Malley nodded. He said he could definitely understand. But he pointed out that after every major hate-crime attack in the U.S., there were similar incidents: graffiti, anonymous threats on the web, all sorts of provocations that posed no real danger.

"So you're not worried at all?" I asked.

"Absolutely not. Of course, we'll check the school's CCTV cameras to see who was in the area, and we'll catch the kids who did it. But I really don't think that whoever wrote those things will try to harm your son. By the way, why, in your opinion, did they mention his name in particular?"

Mikhael gave him a withering look. He didn't even try to control his anger. "What do you mean, why? Because of your unnecessary search of our home. It made all kinds of lunatics think that maybe Adam really is involved in this."

"At no point did we ever say that your son was suspected of anything."

"That doesn't matter. The minute you went into our house with your dogs, people started talking."

"And you're sure they're talking for no reason?"

O'Malley's tone was as polite as before, and that was what infuriated Mikhael. He stood up from his chair.

"I came here to file a complaint, not to listen to your ridiculous insinuations about my son."

"I'm not insinuating anything," the detective replied coolly. "I'm just asking. It's my job."

"Your job is to prevent the next attack on a synagogue and the next act of vandalism, not to encourage dangerous conspiracy theories."

I wasn't used to hearing Mikhael speak in that tone to authority figures, certainly not in America. When he finished talking, I was suddenly afraid that he might have gone too far—maybe he had gotten us into trouble. O'Malley's face was totally unreadable when he said, "Thank you, Mr. and Mrs. Shuster, I appreciate your taking the time to come here."

When we walked to the parking lot, Mikhael was furious. I had never seen him so angry. "I'm going to write the chief of police and demand that they fire that guy."

I listened distractedly. On the way home, my hands shook on the wheel. I pulled over to the side of the road, afraid I would cause an accident. I asked Mikhael to drive. When we walked into the house, Mikhael poured me a glass of water and asked if I wanted to eat something. "No, thanks," I said. "I think I'll take a shower."

At the bathroom door, I called Lucia and told her that I had to cancel my workshop for that afternoon. "I'm sorry about the late notice," I said, and I was a bit surprised by the silence on the other end of the line. "I could try to get there tomorrow instead," I offered.

"Thank you, Leela, there's no need."

The coldness in her voice confused me. "I'm really sorry, Lucia. I know I've taken a lot of time off recently, but we'll meet on Friday as usual and talk about it, okay?"

Another silence. Then: "Thank you, Leela. And about Friday, there's really no need."

When I came out of the shower, Mikhael's suitcase was on the bed, half packed.

"You're still planning to go to Washington?" I asked in surprise.

"I have no choice, Leelo," he replied. "I can't cancel the presentation."

"Did you try to cancel it?"

"No, I didn't." And when I didn't say anything, he added, "It's one of those things that's planned six months in advance. I can't tell them I'm canceling everything because someone is writing graffiti about my son."

The tears began to run down my cheeks. Mikhael left the open suitcase and hurried over to me. He took me in his arms. I melted into them.

"Listen, they'll catch the kid who did it."

We stood there, our arms around each other. Finally, he moved away from me and pointed to his phone.

"It's already appearing on a few news sites: 'A hate crime in Silicon Valley.'" That seemed to satisfy him, as if the fact that a hate crime was publicized was enough to render the hate powerless.

"I called Adam again," he said, "when you were in the shower. I asked him if he wanted to come home early."

"What did he say?"

"He insisted on staying."

I saw on Mikhael's face that he was proud of our son for choosing to stay in school and not leaving with his tail between his legs. I, on the other hand, wanted him to come home, but that morning in the schoolyard, I'd seen how excited he was about joining Yochai and Boaz, who had been standing not far away on the grass. But what had surprised me was seeing the way both of them looked for him, how eager they were for him to join them. Adam had never been the kind of kid that other kids waited for. In day care, grade school, and middle school, he always had to walk quickly to catch up with a group of kids who were heading somewhere without him. That morning, at the entrance to the school whose walls were sprayed with red, two boys had been waiting for my son.

"I really wish I didn't have to go and that I could stay here with you and Adam," Mikhael said and stroked my face.

"Maybe there's still a chance you could tell them to do the presentation without you?"

"I wish I could. If I tell Berman that I'm not going to the Pentagon because of some graffiti on the walls of Adam's school, they'll look for another vice president."

"What are you saying?" I said angrily. "That it's no big deal? That you're not stressed about it?"

"Lilach, of course I don't like it." His voice was cold now, as if he were speaking to an employee who kept making the same mistake when he read the data or to a soldier who was holding his map upside down. "But I think we have to keep things in perspective. A complaint has been filed. I can't stop going to work until they arrest whoever wrote the graffiti."

His phone rang. I waited to see if he'd answer it, and he did. When he spoke, his voice wasn't cold. It was friendly and warm. "Hi, I'm just packing. Tell him we'll meet at the airport."

"Who was that?" I asked.

Bending over his suitcase, he replied, "Jane. Berman asked her to check if we were all on our way." He stopped packing and went to get something from the bathroom. Kelev followed him down the narrow hall. Since this morning, he'd been running all over the house after Mikhael, wagging his tail. He must have sensed the upcoming departure. I wanted to follow Mikhael to the bathroom too, but I forced myself to stay where I was, beside the pile of books abandoned on the night table.

This wasn't how I wanted to say goodbye to him, stuck in this thundering silence. I went down to the living room. Mikhael continued packing. Fifteen minutes later, he came downstairs, suitcase in hand, and kissed me on the forehead. "Uri will drop by later. He asked to borrow my bike for the weekend," he said, already at the door, and we both knew that the bike was only an excuse, that Mikhael had asked him to come by to see how I was. Before he closed the door, he kissed me again, this time on the mouth. "I'll call tonight."

## 53

A SHORT TIME after he left, I received a call from the rabbi of the Reform synagogue. I remembered his face contorted with shock and sorrow by the news on Rosh Hashanah. Now his voice was impressive and compassionate. "This is an insane time," he said. "I didn't believe we would see blood libel against Jews in this day and age." Then he said, "Our community wants to offer our support to you and your family. We would love to have you join us for services some Saturday."

I thought about the wood-paneled lobby of the synagogue. I wondered if Leah Weinstein's parents still went there to pray after what had happened.

After that rabbi, it was the turn of another rabbi, Esther Klein of the Brit-Shalom Reform synagogue in San Francisco. She called and said in a formal voice that their community wanted to offer their heartfelt sympathy. She herself was not the least bit surprised, she said. For quite a while now, she had been warning people about the rise of antisemitic sentiment in America.

A few minutes after her call, the phone rang again. A journalist from the *Jewish News* introduced herself and asked for my response to the antisemitic graffiti at the school. Right after that, there was a call from a correspondent of Ynet, who asked how we felt about the antisemitic atmosphere in America. And then another call, this time from the *San Francisco Chronicle*: Did I feel that the tension between the African American and Jewish communities had reached new heights? I told all of them "No comment" and said that I didn't want to be interviewed. I demanded that they keep our family's name out of the media. "He's a minor," I said. "If you reveal identifying details, I'll sue you."

I turned off the phone ringer. I watered the garden. I tidied the house. I tried to read a book. I decided to clean everything, even though Maria was coming the next morning. I undid all the organizing I'd done so meticulously earlier. I put the chairs on the table. I rolled the rugs to the sides of the rooms. I moved the plants from the floor to a high shelf. Our familiar home looked suddenly like the home of a different family. I vacuumed. I scrubbed. I put everything back in its place—the chairs, the rugs, the plants. I washed dishes. I descaled the electric kettle. When I finished, it still wasn't late enough to pick up Adam. I pulled the curtains closed. I got into bed, sure I wouldn't fall asleep, but only a minute after my body touched the mattress, I was carried off into a long, swampy sleep.

I startled awake from a dream. With a pounding heart, I sat up in bed, my ears still filled with the clear sound of something smashing. I looked around. The room was as quiet as it had been when I fell asleep. The turquoise curtains moved slightly in the breeze. And beyond them, I heard birdsong, a car driving away, the faint sound of bass guitars. I threw off my blanket and went to the half-open window. I moved a hesitant hand over the cold glass. Through the window I could see our yard, a mowed lawn, a small pool, wooden furniture, and the fence Adam had painted last summer in exchange for the skateboard Mikhael promised him. Looking at the white fence, I suddenly remembered the dream, which I had buried under my quilt when I woke up: A white fence, similar to the one in our yard, but higher. Someone had sprayed graffiti on it and I tried to read the words but couldn't, and what upset me more than the graffiti in the dream was the fact that I couldn't read it. Uri arrived and said, *But you're trying to read from left to right.* And suddenly the music from the party grew louder, menacing, and that noise, that loud—

I slammed the window shut and went into the bathroom to wash off the vestiges of sleep. A pale and frightened woman looked at me from the mirror, and I said to her, "Calm down, Lilach, it was only a dream." I smiled at myself, dried my face with a towel that smelled of fabric softener, and spread cream on my cheeks in a circular motion.

I walked out of the bathroom, a vague plan in my mind about a mushroom quiche I would make for dinner. As I walked downstairs, I made a mental list of the ingredients and went into the kitchen to see what I would need to buy. I sat down and scribbled a shopping list. When I raised my head, I saw a red drop on the floor. And another one. And another.

There were very prominent red drops on our light gray wood floor. I stood up and went to get a rag. When I knelt down to wipe away the drops, I saw more red stains, closer to the cabinet I'd taken the rag from. Only then did I notice that I was bleeding.

I checked my feet. A thin trail of blood was coming from my left heel. I sat down on the floor and removed a piece of glass that was stuck in my skin. I pressed the rag hard on the spot to stop the bleeding, which I hadn't felt at all, even though it had left marks on the wood. *I have to put a Band-Aid on it,* I thought. I straightened up, careful not to step on my left heel. And I stopped a fraction of a second before placing my entire foot on a pile of glass shards where the rock had struck.

## 54

I HAVE NO idea how long I stayed there, surrounded by broken glass. The California sun bathed the house from all directions, and in its light, the shards glittered like diamonds. Among all those glittering shards lay the rock, dark and heavy. It was hard to believe that the material, so inanimate, had flown through the air only a short while ago, had risen above its solid nature, above its existence among earth and moss, as it was hurled straight through our bay window.

I picked up the rock and estimated its weight, cradling it the way you'd cradle a baby's head. The hand that had thrown that rock through our window was long gone, and with it, the knife that had carved on it the letters *NOI*—Nation of Islam. *You have to call the police,* I thought, but I remained where I was. And that's how Uri found me when he arrived to borrow the bike—surrounded by shards of glass, a rock on my lap.

"Lilach, what happened? Are you all right?" His worried eyes looked at me through the shattered window that faced the front yard.

"Are you hurt?"

I shook my head, but he was already bending over me. He saw the bloodstained rag and lifted my bare foot to examine it more carefully.

"Just a scratch," I said. "I didn't even feel it until I saw the blood."

He let go of my foot, but the heat of his fingers remained on my skin. "Look at this," I said, and handed him the rock. His large hand brushed mine for a fraction of a second. In Uri's hand, the rock looked much smaller. Gently, as if he were caressing a baby's cheek, he ran a finger over the letters carved into it.

"It's Jamal's friends," he said. "They've targeted Adam."

Tears ran down my face and I didn't have the strength to stop them.

"Hey." Uri came closer, trying to comfort me. "Everything's okay."

I couldn't control the burst of laughter that rose in my throat. "Do you hear yourself, Uri? They smashed our window with a rock. A *rock!* Like in the intifada! And you tell me that everything's okay?"

He smiled in embarrassment, and his expression seemed to say that he would happily let me explode at him if it would make me feel even slightly less powerless.

I didn't say anything more. I assumed that he was about to offer me a tissue or a glass of water. But Uri didn't offer me anything. He waited for my tears to stop falling and said, "I'll sleep here tonight. And tomorrow. Until Mikhael comes back from Washington."

I nodded, even though there was no need. Uri hadn't asked me. He'd told me. "I'm sorry about our last conversation," I said after a beat. "Mikhael didn't tell me that day that you were picking Adam up from school. I went nuts with worry."

"I understand completely," he said. "If I went to pick up my son from school and he wasn't there, I would go nuts with worry too."

Only when I tried to stand up did I realize how long I'd been sitting frozen among the shards of glass. My muscles were stiff and painful, the way they were after a long flight.

"Wait," Uri said. "I'll get your shoes so you don't cut yourself again." He hurried over to the shoe rack at the entrance and came right back carrying my sandals, but when he looked again at the floor, he changed his mind. He put the sandals on a glass-free spot in the living room and walked toward me in his heavy shoes. The sound of crunching glass accompanied every step.

"Hold on to me," he said, and I obeyed. I put my arms around his neck and he lifted me and carried me to the living room without looking at me and put me down in such a way that my feet would slide directly into my sandals. I bent over quickly to fasten the straps.

The patrolman, a chunky guy with a red beard named Officer Stevens, arrived fifteen minutes after Uri called the police and reported the incident. He shook my hand politely and asked an endless series of questions that could have been summarized with *Do you have any idea who did this?* I gave him a cup of coffee and some cookies.

"The fucking Nation of Islam," he said quietly to Uri while I was putting the dishes in the sink. "They make trouble everywhere they go."

We went out to the front yard. Officer Stevens and a policewoman who had been waiting in the patrol car while he talked to me in the house examined the grass. She didn't utter a sound the entire time. Another police car drove up and I hoped that Detective O'Malley wasn't inside it. When he stepped out, I gave him a cold hello and bravely endured Kelev's excited tail-wagging greeting. O'Malley petted him affectionately, turned to Officer Stevens, and asked, "What do we have here?"

"It's his fault," I said loudly in Hebrew to Uri. "That fucked-up search made everyone think that Adam's hiding something."

O'Malley flashed me a look and lowered his gaze, because even though he didn't speak Hebrew, he understood exactly what I'd said. I waited for Uri to signal me to be quiet the way Mikhael certainly would have, with that secret look men have when they're trying to let women know that they've crossed a line. But Uri didn't say anything—just the opposite. He looked at O'Malley sternly, and I, bolstered by his clear anger toward the detective, almost stopped controlling my own fury. I was about to let O'Malley know exactly what I thought—this time in English—when Uri suddenly said to Officer Stevens, "If you don't need us, I think Mrs. Shuster and I will go for a drive."

"Don't you think we should stay?" I asked.

"On the contrary," he said, "I'm sure we *shouldn't* stay. The glazier is on his way. The cleaner is on her way. Let's drive somewhere nice and walk for a bit. It will give you a chance to settle down before it's time to pick up Adam. Go get your sneakers."

## 55

HALF AN HOUR later, we had hiked up a road in an oak forest. The cut on my heel stung. Uri walked in front of me. His silence surprised me. From the moment he moved from the asphalt of the small parking lot to the ground of the forest, he had removed words from himself the way you remove a coat. Every once in a while, he stopped, drinking in the view with his eyes, and waited for me to reach him and catch my breath before going ahead. I tried to slow the pace, but Uri only increased it.

The higher we climbed, the more heavily I panted. To my ears, there was something almost obscene about it, panting that way in the presence of a stranger. In that huge forest, our aloneness was suddenly more conspicuous. I looked at Uri to see if he felt it as well, but his expression was untroubled and open, taking in the full expanse of the view. And as if to confirm my feeling, he said, "Do you feel the taste of the air on your tongue?" and inhaled loudly.

"It reminds me a little of the Galilee," I said. I thought he'd laugh a little—those Israelis who say that the Norwegian fjords remind them of the Sea of Galilee always make me laugh—but Uri actually nodded. We kept climbing. I bit my lip, straining not to fall far behind him, cursing myself for the exercise classes I'd skipped, but Uri was too quick, and now I thought he was moving even faster. Finally, we reached a small clearing in the forest. I collapsed onto a boulder, red-faced and a bit angry. I took off my sweatshirt, wearing only my tank top now. I pulled my hair back into a ponytail high above my sweaty neck. I let the breeze on the summit cool me. Far below, beyond the forest and the hills, I could see the ocean. Uri looked around, his eyes wide. He inhaled the aroma of the forest again with visible pleasure.

A small ant crawled along my leg. I let it. "I think I miss the Galilee more than any other place in Israel," he said. I knew I was supposed to nod now, but I didn't. The ant reached the middle of my calf. It was red, the kind we called fire ants in grade school. Uri noticed my silence. He didn't know whether to ignore it or charge it head on. "And do you miss it?" he asked.

"The Galilee? Definitely not."

He looked at me in surprise. I knew this even though I didn't look at him. I thought he'd ask something, but he didn't. He didn't change the subject either, as I had assumed he would. He kept silent and waited. A few moments later, when the ant reached my knee, I told him about the trip that year, in October. I was at the end of my seventh month, a short time after the third screening test. The nausea had finally passed and Mikhael suggested we take a day off and do some hiking. All the way from Tel Aviv, we talked about the list of lullabies we were going to prepare for Ofri.

That was our favorite game at the time, preparing lists of songs we'd sing to our baby. We sang to her on the way north that day, taking turns choosing songs, and every time I sang out of tune, he spoke to my stomach and said, "Ofriki, don't listen to your mother, she has a heart of gold but a tin ear for music." We wound our way upward on the road, the Sea of Galilee spread out beneath us. It shimmered and dazzled in the sun. I asked Mikhael to drive carefully. Two idiots traveling in the north, as if Israel were the kind of country where you could simply go on a hike without first making sure the path was not in the middle of a battlefield.

We parked not far from the Nimrod Fortress and started walking among the oak trees. I picked up acorns and put them in my pocket and said to Mikhael that one day, we'd turn them into a mobile for our daughter. All the way down the winding path, we talked only about Ofri: what she'd like, who she would be, how we would play the Beatles for her instead of the crap they played for kids today.

"When the explosions began, we were halfway to the Banias River. You know that trail? It's not very steep. Definitely appropriate for a woman at the end of her seventh month. Assuming you walk down it, right? Not if you run down it like a lunatic because you hear sirens and are afraid that rockets are about to rain down on you. I ran all the way down among the oak trees praying not to fall, and I didn't. I reached the Banias parking area, shaking all over. Somehow, Mikhael managed to convince someone there to drive us back to the top. Our original plan had been to hitchhike, but because of the explosions, there was hardly a living soul outside. And Mikhael always knew how to get people to help. I don't remember much about the drive back, only that I couldn't stop trembling and Mikhael kept saying, 'Everything's fine, everything's fine,' and thanking the driver for helping out a pregnant woman. The driver said, 'No problem, really,' and as I was about to get out of the car, he wished me good luck. 'Sweetheart, I hope that by the time your baby grows up, there won't be any more wars.' When I got out of the car, there was a bloodstain on the back seat's upholstery. I walked away from the car and stood behind a tree. I didn't care who saw me. I took off my underpants and saw the blood.

"The nurse in the maternity ward was overflowing with good intentions. She told me that many women miscarried at the end of their seventh month. That they didn't talk about it very much, but it was a very common thing. That in most cases, it didn't mean anything about the next pregnancy, absolutely nothing. She said I would have many more adorable children and that I would come to the ward to show them off. I wanted her to leave me alone, but she stayed, talking cheerfully about the children I would have, asking ten times if I was sure I didn't want to eat anything. *Maternal,* that's the word most women would probably use to describe her. But I didn't want that nurse to be my mother; I wanted to be Ofri's mother.

"Mikhael took time off from work to be with me in the hospital. And more time off from work to be with me at home, because after I was discharged from the hospital, I didn't want to get out of bed. The military tensions continued, and a few days later, Mikhael was called to reserve duty. I lay under the quilt with the blinds closed. Sometimes I turned on the TV and looked for an American sitcom with canned laughter in the background. Once, by mistake, I pressed a button on the remote and came across pictures of a wailing Arab mother, a dead baby in her arms. I pressed again, and Phoebe from

*Friends* appeared like a blond good fairy to take me away from there.

"Our life went on. Our hearts kept beating as they had before. But in the silence between the beats, I always heard her; I heard the silence of a baby who comes out and doesn't make a sound. Mikhael called home whenever he could. 'Are you okay?' he'd ask, and I'd say, 'Yes.' What I didn't say was *Mikhael, the sunlight hurts me,* or *Mikhael, I still feel her moving in my womb even though she isn't there.* Because he was at the front, and I was at the home front, which was supposed to be strong.

"Two weeks later, Mikhael came home. We hugged in the stairwell. He smelled of rifle oil. When we lowered our arms and he looked at me, he was alarmed. 'You didn't eat anything this whole time?' I said not to worry, I'd eat now that he was home, I'd eat and eat and eat. I cooked us dinner. I opened a bottle of wine we'd bought in France when I was in my third month. We'd agreed not to drink it until after the birth. At night, in bed, I thought about that moment under the tree and began to cry like a crazy woman. But I'm not crazy, Uri, that country is crazy, and that's why I don't miss the Galilee or any other place, because I'm not crazy, and no matter how many people told me that I probably would have miscarried anyway, it was clear to me—my baby died because of the Middle East.

"You know," I said and looked into Uri's eyes for the first time since I'd begun to speak, "after we moved to America, I sometimes dreamed that we still lived in our old apartment in Tel Aviv. I loved Israel, I loved it the way a woman loves her abusive husband but understands that she has to get away from him in order to save her children."

## 56

WHEN WE CAME down from the ridge, the sky was going pink. The silence between us wasn't charged the way it had been when I finished talking about Ofri. The walk had disarmed the silence. With every step we took, it was as if something else were tossed away, and when we returned to the paved area, our steps were soft and light. I bent down to wipe the mud off my shoes, but Uri signaled me that there was no need. "It's not that kind of car." And it really wasn't. Uri's car was messy and dirty and smelled faintly of sawdust, all of which made it much more inviting than our sparkling-clean car with its lavender smell that tyrannized your nostrils.

On the way to pick up Adam, we stopped for a moment at Uri's house. I stayed outside while he went in to pack a few things for the night he was going to spend at our place. I looked through the window at the untended yard. At the edge of the lawn, which grew wild, was a large, rusty trampoline. I remembered the picture of the blond boy doing a hand-stand on Frishman Beach in Tel Aviv. Uri came out with a bag slung over his shoulder. I think he noticed the way I was looking at the trampoline, because he immediately turned on the radio, as if he wanted to drown out the silence of the deserted yard.

For a moment, I pictured him there, alone at home. What books did he have? What pictures hung on the wall? I tried to think of him alone in the living room after his evening shower. *Why are you so certain he's alone?* I suddenly asked my-self. *A man like him must surely have female companionship.* But he didn't. I could smell the loneliness emanating from him like aftershave.

When we reached Adam's school, there wasn't a trace of

the morning's graffiti. The wall had been freshly painted in the familiar off-white shade. But the newly painted area was nevertheless slightly different. Instead of the red spray that had been removed, there was a huge lighter off-white stain on the wall.

Adam came out with Yochai and Boaz. When he saw me, he tried to look like his normal self, but a full day of pretended indifference had taken its toll. He was stooped and faded, and his young face looked as shriveled as an old man's. Only when I said that I'd come with Uri did a weak smile cross his lips. When we reached the car, Uri peered at him through the rearview mirror and declared, "You look like someone who needs pizza."

We ate in an Italian restaurant. Uri and Adam sat on one side of the table, I on the other. There were red-checkered tablecloths. The place was full of customers. I looked around, searching for signs of anything suspicious. Because if someone was capable of throwing a rock through our window, maybe he was also capable of attacking us in the middle of a restaurant. The Black guy over there with a peaked cap that covered his eyes—was he looking at us? And his hands, deep inside his sweatshirt—I wanted to see them. All at once, I remembered riding the buses in Haifa during the time of the terrorist attacks, when every passenger who boarded was a potential terrorist. How, whenever we went to the mall, my mother pointed out where the emergency exit was and said, "You run there if something happens." How I once got out of a bus in Hadar just because an Arab guy wearing a coat got on and I was afraid that maybe... I hated Haifa that winter of terrorist attacks. At any moment, a familiar, well-lit street might turn into a fiery jungle. I hadn't felt that way since we'd moved to America. Seventeen years in the U.S. and I'd never wanted to know where the emergency exit was in the mall and I didn't wonder which of the bus passengers might explode. Now I surveyed the faces of the diners in the restaurant. The guy with the peaked cap left, but I couldn't calm down. I looked around, tensing at every movement. Wondering where the wolf was hiding.

## 57

FINALLY, WE COULDN'T delay going home any longer. When we were in the car, Mikhael called again. When I'd told him about the rock in an earlier conversation, I'd heard his voice trying to comfort me through the phone. But he was on the other side of the country, in a snowy airport, and I was here in California, and with all due respect to cell phones, it was just too far away. I'd told him then to call later. I had been in a hurry to hang up. Now he was calling again, asking why I hadn't answered for the past few hours, saying he'd called every time they'd had a break between meetings. I felt the heat burn my cheeks. Maybe, if Adam hadn't been in the back seat, I would have told Mikhael that it wasn't enough for me to be the break between meetings, that if he wanted to know what was happening with us, he could get on a plane and come home.

"Put him on speaker," Adam said, "so we can hear him too." I switched to speaker.

Mikhael, Uri, and Adam updated each other. I looked out the window. Mikhael said, "So, good night, everyone," and ended the call. The three of us continued on our way: Uri driving, me sitting beside him, Adam in the back.

Uri parked in front of the house and turned off the engine. I tensed when I saw the figure standing in front of the garage in the darkness. I nodded my head slightly in its direction. Uri looked and nodded as if to say, *I know, I saw.* We got out of the car and walked along the path to the house. Near the door, I bent to take the key out of my bag, and I thought I saw movement in the bushes. I froze in alarm. I saw that Uri was looking in the same direction and that even Adam, with his headphones on, noticed what was happening. "Don't worry," Uri said a moment later. "Come on, let's go inside."

Maria and the glazier had done nice work. The house sparkled. The glass had been installed. Further proof that, in Silicon Valley, everything happens very quickly if you have enough money. I bent down to the shoe rack and took off my sneakers. "*Yalla,* Adam, into the shower." I thought I heard, or maybe I really did hear, footsteps on the other side of the door. I locked it. Adam went upstairs, protesting mildly, and I thanked Uri for agreeing to spend the night. I told him he could stay in the large guest room. Uri stood at the door to the room as I got it ready. He offered to help twice, but I insisted on making the bed myself, and after standing there for a few minutes doing nothing, he said, "Okay, so I'm going to take a shower."

While he was gone, I spread the quilt on the bed. I fluffed the pillow. I turned on the small lamp. I heard Adam leave his bathroom, and I went up to shower.

How much water do you need to wash off the red graffiti, or Einat Greenbaum's hug, or Mikhael's absence? As I scrubbed my heel, I examined the scratch that the shard of glass from the window had made. The hot water flowed over my breasts, my stomach and back. My thighs hurt from the vigorous climb in the Santa Cruz hills, but it was a good pain, the pain of movement. Silently, I thanked Uri for taking me on that hike. I heard him showering in the downstairs bathroom. The bathrooms were aligned one on top of the other, and based on the slight change in the water pressure, I knew when he turned it off. I remained standing under the spray for a long while, letting the water stream down my body.

As soon as I opened the door, I knew they weren't there. The emptiness of the house hit me like a gust of cold air. Nonetheless, I called, "Adam? Uri?" and when they didn't answer, I called again, louder this time: "Adam? Uri?" The silence was absolute. I went into the bedroom, got dressed quickly, and went straight downstairs. "Uri? Adam?"

The air outside encased my wet hair and still damp ears like a helmet of frost. I looked around. There was no trace of them. *They've just gone out for a walk,* I told myself. *They took Kelev with them.* But our white fence suddenly looked different, as if someone had moved it a bit closer to the house, as if the street had widened into our yard. A strange thought, a crazy one, that made me cross the front lawn carefully. The fence was in its place. I knew that—fences don't move. But something was standing on the left side of it. A figure in a coat. Broad-shouldered. And another person was standing near the garage, his hands in the pockets of his sweatshirt. My heart pounded so hard that Mikhael could probably hear it in Washington. Again I felt the cold on my hair and my ears. Sweat covered my back. I looked around. I thought of shouting, but I didn't know exactly what to shout. And the next instant, the shout solidified in my throat—a pair of dark eyes was looking at me through the fence.

Three people around our house. Maybe they were police, I hoped momentarily, but I knew they weren't. Officer Stevens had complained that they didn't have enough staff to safeguard us. "But after all, there really is no concrete threat, Mrs. Shuster." *So here's your concrete threat—there are three people in the shadows around our house, and from one minute to the next, it's becoming clearer to me that they aren't neighbors. Or passersby. These people are watching my house. Planning something.*

At that moment, Adam and Uri appeared at the end of the block, Kelev beside them. I ran unsteadily toward them. I had to get them away from the house, keep them from getting close. I was horrified to see the figures moving in the same direction. *They'll stab him,* I realized with terrible clarity, *they'll stab Adam right in front of the house.* Just as I opened my mouth to scream, I realized that I had missed my chance. The figures were faster than me. The broad-shouldered one had already reached Adam, raised his arm over my son—and gave him a high five.

I stared at them, stunned. The other two also high-fived Adam and looked at Uri with the same reverence I'd learned to recognize. In the pale light of the streetlamp, I saw the redheaded kid with the kippah, the robust unreadable kid, and Yochai Karin.

I covered the last few steps that separated me from the group and heard Uri say to the boys in his quiet voice, "Have you seen anything suspicious so far?" The red-haired boy shook his head. Yochai puffed out his chest and said that a red Mazda had passed by the house six times already—he'd written down the license plate number.

"That's our neighbor from the end of the block," I said. "His baby girl only falls asleep when they're driving."

Yochai looked disappointed. Uri patted him on the shoulder. "Be alert. The next patrol arrives at nine." They nodded at once, as if it were Uri—not the streetlight—that illuminated them in the darkness of the night.

We went inside. I didn't say anything until Adam went up to his room. Then I whispered angrily to Uri, "Are you crazy? Those kids are playing at protecting us?"

He looked at me in surprise. He honestly and truly did not

understand what I was angry about, and that only annoyed me more. "Didn't you think you should tell me before you brought the undercovers here to patrol?"

"I didn't want to bother you about it."

"They're minors, Uri. Do their parents even know they're here? What if someone from the Nation of Islam really comes and hurts them?"

A half smile spread across his handsome, untroubled face. "I think that the chances someone will really come are very slim."

My fear, I suddenly understood, was only an exercise for him. An opportunity for the boys to flex their muscles. "So why are they here? Why do they have to be outside in this cold?"

"It's an important experience."

"Have you lost your mind, Uri? They're children! Chil-dren!"

The guileless way he stood there, leaning on the kitchen island. From the counter, I picked up the rag still stained with my blood and tossed it into the trash.

"Lilach, I don't understand what's upsetting you so much. Those kids are a team, they have a community, and when some-one from that community is hurt, they mobilize to help him. I think that's a good thing."

"That's exactly what Jamal's friends did when they threw that rock through our window. They were fighting back for someone in their community."

Uri didn't say anything. He didn't want to argue with me. But there was something steely and intractable about his presence in the kitchen now, something that made me feel that, no matter what I said, the man would stick to his guns.

"If tomorrow, one of the kids here decides to retaliate and throw a rock at some Muslim or spray anti-Koran graffiti or God knows what—you want that on your conscience?"

"They would never do anything like that." He looked so sure

that I was almost persuaded. I glanced out the window. There was a chubby kid standing with his back to me at the far end of our yard. "Do they have pocketknives?"

"Even if one boy got carried away and took a Leatherman with him, he wouldn't use it."

"So why bring it?"

Uri poured himself a glass of water and pointed out that if someone in the synagogue had had a pocketknife on Rosh Hashanah, maybe Leah Weinstein would still be alive.

The treetops shook in the wind. I put a hand on the glass. "It's cold outside. You should drive your students home. We'll talk in the morning."

His serene expression wavered for the first time since we'd begun talking. "Lilach, I want to sleep here tonight and keep you safe."

"The California police will keep us safe, Uri. Good night."


## 58


I WAS AFRAID I wouldn't be able to fall asleep, but my sleep was deep, peaceful, and dreamless. Early in the morning, when Mikhael called from Washington to ask how I was, I told him proudly that I had slept wonderfully.

"Great," he said. "It's good that Uri's there."

"In the end, Uri didn't sleep here," I said, aware of the triumphant tone that had slipped into my voice.

His tone was critical when he asked what had happened, why we had changed the plan.

Suddenly I realized that he'd been happy about Uri sleeping at our place not just for me but also for himself, so he would be able to fall asleep in his hotel in Washington. I told him about the night patrol Uri had organized around our house, the sentries he'd posted outside the yard.

"I don't know, Mikhael. Last night I had the thought that maybe Uri has established a kind of underground and is dragging the kids along with him with all that 'We have to fight back' stuff he's feeding them."

Mikhael's silence did not bode well. His doubt spilled out at me through the phone. I could picture him listening to me in his hotel room in Washington, lying in his underwear on the wide bed, his jacket hanging on the back of a chair.

"I see why those patrols annoyed you, Leelo. But I have to say that there's something caring about it. I don't completely understand why you turned on him like that."

"And what if the next stage is sending them to do things other than patrol? Retaliation raids?"

"Tell me, what's going on with you? First you ran away to Mexico with Adam, and now these ideas? It sounds like something from a movie, Lilach. Like the ideas of someone who spends too much time alone with her thoughts."

That's how it is, a small crack opens between you and reality one time, and from then on, everyone treats you like a building marked for demolition. Two months after Adam was born, Mikhael and I smoked a joint that triggered a powerful anxiety attack in me. The combination of postpartum hormones, lack of sleep, and very strong weed landed me in the hospital for four days, diagnosed with a "psychotic episode." For forty-eight hours, I thought our neighbors were plotting to kidnap my baby. I begged Mikhael to take Adam and escape to a safe place with him. The paranoia passed after two days, and two days after that, I was discharged and I never touched pot again. Since then, we hadn't spoken about that episode. I'd never told anyone about the hospitalization, not Noga or Tamar when they came to visit us in America, and certainly not my mother. Mikhael never mentioned it. Even now, despite the clear anger in his voice, he was fair enough not to speak about it explicitly. After a brief pause, he said he'd be back tomorrow. That he missed us. That he thought that when he came home, the three of us could fly to Los Cabos, relax on the beach, and forget everything that had happened.

I heard the door to Adam's room open. "I have to go," I told Mikhael. "Adam just woke up and I want to get breakfast on the table."

I went down to the kitchen and made an omelet. Adam joined me a few minutes later. I noticed how quickly he'd gotten ready. Even his usual ungainliness seemed to have rolled away, and I could see beyond it, perhaps for the first time, to the man he would be.

"Where's Uri?"

That's why he'd dressed so quickly, a soldier who wanted to impress his commander with his punctuality. Surprisingly animated, he took three plates out of the cabinet and placed them on the table.

"He had to go home last night."

All at once, his movements became slower, like a bird shot in mid-flight. He sat down at the table, leaving the plate he'd put out for Uri where it was. I put the omelet down in front of him and took a seat beside him with my coffee.

"Why do you hate him, Mom?"

The blood rushed to my cheeks. I didn't know if it was because Adam was right and the flush revealed the depth of my anger at Uri, or because he was wrong, understanding the intensity of the feeling but not its nature.

"I don't hate him," I said tentatively. Adam smiled bitterly. He maintained his silence all the way to school.

## 59

AFTER I DROPPED him off, I called Shir. She answered immediately. She'd called seven times the day before. Zach had told her about the graffiti and she wanted to see how I was, but this morning, sadly, she couldn't meet me. She was loaded down with work.

"Just a quick cup of coffee," I said.

"You'd really drive all the way to the financial district for a cup of coffee?"

"Of course not. I have other errands to run in the city," I replied, embarrassed about the lie and even more about the loneliness that had caused it.

After my psychotic episode, the doctors recommended follow-up treatment. There were a few Israeli psychologists in Silicon Valley, but I didn't want to go to them. The community was too small—everyone knew everyone else. I chose an American therapist. During the first session, I cried and said nothing. During the second session, I tried to speak and discovered that I couldn't. My English was good, but my inner language was Hebrew. I didn't know how to express myself in another language. During the third session, I told the therapist that the therapy was doomed to fail because of the cultural differences. She said that the language I spoke during therapy made no difference at all. "The real problem is that you don't have a language you can speak to yourself, because I think, Leela, that you feel like a bit of an outsider everywhere, not just in America." When I left her office that day, I planned to return. But then Adam caught his first cold and life moved on.

And now I was a hostage of my own heart. Too many hours at home. Too much time to think unhealthy thoughts that made Adam angry at me and Mikhael worry about me. When I finally got to the financial district, Shir called and apologized—she was in a meeting and couldn't get out anytime soon, but maybe I should do my errands in the city and she'd try to see me for coffee later in the day if she could get away.

I mumbled, "It's okay," and walked back to the parking lot. I suppressed my desire to drive to Adam's school. I drove home. I baked butter cookies from a famous pastry chef's recipe and made the mushroom quiche I'd meant to make yesterday.

Adam came home at eight in the evening. He was all sweaty when he got off his bike, despite the cold outside. An hour and a half earlier, I'd called him to ask if he wanted me to come and pick him up after Uri's class. He said there was no need. The coldness in his voice frightened me. You give birth to a child and the first thing he does when he emerges from your womb is cry in his own voice, which isn't your voice. Until that moment, he spoke from your throat—when he was hungry, he asked for food—and now he's crying in his own voice and you bless that voice, because it makes it clear to you that all is well, that he is breathing without you. You listen to his first babbles, his first mumbles, his first words.

You collect sentences. Until one day, the familiar voice changes. With Adam, it happened gradually. My mother was the one who said, at the end of a phone call three years ago, "His voice doesn't sound like him. Is he sick?"

"No," I told her. "He's becoming a teenager."

Now he locked his bike in the garage and came into the house, letting Kelev in with him. I put the mushroom quiche on the table. I looked at him with satisfaction as he gobbled it down hungrily. "How was Uri?"

"Great."

"What did you do?"

"We ran. Is there dessert?"

"There's ice cream."

Kelev sat down next to the table. Adam petted his head in a circular motion. And I, who wanted to pet Adam's head but didn't know if he would let me, bent down beside Kelev and petted his brown fur too.

When I finished washing the dishes, I got into bed and turned on the TV. I heard Adam and Kelev go out for a walk and come back, and then I heard Adam turn on the TV in his room. And so we sat, he in his room and I in mine, each watching a different show, until the desperate barking and whining coming from the doghouse in the yard startled us into action, and we both burst out of our rooms and raced down the stairs, leaving behind two turned-on TVs.

## 60

WHEN WE REACHED him, he was still alive. His fur was covered with blood and something else (gasoline, I realized a moment later; they poured gasoline on him, they wanted to burn him). Kelev moaned with pain, a low, terrifying wail that made it clear to me, even more than the blood and the sight of his skull where the rock had hit him, that this time, no vet could save him. But my voice didn't give it away. My voice was completely steady when I said to Adam, "Run inside and call Uri."

I was afraid he wouldn't obey me, but he raced inside as if he'd just been waiting for someone to give him an order, to tell him what the hell he was supposed to do. I knelt beside Kelev. The pink skin on his back was now covered in the blood that was flowing from his head. I petted him gently and felt the blood and gasoline stain my hand and my sleeve. He lay there and looked at me. His breathing was very shallow and weak. He no longer had the strength to wail. His head was twisted from the blow he'd received, but his eyes were the same, black and good. "I'm sorry, Kelev," I whispered, "I'm so sorry." He opened his mouth and vomited. I saw his pink tongue, which used to hang from his mouth when he sat beside the table waiting for Adam to slip him something. I looked straight at him and whispered, "Good dog, good dog, good dog," until I realized that he no longer saw me.

At that moment, the moment he died, I didn't feel sadness. In fact, I didn't feel anything. Because even though I knew that the sight of Kelev on our lawn would haunt me for the rest of my life, even though I knew that years would go by before the sound of his wailing would leave me, and even though his black eyes had pierced my breast, at that moment, my heart was closed off and in my mind, only one thought: *Adam must not see this.* Because I had a child in this world, and I was responsible for him. I was responsible for keeping him from knowing the horrific things people could do. That was the only reason I'd sent him to call Uri, because it was clear to me that Commander in Chief Uri Ziv couldn't do anything for us now except dig a large hole in the garden.

I didn't waste a minute. A soldier in the parenthood army, I charged from the lawn to the barbecue grill, pulled off its protective tarp, and hurried back to Kelev to cover him before Adam came back. I draped it over the lifeless body that lay on the grass and was trying to finish covering it quickly when I suddenly heard a bloodcurdling scream from behind me. Adam was standing at the front door, looking at the lawn, at the place where the puppy he had rescued five years earlier lay, covered by a sheet of black vinyl. A frightened, battered puppy he had carried home on his bike that day, who at first could eat only tiny bits of food from his hand, who went with him everywhere and ran to greet him every afternoon when he returned from school. I suddenly realized how absurd all my efforts to cover Kelev were. The black vinyl sheet could conceal the crushed skull and the frozen eyes, but it could not conceal the fact that our dog was dead. Someone had come to our home and killed him.

"Adam," I said, reaching out to him, but he ignored me, raced forward, pulled off the covering, picked up the lifeless body, and screamed his heart out, screamed in a way I had never heard him scream before. I didn't think a human throat could even produce such a sound. He buried his face in the brown fur that was covered in blood and gasoline and sobbed, babbling fragmented sentences into it (all the times I'd seen him whisper soothing words to Kelev when a noise frightened him and he began to bark, and only Adam knew how to calm him down at those moments).

"Adam," I said, kneeling down beside him. I put my hand on his back, but he didn't turn to me. He petted the neck where the fur was thick and soft, petted the scarred back with trembling fingers. *His scar isn't ugly, only the people who gave it to him are ugly.*

"It's because of me," he said in a choked voice. "They did this because of me." And before I could say anything, he threw himself onto the grass and sobbed and screamed, banging his head over and over again on the ground the way he used to when he was having a terrible-twos tantrum, except that he'd been a toddler then, and now he was a teenager, and his outburst was so strong, his loss of control so ferocious and absolute, that, against my will, I drew back, afraid that one of his wildly kicking legs would connect with me.

"Calm down," I whispered, then finally shouted, "Adam, calm down!" But he didn't calm down, he seemed to be crying harder, hurling his body in every direction, the sorrow torturing him from within. It was terrifying, seeing him that way, and it was just as terrifying to discover that I couldn't calm him down. Because when he was two and the tantrums began, I was the only one who knew how to deal with them. "A steel hug" is what Mikhael and I called it. I would wrap my arms around his small body and not let him escape. I'd hold him like that until the frenzy subsided and he came back to himself. But now that he was sixteen, I couldn't force him into that steel hug. I couldn't help him.

I had no idea how long he screamed on the lawn beside Kelev's body. The lights turned on in our neighbors' houses, but no one came out. Every time I thought his crying was beginning to abate, there was a new wave of screams and sobs. My helplessness was heavy and paralyzing. There were moments when I thought Adam would go crazy. Or maybe he already had. Maybe that was what crazy looked like. Something terrible happens and your mind simply shatters, splits into pieces in an instant, and all that remains is your screaming, kicking body.

I couldn't watch him anymore. I couldn't look at his red, contorted face, drenched with tears and saliva. I couldn't listen to him scream that way, like an animal, not like a human being. From minute to minute, he was less my son and more someone—no, not someone, some*thing*—insane.

I looked away from him. I stared at the fence. I covered my ears so as not to hear his screams. I didn't hear the approaching car or the footsteps running on the grass, didn't see Uri until the moment he knelt beside Adam, his large body sheltering my son like a huge eagle. "It's okay," he said and put his hand on Adam's shoulder. Adam continued to carry on, but Uri didn't flinch. He hugged him tightly in his arms.

And in that embrace, in his embrace, my son finally calmed down.

## 61

I SUGGESTED THAT we go inside. I wanted Adam to wash his face, drink something, maybe try to sleep. But Uri said,

"Wait—first we'll bury him." He went into the garage, came back with shovels, and said to Adam, "Let's go, I'm not doing it by myself."

Adam stood up, still panting. Long hours would pass before he'd go back to breathing properly. With shaking hands, he took a shovel and began to dig, together with Uri, in the backyard. They had to change spots twice because they accidentally hit a water pipe.

"Maybe we should wait with this," I suggested. "The police might want to examine Kelev."

This time, it was Adam who insisted. "I'm not letting those cops take him away, Mom. Kelev stays here."

The third time, they dug deep enough. Uri put Kelev gently inside the hole. Adam cried again, but quietly this time, the restrained crying of an adult. Uri put a hand on his shoulder and said, "Come on, let's cover him." Adam obeyed.

We went into the house. I made tea. The three of us sat in the kitchen, not speaking. It was eleven at night. Then Uri went upstairs with Adam and sat in his room with him for almost an hour. Finally, the door opened and Uri came back down, alone. "He's sleeping," he said.

"What did you talk about?"

"I told him about a military operation where I saw my friend killed."

I wanted to throw up, but instead, I washed the teacups. "Thank you for coming," I finally said when there wasn't a single dish left in the sink to wash.

"I'll sleep here tonight," he said.

I nodded. A moment later, I whispered again, "Thank you."

Once again, the guest room on the first floor. The same bedding from yesterday. An extra quilt from the closet. A small bedside lamp. I gave Uri a new towel, and when he went into the bathroom, I took out one of Mikhael's tracksuits that I thought would fit him and put it on the bed.

I went upstairs and dragged myself into the bathroom to take a shower. I took off my sweatpants. I was about to unzip my hoodie when I saw the bloodstains on my sleeve. It was only then, when I knew that Adam was sleeping and wouldn't hear me, that I allowed myself, finally, to cry. I sat on the edge of the tub, my head in my hands. Tears drenched my cheeks. I hugged my legs and dug my nails into the flesh of my thighs to keep myself from screaming.

"Lilach."

Uri was standing on the other side of the bathroom door. His voice was soft and guarded. "Lilach? Are you okay?"

I wanted to say yes, but nothing came out of my mouth. Tears rose in my throat and flowed down my face. He opened the door and found me sitting on the edge of the tub, crumpling my blood-soaked sleeve. His green eyes were soft and kind when he knelt in front of me and put his arms around me.

But Uri's embrace, which had managed to calm Adam, had the opposite effect on me. All the tears I'd held back that evening burst out. Because as long as Adam was awake, I had been the responsible adult, the mother in control, and now that Adam was asleep, I went from being a responsible adult to a terrified child. It was as if only now, the full awareness of the loss of Kelev, all the horrors of the night, hit me.

*Go away,* I wanted to tell him, *your kindness is only breaking me apart,* but I couldn't utter a sound. Uri stroked my shoulder. "Come on," he said, "you're freezing here." I lifted my blood-covered sleeve and showed it to him. He looked at the red stains and said quietly, "Take it off." I remained as I was, on the edge of the bathtub. Uri reached out and unzipped and removed my hoodie, which smelled faintly of gasoline.

"I'll bring you some clothes," he said and walked out. I took off my tank top and underpants and showered sitting in the tub. I didn't have the strength to stand, and the water flowed over me from above, blending with my tears. Finally, I wrapped myself in a towel and got out. Waiting on the chair outside the door were the clothes Uri had brought for me.

Standing in front of the bathroom heater, I put them on.

When I had calmed down a bit, I went into Adam's room and straightened the blanket on his body. Even though he was asleep, his breath was jagged and his body trembled.

I went out of his room and closed his door gently. Uri was standing in the hallway, his eyes questioning. "I just wanted to check that he was covered," I said, and he nodded and asked if he could use the computer in Mikhael's study for a couple of minutes. He had to send a few e-mails and he'd left his phone at home when he ran out to his car.

Lying in bed, the blanket enveloping me completely, I called Mikhael. He didn't answer. I called again, and when he still didn't answer, I called Jane, planning to tell the secretary with the cloying voice that I was sorry for the late hour, but I had to talk to him. Maybe she had the number of one of the other reps in Washington. But she didn't answer either. Desperate, I called his hotel.

"Is Mr. Mikhael Shuster there?" I asked.

"No, ma'am. There's no guest here by that name."

"What do you mean?" I said, shocked. "He stayed the night in Washington."

"That could be, ma'am, but not at this hotel."

I hung up. Why would Mikhael have moved to a different hotel? And why didn't he tell me? I tried to call him again, but my calls went to voice mail.

I called Jane again. True, it was already late, but a beautiful girl like her must be awake at some bar in the city. Because according to what Mikhael said when I asked him, she was supposed to be in San Francisco now. At the last company party, we'd spoken a little, Jane and I. She was wearing the short satin dress whose twin, the one I'd never worn, was hanging in my closet. She had laughed an awful lot. She'd told me proudly that she had more than eight thousand followers on Instagram. I called Mikhael again now, and then Jane again, and when she didn't answer, I looked for her on Instagram. Her last story had been posted from Washington. This afternoon.

How like Mikhael it would be to change hotels so the other members of the team wouldn't see him with her. And even so, I knew it didn't change anything. That's what company vice presidents do here—fuck their secretaries. It's part of the job requirements. Not because he'd stopped loving me, but because he could.

I went downstairs. I had to do something with my hands. My mother always said that when your hands are busy, you don't cry, and unlike other things my mother said, this was absolutely correct. I began to bake so there'd be something for the next day. I took out a bowl and some flour and butter, and when I turned around, I saw Uri.

"You're not sleeping?" I said.

"You're not sleeping?" he said.

"I can't," I said, "so I thought I'd bake cookies."

"Great," he said. "I'll learn the recipe."

I wanted him to go to his room and leave me to myself. I didn't have the strength to talk. But he stood there, and I didn't feel I could ask him to leave. I started making the batter and let him watch. I didn't speak; I just mixed, blended, and kneaded, and he watched me the entire time, learning. Finally, I put the tray in the oven and set the timer.

"That's it. We'll have cookies for tomorrow morning. I'll put some in a box for you to take to the office."

"Thanks."

"I'm sorry for yesterday, Uri. If I hadn't sent you away, maybe, maybe this wouldn't..." All at once, I started crying again, this time in loud, shuddering sobs.

"Shh...you'll wake Adam," Uri said in alarm, and he quickly led me into the guest room and closed the door. He hugged me again, tightly, and I buried myself in his strong arms, in his broad chest with its unfamiliar smell, and he stroked my head. "Shh, it's okay."

His fingers ran through my hair, rising and falling on the back of my neck in a movement that was supposed to soothe but aroused me, aroused him. I felt his groin press against mine, how hard he was, and I knew he could feel my breasts, unrestrained under my shirt, pressing against him. His breathing was suddenly very heavy, and the saliva in my mouth was very sweet, and my entire body throbbed for him to come, to finally come to me.

PART THREE

# MOTHERLAND

# 62

THE DRIVER AT Ben Gurion Airport asked for twelve hundred shekels to take us to Kibbutz Gadot. "That's an outrageous price," I told him, more shocked than annoyed by his audacity.

He smiled broadly and said, "That's the price, lady. Take it or leave it."

Mikhael intended to pay. The years in America had withered his bargaining muscles, and in any case, he didn't have the patience for trivialities now.

"Wait a minute," I said, and I went back into the arrivals hall. I walked around an ultra-Orthodox family with a sign that said WELCOME, EVIATAR, squeezed my way through a group of female soldiers in uniform who were jumping and squealing around a girl with dreadlocks, and went up to two heavyset men who were standing at the coffee counter and quietly offering cheap rides in a gypsy cab.

"How much to Kibbutz Gadot?"

The younger one looked me over, took in the earrings and rings, and said, "Two thousand shekels."

I smiled. He smiled too. Behind him, a little girl in a skirt burst into tears and pointed up to a balloon that was making its way to the ceiling. The younger driver said, "Twelve hundred."

"Twelve hundred is what the legal cab wants."

The older man said, "So, a thousand." And when I hesitated, he added, "*Yalla*, honey, you won't find a better price."

Ten minutes later, we were stuck in a traffic jam on the Coastal Road. I was hot. I hadn't packed well. The phone call had come in the middle of the night, and the flight we'd found was early in the morning, and in the midst of all that, I'd completely forgotten to check what the weather was like in Israel. Now I looked out at the cars. I opened the window and took a hesitant breath.

After sixteen hours in the recycled air of the plane—twenty hours, if you count the connection in Washington—the air outside the taxi was a change for the better. I thought that in addition to the heat and soot, there was something else I was smelling, maybe the citrus groves on the other side of the road. But Adam complained from the front seat, "Come on, Mom. Close the window, it's hot," and I quickly obeyed.

Mikhael called Assi. "We landed," he said. "We're in a taxi and we'll go straight to the cemetery."

The driver peered at us in the rearview mirror. It seemed to me that even before the call, he'd suspected we were the kind of people who came to Israel only because someone had died. Mikhael was withdrawn, sitting with his fist against his mouth. *You should reach out and touch him,* I said to myself. *He needs you.*

Adam sat in the front seat, near the mirror with a hamsa charm hanging from it that swung every time the driver recklessly changed lanes. Mikhael was sitting beside me, and I thought I could still feel Uri between my thighs (because, yes, almost twenty-four hours had passed, but airplane time is a frozen capsule, a forced halt in the flow of life itself). I leaned back against the leather seat. How was it that everyone had always worried about Moshe, with all his angiograms and bypasses and who knew what else, and in the end, it was Dina who went first?

When Mikhael called from Washington in the middle of the night to tell me, I didn't understand at first that he was talking about her. I was sure he was telling me that his father had died. Since Moshe's first hospitalization in the ICU, that possibility was always implied in every call from Israel. No one thought that Dina would precede him, not only because she was always late, but mainly because she didn't seem like the type who died. Her speech was always so frenetic, and her movements were an

endless rattle of bracelets and necklaces and rings. That's why I
hadn't grasped what Mikhael was saying when he called. And
perhaps now, on the way to the kibbutz, I still didn't really grasp
it. I needed to be at the cemetery to believe it.

Dina had died at eight in the morning in Poriya Hospital
in Tiberias, but Moshe and Assi waited before telling us, and
because of the time difference, we didn't hear about it until the
middle of the night. How strange and terrible it was to imagine
the hours that Dina had lain dying in the hospital while we in
California had no idea, weren't thinking about her at all. And all
the hours after that when for us she was still alive, though in fact,
she wasn't.

Assi met us at the entrance to the kibbutz. On the way
to the cemetery, when I said to Yael that it was so terribly
sudden, she looked at me in surprise and said, "How sudden can
cancer be?"

Mikhael was standing not far from me, his fist covered by
marks his teeth had made, and I didn't think he'd heard anything. But in the evening, after all the people who'd come to
give their condolences had gone, I saw him and Assi arguing on
the balcony.

"How dare you keep something like that from me?" he said
in his quiet-Mikhael tone, the one that upsets me more than the
loudest screams.

"Mom didn't want you to worry. What could you have done
with that information there in America?"

Mikhael took a cigarette from Assi's pack but didn't light
it—he just rolled it around on the table as if he enjoyed showing
Assi that he didn't need what Assi was addicted to. "I don't care
what Mom wanted. I'm talking about you. You should have
told me."

Assi put his cigarette out in the rose plant—if Dina had been there, she would have shot him for that—and turned around to face Mikhael.

"Mikhael, with all due respect, you weren't here when I was making the rounds between Mom's radiation treatments at Poriya and Dad's angiogram at Assuta, so don't come complaining to me now."

Distractedly, Mikhael pulled up a few weeds that had grown around the edges of the rose plant, careful not to touch the cigarette Assi had put out in the damp earth, and said, "From now on, you report to me everything that happens with Dad's health, you hear me?"

"Yes, Commander," Assi said, and he smiled. It was clear that he was actually saying *Go fuck yourself.*

## 63

WE WOULD BE sleeping in Mikhael's old room, on the convertible couch. The sheets smelled of myrtle. That was Dina's handiwork. Once a week, she would pick myrtle branches from the kibbutz paths, put them in the closets, and take them out in the morning.

I finally took off the clothes I'd been wearing since the hurried preparations back home. I showered thoroughly in the small shower. I lay down on the sofa bed. Mikhael groped for my hand and I was glad for the darkness that hid my face from him. His body under the blanket was as large as usual, but his voice was very weak when he said, "In the first grade, I went to the harvest with her and she tripped and sprained her ankle. Instead of helping, I started to yell at her to get up. It wasn't because I cared about her—I was only afraid that she wouldn't get up and I would be without a mother again."

In the silence, we could hear the wind roaring in the bulrushes outside.

"Assi was right," Mikhael whispered a moment later. "She had every right to hide her illness from me. I ran away so I wouldn't have to take care of them."

"You didn't run away," I said gently. "You went away to work. That's what children do when they grow up. They leave home."

He shook his head. "Normal children leave their homes and move to Kfar Saba, like Assi, or to Kiriat Ono, like your sister. They don't go to the other side of the planet. Damn it, Leelo, they had to wait a whole day to bury her because of us."

"Everyone feels guilty when their parents die, Mikhael. It's not because of the relocation."

In the middle of the night, we heard Adam crying in the small room next to ours. The others might have thought he was crying about Dina, but I knew he was crying about Kelev. I went to him. I hugged him without speaking and waited for him to fall asleep. I hoped that Mikhael would be asleep when I went back to bed, but he was awake. We barely slept that night. Mikhael tossed and turned on the bed and I lay beside him, trying to stop thinking about Uri. I relived the taste of him in my mouth, the moment he entered me, the way his fingers roamed over my body. For the past twenty-four hours, I'd been afraid that my body would give me away if someone really looked at me: at my flushed cheeks, my eyes still besotted by the sight of another, unfamiliar body on mine. But no one saw. No one guessed. The people who had come to the house after the funeral told Moshe what a beautiful daughter-in-law he had, and they didn't know that I wasn't always that beautiful, that what I'd done had revitalized every feature of my face.

For the next few days, Mikhael cracked sunflower seeds and chewed pastries and was a proper host to everyone who came to the shiva. And at night, he buried his face in my breasts and wept soundlessly. If it hadn't been for the wetness left on my shirt, I might not have known. A bit after dawn, he would get up and go out to run on the road that circled the kibbutz the way he used to, and I would stay in bed, tensing at every sound that meant Adam had awakened. I assumed that Adam would spend the week doing things with Tamir and Aviv, but most of the time, he stayed in Assi's old room, looking at pictures of Kelev on his phone. When I went in, he let me stroke his back and didn't brush my hand away. (It was like petting Kelev's back, I thought. He let you touch the exposed skin.)

I spent the days in Moshe and Dina's small living room, talking with the endless flow of people who came to offer their condolences. Relatives and acquaintances flocked to the house, shook hands, sat on the balcony. They asked Mikhael, "So, how are you doing in America?" They asked where we thought it was better. Over and over again, Moshe took out his phone and showed his guests pictures he'd taken in our house. The phone was passed around, and the visitors looked in amazement at the pool. When it was Assi's turn with the phone, he handed it to the person sitting next to him without looking at it.

We decided to drive to Haifa right after the shiva was over. My mother had suggested we stay at her place, but on the last day of the shiva, I slipped out of the living room and looked for a hotel for us.

"Did you find anything?" Mikhael asked, standing in the doorway to the room that once had been his, chewing one of Dina's olive pastries that he'd defrosted for himself in the microwave. Moshe and Dina's freezer overflowed with such pastries, and it was obvious to all of us that Dina had made thorough preparations for the shiva, had baked everything in advance because she didn't trust Moshe to organize it by himself.

"I think so," I said and handed him the phone so he could see the picture. "It says the pool is heated."

"I didn't tell you about the crazy thing that happened to us in Washington!" Mikhael said. I shrank back into my chair, but he didn't notice. He devoured the pastry in one swallow and continued talking. "The second night, Berman decided we should switch hotels—you're not going to believe this—because he was afraid of industrial espionage!"

"Industrial espionage?"

"In the hotel bar, he recognized a guy who had once worked for him as a team leader and now works for one of our competitors. That worried him, so he did some checking and found out that all the companies that had come to make presentations at the Pentagon were staying in the same hotel. He *exploded* at Jane and Alice—how could they not have asked about that when they booked the rooms?"

Ice water flowed through my veins as Mikhael kept speaking. "I was standing next to Jane when Berman called her. The poor girl started crying! She wasn't even supposed to be in Washington—Alice was, but her kid got sick, and she asked Jane to go in her place. Berman gave Jane half an hour to find another hotel the whole group could move to without disrupting our meeting schedule. It was crazy."

"And she found one?" My voice was metallic and flat, but Mikhael was too intent on his story to notice.

"Yes, at the other end of the city. We waited half an hour for a taxi and wasted away inside it for another hour and a half while it crossed the city at rush hour, all because of Berman and his paranoia.

"Leelo? Is everything okay?" Mikhael asked, leaning down in

front of me. Since we'd arrived here, he'd been wearing only shabby jeans and T-shirts he took out of the old closet he'd shared with Assi. RACE AROUND THE SEA OF GALILEE was written on the shirt he had on now, the letters faded from so much laundering. If someone from work were here now, he wouldn't recognize Mikhael.

"Leelo?"

I didn't cry. I didn't say anything. I sat with my arms wrapped around myself, and Mikhael, who thought it was because of Dina, immediately knelt to hug me and ran his large hand over my cheek, my face, my back.

The hotel in Haifa was full of Frenchmen. Adam and Mikhael imitated them in the dining room, pursing their lips and lengthening syllables and bursting out laughing every time I whispered, "Shh, they'll hear us."

"So let them heee-aaar us," Mikhael said, drawing out the word in a parody of an artist in Montmartre, and Adam laughed so hard that his breakfast juice spurted out of his nose.

"I won!" Mikhael announced with satisfaction. On the last day of the shiva they had made a bet on who could make the other one laugh until whatever he was drinking came out of his nose. I hadn't been there when they made the bet—I was just coming back from a walk around the kibbutz—but even before I approached Moshe and Dina's house, I could hear their booming laughter. Shiva laughter, wild and defiant.

How easily Mikhael slipped back into kibbutz life. Running around the encircling road three times every morning. Olive pastries on the balcony at lunchtime. In the evenings, after the visitors left, Assi, Mikhael, and the boys played soccer, and sometimes friends joined them. Assi said that from now on, they'd do it once a year and call it the Dina Tournament. But on the last day of the shiva, something in Assi cooled off. Mikhael pulled our suitcase out from under the bed and took it down to the car we'd rented. Assi looked askance at the suitcase and said, "So that's it. Back to America."

Mikhael looked at the soccer ball that was lying at the edge of the yard and said to Assi, "*Yalla*, one more game." For a moment, you might have thought he'd never left, that he'd always been here at Friday-night dinners and during the week, at soccer games and during the khamsin winds.

I envied him. The way, at any given moment, he could stop being Mikhael Shuster, COO, and just walk into his childhood room and be that kibbutz kid who plays soccer or that dad who laughs with his son about French tourists in a hotel in Haifa. It didn't work that way for me. Twice, waiters spoke to me in English. Maybe I would never be at home anywhere, neither here nor there.

In the evening, we drove to my mother's. I got lost three times on the way because of the new neighborhoods. When we finally arrived, everyone fell on everyone else with hugs and kisses. Around the table, they all had a lively conversation about a reality-TV star I didn't know who'd sexually harassed a singer I'd never heard of. Adam sat next to my mother, who piled food on his plate as if she needed to compensate him for sixteen years of extreme hunger.

When we'd first arrived, my mother gave Adam such a long hug that it almost thawed the spot of frost in my heart, the one in the middle with her name on it. But then my sister and her husband came in with the three grandchildren and I saw the way she hugged them. It wasn't that she hugged her Israeli grand-children longer. In fact, the opposite was true, maybe because that love was so natural and flowed so freely that it didn't need to make a show of itself.

After we finished eating, I stood up to clear the table. When my mother bent over the dishwasher, she suddenly looked very small, more stooped than I remembered. *I have to ask Nitzan,* I thought. But perhaps my sister didn't notice those changes. For her and my mother, time flowed at the same speed; it was the same river and they changed together. But because I came from far away, those changes hit me suddenly, like a fist.

"So how are you all?" my mother asked over the pile of dishes. "How is Mikhael?"

"He's fine," I said, "trying to take it in." My mother nodded and reached out for the dishwasher liquid.

"And how is Adam?"

"Okay," I said.

"I hope he didn't take Dina's death too hard," she said.

*Not at all,* I wanted to tell her, but I stopped myself. Because just as he hadn't taken Dina's death hard, maybe when the day came, he wouldn't take her death hard either. Maybe that's what she was asking about.

"He'll be fine," I said a moment later, and I arranged coffee cups on a tray.

"And what about that boy from the school who died?"

*Good for you, Mom. Even when you're bent over the dishwasher, busy loading the dirty dishes, you still know how to hit where it hurts.*

"It was drugs," I said.

She straightened up and took dessert dishes out of the cabinet. "Believe me," she said, sighing, "kids today . . . And you say that Adam wasn't too upset?"

*They killed our dog, Mom. They threw a rock into our house.* "No. Not at all. He's in a good place. He's taking a self-defense class that he loves."

"That one taught by the man from the Mossad?"

"Excuse me?"

"On the phone, you said it was some Mossadnik who teaches the class."

"Ah, that's what Adam said once when he'd just started. I don't know if it's really true."

"Too bad," she said. "I've already told everyone at the hairdresser's that my grandson is learning to be a Mossad agent."

We went back into the living room with a tray of coffee and cake. Mikhael didn't touch dessert. He took his phone into a side room and became engrossed in an urgent conversation with Berman. When we drove back to the hotel, he said that he'd moved our flight up to the next day.

"There are rumors about data leaks. Berman is super-stressed that the Pentagon will find out about it and cancel everything. If they decide to go with another company, we'll lose millions."

"Is that why he was so melodramatic about industrial spies in Washington?"

Mikhael didn't smile. "It sounds far-fetched, but it's not completely unreasonable. I don't think he really believed someone would spy in the hotel, but seeing the competition's entire team walking around in the lobby really spooked him."

"What could they actually do?"

"There are conversations, there are rehearsals for the presentation we wouldn't want them to hear. Some idiot might leave his laptop open for a minute when he goes to the bathroom."

And I remembered Uri's expression when, after I had checked on Adam, I stood beside him in the middle of the night in the study in front of Mikhael's computer, his beautiful face glowing in the light of the screen. *I have to write a few e-mails,* he'd said in an apologetic tone. At that moment, it made sense. And when he asked if I happened to know Mikhael's password, I went over and typed it in for him. Mikhael's password: Adam's birthdate in the Hebrew calendar. It had seemed reasonable to me. But now, on the drive down from Haifa, I suddenly felt my knees begin to tremble.

## 64

THE CLERK AT the airport asked if we had packed our suit-cases ourselves. Behind her hung a huge poster of a beautiful woman wearing sunglasses. The model's glowing complexion only accentuated the red blemishes on the clerk's face when she leaned over to put the tag on our suitcase. We walked toward the duty-free shops, passing huge pictures of the Israeli landscape on our way: soldiers crying at the Western Wall, an aerial photo of Masada, anemones in Gamla.

We had time before the flight, and Mikhael went into one of the shops to buy overpriced halvah to take back to the office, a present from Israel. A saleswoman for Ahava products offered me a bag of Dead Sea mineral mud that was on sale for twenty-five dollars. Adam wanted to buy a package of chocolates to bring to his friends from Uri's class.

When the plane took off, I closed my eyes and leaned back. I wanted to sleep but couldn't. Some people are afraid of flying, but I was afraid of landing. *When we get home, Kelev won't be there to welcome us. When we get home, I'll have to ask Uri what he was looking for on Mikhael's computer in the middle of the night.* Uri. His name made me sweat despite the frigid air of the plane. And Mikhael, as if he sensed my apprehension, suddenly said, "Uri and I agreed that he would pick us up from the airport."

"Are you crazy? We can take a taxi."

"He offered a few times this week. Why not, Leelo? He's like family."

Only then did I understand that he'd been there with us for the past few days. Mikhael had spoken to him on the phone almost every night, had written him WhatsApp messages during the day. The TV screens on the plane updated us: We were cruising at thirty-three thousand feet. Under us was a black, opaque sea. Around us was the smell of dinner rolls heating up in the microwave.

"What do you even know about him, Mikhael?"

He sighed, not understanding my renewed outburst of resentment. "I know that during the shiva, he called every evening to ask how we were and that he handled two projects that, without him, would have been canceled."

"Was one of them MCJ?"

He looked at me in surprise and shook his head. "He doesn't have the security clearance for MCJ. Berman agreed to put him on the team, but only on the third level."

*Your computer, Mikhael. What was on your computer?*

He waited for me to respond, and when I didn't say anything, he went on. "But except for MCJ, he handled everything for me."

"If Jamal Jones hadn't died, he would never have gotten that position."

Mikhael looked at me, stunned. Even more than that, horrified. He thought I'd lost my mind. Adam was sitting across the aisle, his eyes closed, his legs stretched out in front of him, his earphones playing hip-hop at full volume. Mikhael looked at him, then back at me.

I spoke quickly, in a whisper, not giving him a chance to shut me up. "Berman was afraid of industrial espionage. Maybe he knew what he was talking about. You work in a company that has one of the highest security clearances in the Valley. No one can get in—but for Uri, you rolled out the red carpet."

"You've really lost it. First you thought he'd established an underground, and now you think that—that what, actually?"

"Weapons systems that interest the Pentagon also interest the Mossad."

He opened his mouth in disbelief. I whispered quickly, "Uri

said that Adam called him when Jamal died, but what if Uri was at the Harts' place before Adam called? Or what if Adam didn't call him at all?"

"Do you have the slightest idea how crazy you sound?"

"Someone tried to frame Adam for something he didn't do. I thought it was Netta who'd talked to the police, but maybe it was Uri. Think about it, Mikhael—the more we worried about Adam, the more we let Uri insinuate himself into our lives."

"Enough," he said firmly. "This conversation is over." He leaned back in his seat and closed his eyes. He kept his eyes closed for thirteen hours. Thirteen hours during which I watched the small TV screen detail the plane's progress: how many feet separated us from the large sea below, how long until we'd reach home.

And while the plane flew straight, my thoughts flew in circles. They plummeted. They skyrocketed. People around me went to the restroom. Stretched their legs. Watched movies on the small TV screens they were connected to by black umbilical cords the airlines had supplied. Warmed-up meals were served on plastic dishes. Glasses of water were poured. Books were read. Passengers slept with open mouths, closed mouths. I was outside of time, no longer on Israeli time and not yet on American time. My eyes were wide open, my tongue was dry in my mouth. *Did you throw the rock, Uri? Did you spray the graffiti?*

*And Kelev—was that you, Uri? And Jamal?*

## 65

AS SOON AS we landed in San Francisco, Mikhael turned on his phone and checked that the time zone was correct. My phone still showed Israeli time. I didn't fix it. (For the next few days, six in the evening was four in the morning. Dawn was sunset and vice versa. And considering everything that had happened, it made perfect sense.)

When we left baggage claim, Mikhael looked around for Uri. We were standing with our bags and the presents we'd bought in the duty-free shops. On the plane, we still heard Hebrew coming from every direction. The language enveloped us the way the scent of Dina's myrtle branches had. But outside the airport, the Hebrew faded and was lost in a hodgepodge of English and other languages. Not far from where we were standing, I saw a family that had been on the plane trying to bargain with a taxi driver. The driver stared at them in disbelief and repeated the price he'd just given them. They looked as if they'd come for a bar mitzvah trip. Their son stood beside them wearing a Barcelona shirt. The older girls were taking selfies with their phones.

"Where is he?" Adam asked, looking around. He was eager to see Uri. I was afraid of the moment he would arrive. I pictured him appearing from behind every man I saw, wearing the faded jacket I'd first seen on him the night of the party or the elegant jacket he'd bought a short time after he began working at Mikhael's company. In a moment, I'd be standing in front of those green eyes of his again. Eyes that had looked at me from so close up that night when I came. In a moment I'd politely shake his large hand, the hand that had covered my mouth so I wouldn't scream in pleasure, then stroked my cheek with a gentleness that surprised me.

But Uri didn't come. Mikhael went to the restroom, brushed his teeth, and exchanged the T-shirt from Israel for a button-down shirt. Adam also went to wash his face and returned a short time later with his hair combed back. In the end, I went as well, stood in a quiet, orderly line of American women, peed without sitting down into the toilet that gleamed with bleach, then put on makeup. I expected to see him when I came out, but Mikhael and Adam were still standing in the same spot, alone.

"Let's call him," I said.

"He doesn't answer," Adam said. "Dad tried twice."

I took out my phone and called him too, with no response. "Maybe he forgot," I suggested.

"Maybe he's in a traffic jam," Adam said. "Or got the time wrong."

"Should we call a taxi?" I asked.

"Hold off on the taxi," Mikhael said. "Let's make sure he's okay first."

I stood there, rebuked, while Mikhael tried to call Uri again. I turned my back to both of them. The last of the passengers from our plane had already been swallowed up into taxis and had gone on their way.

"Hello," Mikhael said. I turned back to him quickly. I thought Uri had finally answered. "Jane, it's Mikhael. We just landed, and Uri Ziv was supposed to pick us up. Do you happen to know where he is?"

Adam and I stood beside him. Uri might come on the line at any moment and apologize, saying he forgot. *It could happen to anyone,* Mikhael would assure him, *it's fine.*

But with each passing second, Mikhael looked more worried. Adam ran his fingers through his hair nervously.

A few long moments later, the secretary came back on the line. I heard her voice through the phone Mikhael was holding to his ear, too faint for me to understand what she said. But I didn't have to hear her. The shock on Mikhael's face was enough. He ended the call without saying goodbye.

"Uri's been arrested," he told us, his face pale. "The police took him in last night."

He was the first to recover. He ordered an Uber to take us home.

While we were loading our bags, Jane called again and asked if Mikhael could come to the office now. Berman was stressed about the Pentagon. Mikhael said yes and ordered another Uber for himself. When we said goodbye, he promised to update Adam the minute he knew what was going on.

Adam and I spent the ride home trying desperately to get information. He called his friends from the self-defense class, but they were all in school, and the one kid who answered didn't even know about the arrest.

When we finally reached home, Adam sat down on the living-room couch and kept making calls, and I closed myself up in the bedroom and tried to unpack. After ten minutes, I called Mikhael. I decided that when he answered, I would tell him everything. I wouldn't wait for tonight. I should have done it much sooner. The call didn't connect, but I didn't give up. I called again and again, nagging him with the constant ringing until he finally answered. He spoke to me in English. His voice was strange and distant when he said, "I can't talk now, Lilach. The police won't let me."

## 66

INDUSTRIAL ESPIONAGE. THAT'S what our lawyer told us after hours of waiting. "Your husband, Mrs. Shuster, is suspected of industrial espionage."

My eyes were drawn to the lawyer's long eyelashes. I found it difficult to focus on what he was saying. The words couldn't penetrate the milky membrane that encased me. From the moment I'd arrived at the police station, I noticed everything and nothing. I was aware of the pungent odors, the background noises, the small hole in the upholstery of the chair in the waiting room. But the words that were said to me by the people who spoke to me—those I found difficult to concentrate on. The lawyer could tell. Perhaps that's why, as we sat down in the coffee shop across from the police station, he repeated the charge: "Industrial espionage."

He waited for me to object, deny, and ask, *What? Why?* but all I did was stare in shock at his long eyelashes. He responded to my unasked questions as if they had been spoken aloud.

"The police arrested your husband after they found documents during a search of the computer belonging to his friend Mr. Uri Ziv."

His words seeped in slowly. They had arrested Uri when he tried to sell information to the competition. They'd found a great number of commercial secrets on his computer, information that only Mikhael had access to.

"He's not his friend," I finally said.

"Excuse me?"

"Uri and Mikhael, they aren't really friends."

We were sitting in the corner of the nearly empty coffee shop. The lawyer wrote down what I said on a small pad, the kind people no longer own these days. He wrote down every word I said.

"But your husband fast-tracked Uri Ziv's entrance into the company. He vouched for him."

"Mikhael didn't help Uri with any espionage," I replied firmly. "Even if Uri did something, Mikhael definitely had no part in it."

The lawyer's eyelashes fluttered quickly behind his glasses. His tone was very serious, the tone of a doctor delivering bad news about a biopsy: "The investigators' current working premise is that Mr. Shuster knowingly planted a mole in the company and passed commercial secrets on to Mr. Ziv. There are confidential documents on Mr. Ziv's computer that only your husband could have sent him."

(His green eyes shining in the light of Mikhael's computer. His large body in Mikhael's tracksuit that I'd lent him. The smell of me still on his fingers when he got up in the middle of the night to type on the keyboard some more.)

"Uri slept at our house when Mikhael was in Washington. He had access to my husband's computer."

The lawyer's hand lingered over his pad for a moment before continuing to write. He didn't raise his eyes when he asked, "Could you give me details about the circumstances that led to Mr. Ziv's spending the night at your home when your husband wasn't there?"

I wrapped my arms around my body and said, "He came to help."

Now the lawyer looked up and removed his thin-rimmed glasses. "Mrs. Shuster—"

"Lilach."

"Leela, look, I'm here to help you. But you have to tell me everything. Believe me, there's nothing I haven't heard before."

"My son was being bullied," I said, averting my eyes. "The night that Uri slept at our place, they'd killed our dog. The day before that, they sprayed graffiti about my son on the school walls. They threw a rock through our window—that's documented; we called the police." (*There's no evidence of the other things, Mr. Lawyer, and I don't think we'll speak about them. Even though, behind those glasses and odd lashes, you actually have kind eyes.*)

The lawyer leaned slightly in my direction. "Do you know who did it?"

I shook my head and said, "The police assumed it was a hate crime," and before he could show his puzzlement, I added, "We're Jewish, from Israel. My son was targeted by boys from the Nation of Islam."

He intended to write, but his fountain pen stopped working. He mumbled an apology and took another one, no less expensive, out of his pocket. "So the police considered it a hate crime carried out by teenagers?"

I nodded. I wondered if I should tell him about Jamal and Adam or if that would only complicate matters more.

"And in order to protect you and your son from that kind of threat, Mr. Ziv slept in your house?"

"Yes," I whispered, and beyond the hum of the coffee shop, I could hear the sound of shattering glass that had awakened me that day. "I gave him the password for my husband's computer. He said he needed to send some e-mails."

He wrote in his notebook. "Excuse me for repeating this: You're saying that Mr. Ziv arrived to safeguard you in your husband's absence, and that definitely sounds as if they were good friends."

He waited for my response.

I took a deep breath. "No," I said. "Mikhael thought they were friends. He was wrong."

The lawyer asked me a few more questions. His initial conversation with Mikhael had been short and fragmented. He wrote everything down meticulously. Then he asked if I wanted to drink something. When he stood up to get me water, the pad fell open, and I saw that there were small drawings on the margins of some pages, which were otherwise filled with his crowded handwriting. He noticed my glance and was embarrassed. He picked up his pad and, a minute later, came back with a glass of water.

"Your husband will have to take a polygraph test," he said as he sat down beside me, "but what you said can definitely work in his favor. If everything you said is true and the polygraph supports it, I absolutely believe that it will be—"

My chuckle interrupted him. He looked at me, slightly offended.

"I'm sorry," I said. "I interrupted you. You were going to say that you believe everything will be fine."

## 67

"WHEN IS DAD coming home?" Adam asked that evening. I replied that I didn't know. He asked many other questions, and I answered them all the same way. But the next morning Adam came downstairs, and even before he opened his mouth to ask, I said, "Come sit with me."

I'd made myself coffee and squeezed orange juice for him. "Drink it before the vitamins fly away." I thought he'd argue with me, but he drank it. Adam was being as careful with me as I was with him. The window faced our backyard, and we both looked out at that place where new grass was growing. Adam rubbed his hand over the sparse stubble sprouting on his cheeks. I asked him if he knew what industrial espionage was.

He knew more about it than I did. "Still," he said, "even if that's what they think, don't they have to either charge him or let him out?"

"Well, it's not only a case of industrial espionage. The system that Dad developed for the Pentagon is more than a commercial secret. There are serious security ramifications involved."

"Like, because it's weapons?"

"Yes."

"So they think Dad sold arms to the Iranians or something?"

"Not exactly," I said, trying to decide how much of what the lawyer had told me I could tell Adam. "At first they thought he was spying for the Mossad."

Adam's eyes lit up. If there was one thing he understood from all the thriller movies he'd seen, it was that the Americans and the Israelis worked together. He was too young to have heard about Jonathan Pollard. For one sweet moment, he thought his dad was really cool.

"Did he do it?" he asked excitedly. "Did Dad work for the Mossad?"

I shook my head. The light in his eyes went out, then lit up again as he searched my face for the secret he hoped I was hiding from him. To extinguish that spark once and for all, I added, "The lawyer says that the investigators have dropped that line of inquiry."

Adam looked disappointed. From what I understood from the lawyer, Uri had denied any connection to the Mossad from day one, but of course, no one believed him, and because of what they thought about the relationship between Uri and Mikhael, they didn't believe Mikhael either. Clarifications from the Mossad, if there were any, would not have placated the Americans, because no self-respecting espionage agency would be in a hurry to admit that one of its agents had been caught.

Deep in thought, Adam drank the rest of his juice, then abruptly put the glass down on the table and, his face shining, said, "But, Mom, the kids in the class told me that Uri works for the Mossad!"

I listened as he tried to convince me, waving his hands in the air, his voice full of hope, that Uri and Mikhael were secret agents who had spied together for the sake of Israel's security. The more he struggled to defend Uri, the more obdurate I became. Finally, I told him, with a tinge of coldness in my voice, that it was actually the boys from the self-defense class who had cleared Uri of the more serious charge of spying for a foreign country. After speaking to them, the investigators were convinced that Uri Ziv was far from being a spy—a real agent would not have revealed himself to a bunch of sixteen-year-old kids.

Adam didn't say anything. The hurt showed on his face. Tears and restraint fought each other in his eyes, and restraint won. He didn't cry, but he finally asked quietly, "So what do the investigators think happened?"

"You're sure you want to talk about this now? I know how much you love Uri." His slender, pale hand clenched into a fist on the table.

"Go on, Mom, tell me."

The coldness was gone. I was as gentle as I could be when I told him about Uri's debts. The huge mortgage he'd taken out right before the collapse of the company he'd founded. "His kids went back to Israel and he was stuck here."

"But I don't understand, Mom," he said, and the weakness in his voice now made my body stiffen. "If Dad got Uri a great job, why didn't Uri just save up his salary? Why did he have to put himself in danger like that?"

I thought the reason was clear. In Silicon Valley, a programmer can stay at the same job for three years before getting a promotion. And Uri didn't have three years. He was supposed to have been made chief of the general staff a long time ago.

"He wanted to be near his kids," I said, "and to do that, he had to get his hands on a lot of money, and fast."

When the investigators realized that, they went easier on Mikhael, but they still didn't release him. The police found it hard to understand why he'd gone out of his way to secure such a sensitive position for someone he didn't actually know.

I finished my coffee. I drove Adam to school. On the way, we stopped at the animal shelter. Adam wanted to donate the bags of food we'd bought for Kelev and no longer needed. At the shelter, he asked me to go inside and give them the food while he stayed in the car.

"You don't want to pet the dogs?" I asked.

He shook his head.

In the school parking lot, he surprised me with a kiss on the cheek before he got out.

On the way home, I called the lawyer again. If he was tired of my calls, he made sure not to show it. "They still think your husband is involved," he said apologetically. "They're sure he had something to gain from it. Otherwise, why would he have made such an effort to get Mr. Ziv into the company?"

From his question, it was obvious to me that Mikhael hadn't said anything to the investigators about how close Uri and our family had become. I assumed he didn't want to raise other questions about Jamal, especially since the police had finally closed the case and determined that the death at the party was the result of a self-administered overdose. Another man who found himself under arrest might have felt pressured enough to blurt out the information, but Mikhael was one of the most self-possessed people I'd ever known. That's how they trained them in the elite combat unit. And that's why, when they asked him why he'd gone all out to get Uri into the company, Mikhael talked about the comradeship of soldiers in the Israeli army. In our culture, he told them, we're like brothers.

In the end, they were persuaded. They returned his watch and his jacket and told him he was free to go. Adam and I picked him up. The three of us hugged. When we were still in the parking lot, Berman called to tell Mikhael that he should take a week off. He had to decide whether to let him back in the company offices.

"You're not a spy, Mikhael, but you're a fucking idiot," he said. "The Pentagon just heard the whole story and kicked us out on our ear."

We drove home in silence. At the highway exit, Adam asked if we could listen to Lil Nas, and Mikhael said, "No way. I'd rather go back to jail."

And for a moment, just a moment, everything was a drop less terrible.

## 68

THE END-OF-THE-YEAR award ceremony was supposed to take place outside, but at the last minute, they switched it to the gym because of a storm. Shir Cohen waved to me when Adam and I entered and pointed to the spot she'd saved next to her on the bleachers. I made my way over to her, and Adam went to join his friends. Einat Greenbaum was sitting in a nearby row and taking pictures of everything with her phone. The kids were standing around, holding the report cards they'd just been given. The school band was playing a song I didn't recognize. Girls in cheerleader uniforms were dancing.

Shir tilted her head in the direction of the entrance. Annabella Jones was standing there. She wore the same black dress I remembered. The same gold locket hung around her neck. I couldn't take my eyes off her. Other parents were standing with Annabella. Some spoke to her, others patted her shoulder in encouragement. I couldn't tell whether she replied to them. The principal hurried over eagerly to Jamal's mother. She took hold of Annabella's hand and led her to the first row. The band continued playing and the parents continued to snap photos, but it seemed to me that they were trying not to include the silent woman in their shots of the decorated gym.

When the ceremony began, the principal announced that the school would award an annual scholarship for excellence in Jamal's name, and she asked Annabella to stand at her side and make the first presentation. Jamal's mother stood up and made her way heavily and too slowly toward the dais that served as a stage. When she finally took her place at the lectern beside the principal, she reached into her bag and removed a folded piece of paper. At the sight of it, the principal exchanged a glance with her vice principal, standing at the back of the makeshift stage. They hadn't expected that. Annabella Jones was just supposed to present the scholarship for excellence in her dead son's name and go back to her seat. Unplanned speeches might lead to crying. Crying might lead to collapse. And a mother's collapse was inappropriate for an end-of-the-year award ceremony for 397 teenagers. Annabella Jones's mourning was supposed to remain restrained. She was supposed to lead it out in public the way you lead a horse, display it, and return it to its place.

"I want to read you a poem that Jamal wrote," Annabella said. Her pianist's fingers unfolded the paper and smoothed it out several times even after it was spread on the lectern. The principal stepped back to give her space. "Maybe it's a rap song," Annabella said, "but I don't do rap, so . . . I'll just read it like a regular poem, okay?" The audience nodded at her in unison. It was a long, callow poem, but we listened respectfully because we knew there would be no more poems. *Your blue eyes* . . . he had written. *Someday we'll be one* . . . he had written, and we didn't know to whom he'd been writing or why, but we listened carefully to every single word.

Annabella folded the page so suddenly and sharply that it surprised the people in the audience. It was such a strong contrast to her soft tone, to the movements of her body, which were reminiscent of, more than anything, the sinuous movements of an underwater creature.

"That's it," she said. I wasn't sure if she meant it was the end of the poem or that the poem went on but she had decided to end it there. The principal hesitated for a moment, then went back over to the lectern. I thought I saw relief in her narrow lips, which had pursed when Annabella began to read but now parted slightly.

"Thank you, Annabella," she said. "Now it's time to award the Jamal Jones Scholarship for Excellence."

The principal gave a piece of paper to Annabella, who read out the winner's name. A black-haired girl went up onto the stage, her expression serious, as the occasion demanded. Annabella handed her a golden envelope and shook her hand formally. Projected onto the wall behind them was the picture of Jamal that I remembered from Annabella's living-room table. His face—open, bright—shone at us from the other side of the gym.

I looked at Adam, and I wasn't the only one. Parents and students stared at my son. He was standing, flanked by Boaz and Yochai, busy reading his report card. I felt like getting up and taking him out of there before those intrusive glances could stab him, but when I stood up and hurried down the bleacher steps toward him, he turned his face to me and flashed me a warning look: *Don't*.

I continued down the steps, but I didn't go over to him. I walked away from the bleachers and out of the gym, leaving behind the principal's speech and the school band, and went to the bathroom. The door of the stall was completely covered with nasty and hurtful graffiti: *Taylor is a whore. Amy's easy. Amanda is full of shit*. Everyday cruelty, ancient and familiar. The only difference between America and Israel was the scrawled names of the humiliated kids.

I sat on the closed toilet seat and breathed deeply. I looked at the scribbles on the bathroom door for quite a while. When I came out of the stall, Annabella was standing in front of the sink. Her face filled the mirror. Under her arm, she held a piece of paper—Jamal's report card, I understood.

"Hi," I said.

"Hi," she said.

I walked the few feet from the toilets to the sink. What torment this must be for her, coming here today. Seeing all his classmates receiving their report cards. Hearing them making plans for next year, for the summer.

"The poem you read was lovely," I said. I waited for her to say something, but she didn't. I turned on the faucet. The water flowed over my hands. I scrubbed my fingers with soap, even though there was no need.

"I heard about your dog."

*How? From whom? Did the rumor crawl to you slowly, the way snails crawled across the newly painted school walls?* I turned off the water. I looked for paper towels to dry my hands, but there weren't any. Annabella looked at me while I dried them on my pants, my fingers leaving long, wet stripes on the fabric.

"Will you stay for lunch?" I asked. I knew that the parents' association had ordered food from a high-end catering service, and folding tables had been placed at the back of the gym.

"I don't think I can bear it," she said.

I reached out to touch her shoulder, but the sharp look in her eyes stopped me. And after a moment, Annabella walked out the door.

I followed her back to the gym. The physical distance between us was strange and awkward. We weren't two women walking together, but we weren't just two women who had happened to come out of a public bathroom at the same time. She walked faster. I walked faster. She reached the door of the gym just ahead of me.

"Annabella! There you are." Two Black women who had been standing with Annabella earlier walked toward us.

"Come sit with us, baby," one of them said, opening the door for Annabella and putting her arm through hers. They didn't look at me. Maybe they hadn't seen me there.

I waited a few moments and then walked into the gym and

returned to my place next to Shir to watch the rest of the ceremony.

## 69

**WHEN I FINALLY** went to visit him, he looked thinner than I remembered. His cheeks were covered with a thick beard, and his alert green eyes were faded and dull. I thought he would be surprised to see me, but there was no surprise in his face. He studied me slowly. He'd known I'd come.

I didn't say anything. Neither did he. Not far from us, another prisoner kissed his wife and children goodbye through the glass partition. Uri looked at them. He seemed to suddenly empty out. *He's alone in here,* I thought. *No one comes to visit him.* I wondered if his children knew he was here. I remembered the little blond boy and the chubby teenage girl on Frishman Beach. I hoped, for his sake, for all their sakes, that they would never know. I pictured Tali Ziv, beautiful and poised, and asked myself if he'd already told her.

He watched the other prisoner's family as they made their way to the exit. A curly-haired toddler let the stuffed dinosaur he was holding drag on the dirty floor. When he reached the door, he turned around and looked at the man behind the glass, waved, and gave him a broad smile, as if this were a routine farewell at the kindergarten door. The boy's mother put a hand on his shoulder and pushed him forward. The dinosaur dragged behind them as they walked out.

Uri looked back at me. "They come every week, the little boy and his mother. The older siblings sometimes skip the visit, but the little one comes every week."

I nodded. So many questions I was afraid to ask collided in my mind. *Why did you keep silent, Uri? Why didn't you tell him? Which one of us did you want to protect?*

"Thank you," I finally whispered.

The fat guard in the corner looked me over curiously. My jewelry, the white silk blouse—I didn't look like the other women here.

"You didn't come here just to say thank you," Uri finally said, and he gave me a baleful look. It was as if I had entered a tunnel I thought was empty, and suddenly, a pair of glittering eyes flashed at me in the darkness. "You're not here for that."

"You're right," I said after a beat. "I'm not here for that." And before my courage deserted me, I leaned toward him and said, "I wanted to ask you about Jamal."

I recognized a familiar green spark in his eyes, the one I'd seen the first night when he was near the Hart home. "Did you do something to him? You can tell me. I swear I won't tell anyone." My temples throbbed as if I were in the midst of a mad run. Uri sighed and rubbed his forehead, and I saw that his nails were bitten.

"Lilach, your son hated that boy. You don't have to believe me—he told other people about it."

"That's the only thing I know for sure. All the rest are things you said."

He looked down, a gesture that confused me. I leaned toward him. If it were possible, I think I would have touched his shoulder.

"You told us that Adam searched sites on how to make meth and made it sound as if you were helping him when you in-structed him to delete those searches. But I don't think there was anything really terrible on Adam's phone or computer, Uri."

He still hadn't looked up from the floor of the visitors' room. His hands rested on his thighs, just as several weeks before, they had rested on mine. His face remained unreadable when I said, "You poisoned Jamal and made us suspect Adam so you would have an opening to us through him. And when that wasn't enough, you threw a stone through our window. You killed Kelev."

"In a minute, you'll say I disguised myself as a Black kid and beat up Adam."

"Jamal beat up Adam. That I know."

"And I used it, you're right about that. But I never touched that boy." He spoke quietly. I had to lean forward to hear him. He saw this but kept his voice low. "When Jamal collapsed at the party, Adam called me. Maybe because he was terrified when he saw a boy die. Maybe because he himself killed Jamal. I didn't ask him. It didn't matter to me."

"It didn't matter to you?" I fought not to raise my voice and get sent out of there.

"No," he said simply. "Adam had told me where his father worked. I saw an opportunity to get close to Mikhael—and I grabbed it. I rode the wave, but I wasn't the one who created it."

"You're lying!" My whisper was in Hebrew, but you couldn't miss the tone. The couple sitting at the table next to us looked at me for a fraction of a second and went back to their business. I forced myself to calm down. This wasn't how I'd planned for the conversation to go. Uri rubbed his new beard with his huge, bearlike hand, which emerged from the sleeve of his prisoner's shirt.

"Look, Lilach, it could be that your son went to that party like any other kid and had nothing to do with Jamal's death. And it could be that for once in his life he was tired of being a victim. You know, maybe he didn't even mean to kill him. Maybe he just wanted to get Jamal into trouble with drugs so they'd throw him out of school and the bullying would stop, but somehow things got out of hand and he had to cover himself. You'll have to decide which option you believe."

Now I couldn't help but raise my voice. "From the first minute, you tried to make me believe it was Adam!" I choked. Too many possibilities. Too many question marks.

"If it were my son," Uri said in a different, quieter voice, "I think I would have asked him." His eyes were distant, fixed on an invisible spot in space. "But they say that's the kind of thing a mother just knows, right?"

## 70

ON THE DAY of Adam's flight, Mikhael didn't come to the airport with us. "A job interview," he'd told me in an apologetic voice. "I have to prepare." Adam put his large suitcase into the back seat and asked if we could listen to hip-hop on the way. When we pulled out of the driveway, Mikhael was standing in the yard waving goodbye. His image shrank as we drove along the green, quiet street that intersected with the green, quiet avenue in one of the greenest, quietest, and safest cities in America.

When we finished at the check-in counter, the sun was shining through the large airport windows, blinding us. "Don't forget sunscreen," I said. "It's really easy to get sunburned there."

"Come on, Mom, you can get sunburned anywhere." (And I remembered the morning in Tahoe when I went out to ski with Uri, and because of the cold, I forgot to slather on sunscreen, and both our faces burned. His green eyes above the snow.)

The group of teenagers standing in front of us moved toward the security checkpoint. Their cheerful giggling remained behind, like a cloud of perfume, and we stayed inside that cloud, silent and still. The departure board hung above us: Paris. Tokyo.

Rome. An endless number of flight routes spread out in the sky, and of all the possibilities, he'd chosen this one. Israel. My son was returning to Israel. And it didn't matter that it was only for three weeks. It didn't matter that the leader of the Birthright Israel group had promised in four different conversations that, no matter what, my son would land back in San Francisco on July 3. ("He's a minor," I warned the man on the phone. "If anything happens to him, I'll sue the pants off you," and Mikhael took the phone and asked him to excuse his wife. Like every mother, she was a bit upset. It was clear to us, he said, that this was an educational tour that would end on time, and of course he had our permission to go.) It didn't matter. Because I knew that he wouldn't really come back from the trip. When it ended, he'd tell us that he wanted to make aliyah.

On the departures board, the words *Tel Aviv* moved up as earlier flights left. Boarding was starting soon. Adam put on his backpack like on the first day of school. From behind, he looked like a fourteen-year-old, but anyone who looked at his face would suddenly be confused by the mature eyes. And perhaps he was confused as well, the adult and the boy fighting within him, because his sweaty hand grabbed mine and pressed it with the same desperation I remembered from his time in day care and the beginning of grade school, the don't-leave-me-here grip.

"You want to come back home?" I asked, and immediately regretted the question, because simply asking it might make him drop my hand. He shook his head resolutely but didn't move. I knew that I shouldn't look into his eyes now, that doing so could only destroy this rare moment when a sixteen-year-old boy was willing, however briefly, to hold his mother's hand. Instead, I looked at his fingers, gentle and slender, wrapped tightly around my hand. Right after he was born, I hugged him—pink and smooth and perfect—and counted the tiny fingers to make sure they were all there. Now I looked at those fingers and asked myself if they were the fingers of a killer. And perhaps sensing that, he let go of my hand all at once, stood a bit straighter, and said, "I have to go."

We stood in front of the security line. His eyes were dark and turbulent like the sea in Tel Aviv in winter. Jamal's eyes in the picture in Annabella Jones's house were dark as velvet. Adam's left eyebrow twitched slightly. His mouth opened, maybe to speak. If I asked now, at this moment, he would certainly answer me. I leaned toward him, put my hand on his shoulder, and said, "Take care of yourself."

AYELET GUNDAR-GOSHEN was born in Israel in 1982. She is a practising clinical psychologist, has been a news editor on Israel's leading newspaper and has worked for the Israeli civil rights movement. *One Night, Markovitch*, her first novel, won the Sapir Prize for best debut. Her novel *Waking Lions* was a *New York Times* Book of the Year and won the Wingate Prize, and her novel *Liar* was Editor's Choice in *People* magazine. All of her novels are available from Pushkin Press.

SONDRA SILVERSTON is a native New Yorker who has lived in Israel since 1970. She has translated works by Amos Oz, Etgar Keret and Eshkol Nevo. Her translation of Amos Oz's *Between Friends* won the 2013 National Jewish Book Award for fiction.